Coal is the hard, black heart of the mountain town of Stillwater, West Virginia, but far beneath it lies something much darker, an evil beyond time, waiting to rise and bathe the world in blood and fire once more. When unwitting miners dig into its tomb, only Kyle - Stillwater's prodigal son - and paranormal investigator Maya stand between humanity and Hell. Time is short and evil runs deep in...

STILL WATER

"In STILL WATER, Justin R. Macumber brings all the vivid Americana of Stephen King and all the creeping evil menace of Lovecraft, to a claustrophobic tale of horror lurking in the deep parts of the world. The lush prose pulls you in and carries you along at a mounting pace until a confrontation so bloody, you can feel the claws raking you." -Kane Gilmour, Bestselling Author of RAGNAROK and THE CRYPT OF DRACULA

"You'll want to leave the light on long after you've turned the final page of this dark thriller! " -Jeremy Bishop, author of REFUGE.

"Justin Macumber excels in the dark. STILL WATER will trap you and never let go." -Edward Lorn, author of CRUELTY

"Macumber's Stillwater marries Lovecraftian-dread with a character driven thrill-ride that will leave you shivering with fear." -Paul E Cooley, author of GARAAGA'S CHILDREN.

Books by Justin R. Macumber

Novels and Novellas

Haywire

Titans Rise (forthcoming)

A Minor Magic

A Broken Magic (forthcoming)

Still Water

The Ties That Bind

Short Fiction

That Old Hell Magic

Dark Running

The Dame Wore White

Pirates of the Crimson Sand

STILL WATER

JUSTIN R. MACUMBER

Gryphonwood

Gryphonwood Press

STILL WATER. Copyright 2014 by Justin R. Macumber.

Published by Gryphonwood Press
www.gryphonwoodpress.com

Cover design by Scott Macumber

This book is a work of fiction. All names, characters, places and incidents are the product of the author's imagination, or are used fictitiously. Any resemblance to actual events or persons is entirely coincidental.

ISBN-10:   1940095158
ISBN-13:   978-1-940095-15-8

Printed in the United States of America
First printing: April, 2014

DEDICATION

I listened to podcasts before they even had a name, and about seven years ago I considered doing one of my own. That podcast ended up being The Dead Robots' Society, which at this point is well over 300 episodes strong, with extraordinary guests and convention panels aplenty. The podcast never would have lasted this long, though, were it not for the amazing people who stepped in and co-hosted with me. In particular I want to give a special shout-out to Terry Mixon, Ryan E. Stevenson, Paul Elard Cooley, and Eliyanna Kaiser. Each of you has a place in my heart, and I know my writing has been made better by your input and friendship. Thank you all so much.

ACKNOWLEDGEMENTS

First off, a big Texas-sized thank you to my editor, David Wood. The book you hold was written by me, but his notes and edits made it so much better than it was originally. Granted, that's his job, but I still think a word of thanks is in order. ;)

I would also like to thank Akira Yamaoka. When I write I like to listen to music; it creates a mood that makes writing easier. For this book I needed an atmosphere that was especially dark, and there was no one else who created it better than Akira Yamaoka, famed composer of the Silent Hill video game soundtracks by Konami. Those scores got me through many a sunny day when horror should have been a million miles from my brain.

"Rain fell on the roofs of the just and the unjust, the saints and the sinners, those who knew peace and those in torment, and tomorrow began at a dark hour."

Robert R. McCammon, MINE
(used by permission of the author)

PROLOGUE
IN THE DEEP DARK

The mine was cursed. Ash hated thinking that way, but there wasn't any other explanation. Never in his life had he seen a mining operation struggle so much, and the rate at which people were getting hurt or quitting was enough to ruin what little sleep he managed to get between shifts.

The sun – nearly hidden by approaching storm clouds – crept toward the horizon as Ash turned off Sewell Road and drove down the dirt path leading to the mine's gravel parking lot. Rounding a sharp bend, the sight of a dozen men crowded together in a mob ruined the start of his day. He steered for the nearest open slot, slammed the transmission into PARK, and climbed out of his truck.

Angry voices churned the air as he stomped across gravel. No one looked his way as he approached, but they knew he was there when he broke through their ranks with a broad shouldered shove he'd perfected during his high school football days. "What the hell is going on here?"

To his surprise he found his boss, Ray Dennings, leaning against the mine's low-slung electric cart with his arms held up in front of him. Normally the Badger Mining president was calm and tidy, but today that wasn't the case. Coal dust and black handprints covered his light gray shirt and the blue paisley tie hanging half-torn from his neck. Bright red carnations bloomed on his left cheek, the beginnings of ugly bruises. The final touch on the surreal scene was blood dripping from his split lower lip. When Ash appeared, he heaved a massive sigh of relief. "Oh, thank Christ. I never thought I'd be so glad to see your ugly face."

"Don't defend him, Ash!" a voice shouted from the back of the crowd. More shouts went up behind him, their angry words overlapping each other like storm clouds. Hands pushed and pulled at his back.

"Yeah! Don't get in the way!"

"Goddam suits are stealin' from us!"

"We ain't gonna stand for it!"

Sick of the noise and jostling, Ash whipped around and glared at the mob. "Shut the fuck up!" The command thundered over the angry crowd, bringing everything to a standstill. Taking advantage of the brief moment of quiet, Ash turned back to Mr. Dennings. "What's going on?"

"They've gone insane!" The president's thin arms shook as he kept them raised in front of him. "And they should be damn glad I don't have the police here arresting the whole lot of them."

"We ain't the criminals here," someone said.

Mr. Dennings cast around for the man who'd spoken out, but after a moment he shook his head. "That so? I have a split lip that says otherwise. I know all of you are angry. I'm angry too, but I can't grow money on trees, dammit. Get mad at your co-workers who haven't been showing up, who've called in sick day after day. Every man we're down means that much less coal gets cut. Less coal means less money, simple as that."

"I don't blame 'em." An older man stepped forward. From the corner of his eye Ash saw Gus Mason, one of the day shifters responsible for bolting the cave ceiling after a section of coal was dug out of the mountain so it didn't cave in and kill everyone. "This place ain't right. You haven't been down there, but *we* have. This whole mountain is... It just ain't right."

Encouraged by his words, the intensity of the crowd picked up again. It crackled against Ash's skin like static electricity. Gus was normally a tough old cuss, sometimes too tough, so to hear him sound afraid threw Ash for a loop. But Gus wasn't the first person to talk about the Bluestone Mine like it was haunted. When Badger Coal first came to Stillwater promising that their new mining technology could reopen old mines, they'd been greeted as saviors sent by God Himself. And to their credit, for the first couple of months things had been right as rain. Coal went out, and money came in. But, as they dug further into the mountain, Ash started hearing whispers among the men, talk of strange sounds and shadows that didn't move right. He hadn't seen or heard anything out of the ordinary, so he'd blown it off as idle chatter, but idle or not he wasn't about to let the day shift crew use it as an excuse to riot. "Come on now, Gus. We're all reasonable men here, so let's *be* reasonable."

Gus turned to look at him, and a shadow passed over the miner's eyes, sending a shiver down Ash's spine. It only lasted a second, but the sense of...of *otherness*...lingered. "Don't talk down to me, Ashley Franks. You've been in that darkness. Tell me you ain't felt it down there, in the places we don't—"

"Enough!" Ray's voice exploded in their midst like a grenade.

Ash was thankful for the distraction. He didn't want to hear Gus say another word, didn't want to look at him or see the mountain's shadow in his eyes.

Mr. Dennings pushed away from the mine cart and stood up, then straightened his tie as best he could and smoothed the rumpled material of his shirt. "Though I doubt you want to hear the 'suit' complain about how much money he's lost in this place, we are *all* hurting, and it won't get better until we get coal production up. If you want to quit because some animal wandered into the mine and hissed at you from the dark, fine. Come back tomorrow and I'll cut your final check. Understand, though, that as soon as you're out the door I'll be hiring your brother and your best friend, and they'll be the one with a job while you're out drowning your sorrows."

Without waiting to see how the men reacted, Mr. Dennings pushed his shoulders back and walked toward the office trailer. The mob parted like the Red Sea. Some of the men were still angry, but most cast their gaze around like they weren't sure where they were or what was going on.

After the company president disappeared from sight, a few chuckles dropped from the day crew while the rest grumbled and walked to their waiting vehicles. Gus, though, remained where he was, his gaze now shifted to the mine entrance. Ash couldn't tell from the older man's expression if he was glad to be out of it or if he wanted to go back in. After a moment Gus glanced at him, and again darkness flittered across his eyes like a crow flying past the sun. The two men stared at one another for several long seconds before the day shifter ambled away to his dirty brown pickup. As the parking lot emptied, Ash knew he should feel relieved, but he wasn't.

With the crisis averted – at least for the time being – Ash walked to the sign-in board to see what bad news might be waiting for him. Sure enough, two night-shift names had 'Out sick' written in blue ink next to them. Wilbert and Tyler. Damn. They were good workers. An invisible weight pressed against his chest, adding to the load of worry he already carried.

Two sets of headlights appeared around the bend, catching his attention. A third followed soon after. The night shift was on its way, passing through shadows growing longer by the moment.

Taking a deep breath, he hitched up his pants and awaited his crew. He didn't have to wait long.

"Okay, listen up," he said when all his men were gathered. "Wil and Tyler called in sick. I need y'all working hard and working smart. The more cuts we make, the more money we make. If you need anything, let me know. Otherwise, get moving."

The crew drifted apart like ocean wreckage, but they all moved in the same general direction of the sign-in board. As soon as enough had added their names, they turned on the electric cart and one of the men got behind the wheel while others took a seat and leaned back. The cart sat only a few inches off the ground, so it was a pain to get in and out of if you had bad knees or a sore back – which nearly everyone did – but any higher would have meant decapitation as it drove into the four foot high mine entrance.

Ash glanced up as the sky continued to fill with black clouds and night claimed the mountains. He'd lived his entire life in their shadow, and not once had ever felt afraid. It was his home, more than the double-wide trailer he hung his hat in. The narrow roads and sheer drops might frighten lowlanders, but they were the topography of his youth. He knew Stillwater and the peaks around it like he knew the cracks in the vinyl of his truck bench seat. There wasn't anything to fear.

Was there?

"Yo, boss!" a voice shouted. "You ready to get dirty?"

Ash nearly jumped out of his skin, then turned like a child caught licking icing off a cake that wasn't his. Dean Cotton sat in the driver's seat of the mine cart. All the other seats were empty, which meant everyone else was in the mine and this was the cart's last run. Ash frowned, unsure how time had flown by so quickly, then waved and dashed over to his truck to get his lunch pail and bright white hardhat. After scooping them up and jogging to the cart he tested the hardhat's forward-facing light to make sure it worked. He'd put fresh batteries in the day before, but better safe than sorry when hundreds of tons of mountain were waiting to crush the unwary. The headlamp shone bright and steady as he bent down and settled into the cart. "Thanks for waiting."

Dean nodded and pressed the acceleration pedal. Overhead the dark clouds broke open, and heavy raindrops splattered to the ground. The cart's occupants barely had a chance to taste the storm as they slipped into the mountain seconds later.

A rough-hewn cave ceiling squatted mere inches above Ash's head. The cart's headlights lit the way ahead, with more light thrown by the hardhats they wore. It made for a bright scene, but Ash wasn't fooled. The ravenous dark seemed, capable of consuming all the light you gave it, and when you didn't have any more it would reach out and swallow you whole.

After a few minutes of rolling over broken earth and bits of rock, Dean turned the cart to the right, kept things steady for a moment, then made a left. A rumbling sound began vibrating the air, soon joined by a tumbling fog of dust and coal soot. When the cart's headlight turned right a second time, it lit up the hard working night-shift crew.

"Digger's really givin' her hell!" Dean yelled once the cart was stopped next to the roofbolting rig. Billy Simms was already prepping the machine and locking yard long drill bits into place. "Let's get this done, 'cause I want to get outta here

A.S.A. fuckin' P!"

Despite not wanting to give the miners' paranoia credence, Ash couldn't help but agree. "You and me both."

Dean backed the cart up, turned left, and pulled forward until he and Ash were stopped next to the scooper, which was Dean's duty to operate.

After getting out of the cart, Ash stood up as high as the mine allowed — a painfully pitiful height — and made his way toward a group of men kneeling together and talking while Doug "Digger" Renfro sat with his control panel and operated the continuous miner from a safe distance. The mechanical beast chugged along, scraping out coal with its rolling drum of tungsten carbide teeth. Despite Tyler and Wil calling in sick, work was off to a good start.

An hour into the shift coal rolled its way out the mine and Digger was into his second cut. Ready to do his job and make the way forward safe for everyone, Billy drove the roofbolter from controls at the back while his partner Sam guided from the front. Two young guys who'd been hired barely a month ago lugged the continuous miner's electrical cable by hand, making sure it didn't get crimped against a wall or dragged under the machine's treads. They looked to be doing a good job, but suddenly the miner's lights went dark and it ground to a stop. As Ash looked around to see what went wrong, he noted the conveyer belt wasn't rolling and the ever-present hum of distant ventilator fans was gone too.

They'd lost total power.

Ash duck-walked to a phone loosely secured to a nearby wall and picked up the handset to call their man outside the mine. "Chester? We've lost power! What's going on out there?"

The phone's earpiece spat out a blast of noise that made Ash's teeth ache. Through the squealing static he thought he heard the outside man say, "This rain... Crazy! Like...end times! ... check- ... right back!" Mercifully the noise cut out as Chester hung up.

Ash glanced over at the scoop operator sitting idle a few yards away. "Dean, head out there and see what's going on."

Dean nodded and backed down the tunnel, his headlights chasing after him. Once he was turned, the darkness of the mine crept in closer.

As the men stood around waiting to hear news, Ash looked at his lunch pail and wondered if it was too early to eat. He wasn't hungry, but if the generator was having a problem their schedule was about to get screwed, and who knew when they'd be able to stop and eat. He told the men to start their lunch break early. Low cheers tumbled weakly through the mine.

Several minutes later the phone rang, the sudden sound of it nearly driving Ash's heart from his chest. When he had the handset to his ear he heard Chester yelling over the storm. "Boss? You there?"

"I'm here, Chester. What's goin' on?"

Rain and wind squealed from the earpiece like a hurricane. "Hell if I know! The genny looks fine, so I'm gonna need to open her up and take a deeper look! Can you send somebody to help?"

Ash looked at the phone like it was an alien artifact dug out of the ground. When he glanced down he noticed a thin stream of rainwater trickling past his feet. "What? I already sent Dean up there. Ain't he with you?"

"Dean?"

"Yeah, Dean. He ain't there yet?"

"No."

"He should be. Go check the entrance. We're gettin' some water down here, so maybe the scooper's wheels got stuck in some wet grit."

"Okay, boss. Be right back."

Standing around waiting was not one of Ash's strong suits, but at that moment it was all he could do. The men sat together, eating and chatting in soft voices. Some made jokes, but the laughter that followed sounded hollow. Ash opened his mouth to offer a few reassuring words for his crew, but the phone rang again, interrupting him.

"Boss! There ain't no sign of Dean! I looked as far into the mine as I could, but I don't see him or the scooper! He must've got turned around somewhere!"

Ash didn't believe that for a second. Between the scooper and the mine cart, Dean knew his way through the mountain like a rabbit knew its own warren. But, if he wasn't lost, then where was he?

"All right," Ash said. "Get back to the genny. I'll send a couple more guys out to help. Hopefully they'll find Dean along the way, and then y'all can get this problem sorted out."

A squall of noise blasted from the handset. "Sounds like a plan, boss!"

Ash hung up and turned to the two young cable carriers. "Either of you know how to operate a mine cart?"

Both boyish faces nodded.

"Like drivin' a go-cart, sir," said Dale, a blond with a too-easy smile The lanky brunette next to him was Ricky.

Ash wished his confidence level was higher. "Well, head on out then to help Chester. When you see Dean, pick him up too. Think you two can manage that?"

Dale and Ricky nodded like dashboard bobble-heads.

"Then get going. You help Chester get that genny running in the next thirty minutes, and I'll buy you both a pizza when we get out of here."

Needing no more encouragement than that, the two kids bumped fists and walked to the mine cart. The battery powered engine sounded like a cat getting kicked off the back porch as they spun the wheels and took off.

"Okay, y'all," Ash said to the rest of his men. "Hopefully we'll get this fixed up shortly."

The night shift crew nodded over their meals. Out of habit, Ash did a quick head count. When he came up one short, he blinked. Scanning through the gritty faces wasn't easy, so it took a moment to see who wasn't there. "Billy, where's Sam?"

The roofbolter sat on the ground and chomped into a sandwich. The bread appeared gleaming white compared to his blackened fingers. After gulping down a big swallow of sliced ham, he shrugged his shoulders. "I think he went to take a piss."

There wasn't anything unusual about that, but a small chip of ice dropped into Ash's stomach.

"Wasn't that like six minutes ago?" Digger asked over the lip of his thermos.

Billy looked at the miner operator, and then at Ash. "I guess. I didn't think about it. Sorry, boss."

"Don't be sorry, be fuckin' smart." Ash suddenly had the urge to grab the man and choke him to death. Instead he tilted his head up and called into the darkness. "Sam? Where you at? You better not be taking a shit!" His words echoed through the lengthy system of coal cuts, the sound reflecting at odd times and strange pitches. No other noise came back but the dwindling whine of the mine cart. When several seconds went by without an answer, Ash pointed a thick finger at Billy. "All right, numbnuts, he's your buddy, so go find him."

"What?" Billy's eyes went wide and round. "But—"

The earth suddenly rumbled and a roar filled the mine with horrendous noise. Rocks ground together, metal squealed, and beneath that the faint high-pitched warble of human throats screaming in agony. Coal dust billowed toward the miners like a hellish fog from the direction the cart had gone.

Ash took off in a stooped run. "Come on!"

The men ran with him, their heavy breathing loud in the tunnel. Half a dozen beams of light bounced crazily off the tunnel walls, jittering so much they were nearly useless. A minute later red and white reflective tape flashed ahead of them.

"Hurry!" Ash pumped his arms and legs as fast as he could. He barely had enough breath in him to shout. By the time he made it to the cart he felt ready to pass out.

A massive slab of shale smothered the mine cart, its orange paint and crumpled metal frame barely recognizable under dust and loose bits of rock. It had fared much better than the two men in it, however. One body lay half out like he'd tried throwing himself out of the way, his face beaten to an unrecognizable bloody pulp. All Ash could see of the other was a purple-shaded hand peeking out from the left side of the cart. He rushed to the rock and started lifting.

I think that's Dale, he thought as his helmet light swept across exposed dirty blond hair. He couldn't remember which kid had sat on which side of the cart, but Dale's hardhat – while doing nothing to save his face from being mangled – had protected his skull enough to make identifying him possible.

"Hurry!" Digger shouted as he leapt in next to Ash. "I think this un's still alive!"

Ash's arms and legs strained to move the block of shale, but his eyes never left Dale's ruined face. Deep cuts ran down his forehead and cheeks, and blood dribbled off his chin in thick drops. His left eye was destroyed, leaving the socket behind it a vacant dark red hole, but his other eye seemed okay as it moved in small, jittery motions. A deep gouge tore through the soft tissue of his nose, flaying open his left nostril like a butterfly shrimp. Below it his lips were battered strips of flesh that couldn't hide his shattered teeth and bloody gums. Weak sound bubbled from his throat.

Every available fiber of muscle was put against the shale slab, every hand and shoulder. The mine filled with grunts. The men knew it could have easily been them under that shale, dead or dying, and if it had they'd want their friends and coworkers to do all they could to save them. So they did, grunting and crying and cursing all the while. But, try as they did, the rock didn't move an inch. It easily weighed a thousand pounds. To save Dale's life they needed help.

"I'll be right back." Ash turned and ran back to the phone.

His helmet light swept the darkness in crazy swings as his tired legs pumped, lighting the dark yet revealing nothing. As he neared a turn, his light touched a pair of brown work boots peeking from a corner. The uneven wall hid who wore them. Panicked that someone else might be hurt, Ash scrambled toward the boots. When he rounded the turn he saw Sam standing in the dark. His face was calm, his eyes still and unblinking.

"Sam!" A wave of relief washed over Ash. "Thank God!

Come on, we need your help!"

Sam didn't move, didn't say a word. All he did was stare.

"Did you hear me? We've got people hurt over here, so snap out of it and let's go!"

But Sam didn't snap out of it, or move, or speak. His eyes were immovable as they bored into Ash. The bolter didn't seem hurt, he wasn't bleeding or bruised, but his skin – where it could be seen past clothing and coal dust – was porcelain white, while his lips and the skin beneath his eyes was dark, as though cave shadows had settled on his face and refused to leave. And his eyes, which Ash could have sworn were blue, seemed as black as the mine around them. He looked sick, cold, almost…drowned. Gooseflesh broke out on Ash's arms and back.

"Sam, talk to me." He took a small step forward.

Sam moved backward, the motion so smooth it seemed as if his feet didn't move. Then Sam's lips parted, the graying bits of flesh forming words Ash instinctively knew he didn't want to hear. "I've seen it, Ash. I've seen the heart of the mountain in my dreams. It's so beautiful."

Pain lanced through the center of Ash's head, making him wince. He suddenly felt loose, untethered. Nothing made sense. Death lay behind him, and ahead of him lurked something… other. His thoughts were hard to control, keep order of. Desperate to feel something real, he curled up his right hand and punched the stone wall nearby. The pain was intense but clarifying.

"Sam, I don't know what's going on, but we're getting out of here. When the sun comes up we'll get this mess sorted."

Instead of doing as he was told, Sam smiled, his steely lips bowing in a way that made Ash nauseous. "No more." Sam glided backward into the darkness as smoothly as fog drifting from a lake to blanket the shore in wet silence. "No more sun for us, Ash. Only shadows…forever."

A new jolt of pain hit Ash's head, striking through his forehead like a spike. He clenched his teeth and howled, but the sound was lost as the mine trembled under the falling of more stone.

The miners behind Ash screamed, the mountain screamed, and Ash couldn't tell one from the other as dark rock tumbled from the ceiling to pound the cave floor. He saw movement everywhere, legs and arms and rock, dust washing over everything like nuclear fallout. Ash ducked his head and ran without knowing where he was going, his hardhat light useless in the dusty chaos. He was blind, confused, chasing ghosts.

"Stop running." Sam's whisper rang loudly in Ash's head. "The Ancient awakens."

Ash spun around and swung his hands out to push Sam away, but no one was there, and he tripped over his own stumbling feet. His elbows crashed into the ground.

"Digger!" he yelled. "You out there? Digger! Billy! Anyone!"

The only replies were distant screams. As he turned down one cut section of mountain and then another, the sound of roaring changed. It was hard to tell at first, as it all seemed like one long grinding noise, but after a few seconds he heard a mechanical sound beneath it.

The miner, he thought. *The continuous miner's on! We have power!*

Latching onto that thought like a man reaching for a branch as he careened down a raging river, Ash stopped to gauge where he was. With practiced ears he turned left and right, noted a slight change in the noise to his right, and ran that direction. Shadows pulled at him as he ran, inky fingers grasping for his clothes, his arms, his legs. His light crossed from rocky wall to floor to ceiling, but the center of his vision was dark, a hole that had no end. All he could do was run.

Eventually lights appeared in the far distance. They were dim, like the first stars at dusk, but to Ash they were the most beautiful things he'd ever seen, and with that wonderful sight came the relief of the cave finally seeming to settle. As he got closer he saw they were the safety lights on the back of the continuous miner. At the front of it was the rolling drum of metal teeth as it churned deeper into the mountain. In confusion Ash looked around to see how or why the metal beast was operating, and as his hardhat light swept to the right what he found hit him like a punch to the gut, dropping him to his knees.

Bodies littered the ground like empty fast food containers. Some were crushed by rocks, their heads reduced to pulp or their chests caved in so savagely internal organs erupted from their mouths. Others looked normal save for their pale skin and vacant stares. The worst of it was Digger. The miner operator sat on the floor, his legs crossed and his hands on the continuous miner's control panel sitting in his lap. He faced away from Ash, and Ash was glad for that. He didn't want to see the miner. The Bluestone Mine was filled with the stench of the dead, and shadows crept over it all, even him.

The continuous miner suddenly emitted a horrific sound. In it he heard dogs barking, rotted trees crashing in deep woods, glaciers cracking in half, meteors screaming to the ground. It was a noise like the end of the world. The digging drum rolled and rolled until the mountain in front of it gave way beneath a rushing wave of water as dark as the shadows around it.

His mind overloaded by pain and terror, Ash couldn't move as the water reached for him with wet, hungry fingers. Seconds later the wave crashed into him like a wrecking ball, and his body pounded against the mine's walls, scraped against the floor and ceiling. His bones shattered and his flesh tore, and through it all he screamed. When he had no more breath left, the mountain water rushed down his throat, filling his lungs, his throat, his stomach. The darkness was within him and without. Death laid cold fingers on his chest. But, before his heart could stop beating, he heard a terrible voice whispering in his mind, telling him secrets older than time, and as dreams of flame and flood filled his head, his body became something new, something else.

In the darkness of the water he smiled and stared with dark eyes into the heart of the mountain.

CHAPTER ONE

PLEASE COME HOME. IM SCARED.

Kyle looked down at the text message on his phone for the fifth time in an hour as he drove the rented Jeep Wrangler north on Highway 856. A sign reading STILLWATER - 5 MILES flashed by on the right in a green rectangular smear as rain clawed jagged streaks across the windshield. Six years ago he'd put that sign in his rearview mirror with a promise that he'd never look at it again, and now here he was, going back on his word. His sister Taylor was the only person who could make him return to the one place he swore he'd never come back to.

The text message was only the latest in a month-long string of messages from his little sister about their dad. Those who lived in the shadows of the Appalachians were a hard people, and those who made their livelihood in the cramped darkness of the coal mines were harder still, but Gus Mason was a hard man even by those standards. A young Kyle had often watched his dad wash away a long day down in the dark with a six-pack of Pabst Blue Ribbon, his eyes glued to the blurry images on their television while the rest of the world faded away. A lot of abused children would have seen Gus's apathy as a blessing, but Kyle didn't. He knew, deep down in his heart, that his dad didn't love him or his sister, probably didn't even love his wife, and the sting of that apathy hurt as much as a slap to the face. If the emails and text message were right and their dad had become physical, then the situation could quickly become more serious than what Taylor had told him about.

Since Kyle's Army unit was Stateside and not due to head back to the sand for months yet, taking some annual leave had been as simple as filling out paperwork and handing it to his platoon's First Sergeant. Two plane rides and a car rental later, here he was, driving back to Stillwater, West Virginia, wishing like hell he wasn't. Fat gray clouds overhead pissed on the world, mirroring his mood.

Ahead of him a car sat parked on the side of the road with its hazard lights flashing. It was the first vehicle he'd seen for miles – either coming or going – so the sudden appearance of the broken down car was surprising. Kyle wasn't sure what sort of tools the rented Jeep came with, but he had his two hands, and was always willing to help if needed. He lifted his foot off the gas pedal and let the vehicle coast to a stop.

Seen up close, he wasn't sure where to even start figuring out what might be wrong. The Honda Civic looked like it was twenty hard and weary years old, the red paint faded and chipped where it wasn't freckled with Bondo spots. The balding tires were small enough to dunk in a cup of coffee, but as he looked the car over he noticed that the front passenger side was dipped, indicating a flat tire. It was a good thing he'd come along, because if there wasn't a spare in that clunker's trunk, the walk to anywhere able to help was a long one, especially in the rain.

In the driver's seat sat a woman with a cell phone up to her left ear and her free hand pummeling the steering wheel. Whoever was on the other end of the call was getting a scorching earful. She was pretty, from what little he could see of her face, with skin a creamy coffee color and hair a riot of black curls that fell to the shoulders of a silky black blouse. When she turned and noticed his parked Jeep, strikingly blue eyes lit up in surprise.

"Need any help?" He gave a friendly wave and exaggerated his pronunciation so that she could tell what he was saying.

The skin between her eyes bunching together as her upper lip twitched. He thought she was mad at him for having the gall to stop and attempt to be helpful, but she quickly turned her head and hit the steering wheel again as she pulled the phone around so that she could yell directly into the mouthpiece. Once she was done speaking her shoulders sagged and her eyes closed. When she reopened them a moment later, she turned back to Kyle and waved him forward repeatedly while shaking her head hard enough to send her curls bouncing.

Kyle paused, the Good Samaritan in him unwilling to leave a stranded woman on the side of the road, but she was a big girl, and if she didn't want his help, he wasn't going to push it on her. It was the Twenty-First Century, after all. He waved back and nodded, then slipped the Jeep into DRIVE and rolled away. He had enough problems without carrying other peoples' burdens. In a few miles he'd be back in Stillwater, and soon after that he'd be knocking on his parents' door. He wasn't looking forward to any of it, so the sooner he got there and sorted the situation out, the sooner he could put the town behind him once and for all.

"An hour?" Maya fumed. "To come out and change a flat tire? Are you fucking kidding me?"

Her left hand ached from the tight grip she held on her cell phone, and the heel of her right palm was red from repeatedly hitting her car's steering wheel. If she'd had a neck in front of her she'd have strangled it with a smile, especially the neck of the idiot on the other end of the phone.

From the corner of her left eye Maya noticed headlights come to a stop next to her window. She turned her head hoping it was the insurance company's courtesy truck pulling up in spite of what the agent just said, but it wasn't. Instead she saw a guy sitting in spiffy looking Jeep waving at her and talking like she could hear him. Part of her was glad that someone was nice enough to stop and offer help, but a larger part – despite being nearly twenty-four years old – remembered all the warnings her parents had given her about strange men, even the friendly looking ones.

"There's no need for that kind of language, ma'am." The voice's prissy tone drove into her ear like a long, rusty nail. "I'm only trying to be of assistance."

A sharp laugh shot out of Maya's mouth. "Yeah, right. My insurance company telling me I have to wait an hour to get someone out to help me isn't exactly what I'd call *assistance*."

"I understand your frustration, ma'am." The customer

service agent's placating tones made her want to scream. "The closest courtesy truck to you is in Welch, but at the moment they're helping another customer, so the best estimate I have of how quickly they can get to you is an hour. You might get lucky and get help sooner, but I'd rather not underestimate the time and have you angry even more."

Maya's jaw muscles jumped as she pressed her molars together. "Trust me, I don't think it's possible for me to be more angry than I am right now."

A distant sigh fluttered against her ear like a moth batting its wings in a jar. "I understand, ma'am. Let me see if our service technician thinks he can hurry along to you a bit faster. Please hold."

Maya took the phone in both hands like it was a lifeline being pulled away from her. "No, please don't put me on ho—"

A loud click followed by soft jazz cut her off. She closed her eyes and wondered what the universe had against her. Whatever she'd done in a past life, she was sorry as all hell for it.

When she reopened her eyes, the Jeep was still beside her, and the guy driving it looked at her like a dog eager to please. His dirty blond hair and blue eyes set off a handsome face, and to her surprise she noticed a barely perceptible aura the color of sun-dappled water glittering against his skin. It was a good sign. Most people didn't have auras strong enough to see, and if they did they were usually grim and dark. In any other situation she would have been tempted to roll down her window and flirt. Flirting, though, was the last thing on her mind. All her energies were focused on getting her insurance company to provide a service she paid them for; paid – she might add – just so she could avoid dicey situations like this. So, hoping he understood her and didn't take offense, she waved him off and pointed in the direction they were both headed. He didn't leave immediately, so she waved faster until he eventually got the hint and drove on. As taillights pulled away she hoped she hadn't made a huge mistake.

"All right, I think I have good news for you." The

customer service broke through a sleepy rendition of "Dream A Little Dream Of Me." "Our service technician informed me that he has completed his job in Welch and will be on his way to you shortly. He should be at your location in thirty minutes."

Maya's mother once told her that she should be grateful for favors, even the small ones, so she resisted the impulse to curse and bang on the steering wheel again. "Alright, if that's the best you can do. It's not like I have much choice."

"Very well then. Before we disconnect, I'd like to ask you a few questions about the level of service I've provi—"

Maya hung up before he could finish. She'd gotten all she could out of him, and hearing him drone on was something she refused to do. With the call over, she plugged her phone into the car charger and set it down in a cup holder to cool off. She was half surprised it wasn't crushed. She then turned on the car radio and settled into her seat to wait out the minutes until help arrived. As she thought about the service tech, her mind went to the flat tire, then went to the spare tire hidden away in the hatchback, then to the pile of equipment sitting on top of it.

"What did I do to deserve this?" she asked the empty air before reaching for the latch that unlocked the hatchback. The last thing she needed was some mechanic seeing her gear and asking what it was for. She didn't like talking about her job, especially with strangers, so if she wanted to avoid an awkward conversation she knew she'd have to move all of the cameras, laptop, night vision goggles, and EM meters to the back seat. That meant getting out into the rain and walking around in sandals that weren't meant for muddy potholes. Hoping to avoid that had been half the reason she'd called for help in the first place. Not knowing the first thing about changing a tire was the other half.

Knowing that she had no other alternative, Maya sighed, grit her teeth together, and opened her car door. The only bright spot in that dismal moment was knowing that somewhere up above her father was chuckling his ghostly ass off.

"Real funny, Dad." She put her feet through the door and stood up. "Real damn funny."

As the last word passed her lips, the drizzle of rain turned into a downpour. The noise it made hitting the roof of her car sounded oddly like laughter.

CHAPTER TWO

Stillwater looked worse than Kyle remembered, an aging coma patient waiting for someone to come along and pull the plug. It hadn't always been that way, though. To hear the old timers tell it, Stillwater had once been a boomtown riding a coal train to fortune and glory. Once prospectors saw how rich the area was with coal, they built a dam across Stillwater Creek to create a water reservoir, and erected the town of Stillwater on the other side. In those early days, a lot of coal was dug and a lot of money was made, though those who did the digging never seemed to get a fair amount of the riches made from their sweat and broken backs.

Eventually, though, the veins of coal died out, and the town died out with them. In West Virginia, this was nothing new. The state is riddled with empty towns populated by ghosts and the faint oily scent of coal. Those who could afford to pack up and move did so. Those who couldn't, like his family, turned to the mines that were still operating in the surrounding counties. It made for long drives, but folks did what they had to do.

Kyle's folks had assumed he would work in the mines when he graduated, slogging away in the dark with his dad. Kyle had assumed the same thing until the day his father came home early with a back so hurt tears poured down his face. It was the first time he'd seen his dad cry. There'd been a lot of self-pity in those tears, and more than a little anger and resentment.

Rita Mason was the glue that held the family together, a fair woman who deserved better but didn't have the good sense to know it. Kyle loved her, but he hated her too. She'd lived under the same roof, felt the same apathy and neglect, but instead of taking her children and striking out for a better life – and, really, anything would have been better than living with Gus Mason — she lowered her chin and took it. Her children took it too.

Taylor had been the one shining light in their house. Eight years younger than Kyle, she'd been light and happy and joyful, a dandelion floating on her own breeze. Kyle had done all he could to care for her, gave her the love she needed, bought her what toys and trinkets he could afford. She was the only reason he'd considered staying in Stillwater. In the end, it hadn't been enough. The memory of his father, broken and hurt and miserable, was just too powerful. What made leaving bearable was knowing that she was strong, like him, and she'd be able to deal with their father until her own moment of freedom came. But now something felt different. Their father had changed, and he wanted to find out why.

Kyle turned down one street after another, driving mostly on muscle memory, until he eventually crossed onto King Drive His parents' house lay two driveways down on the left. He'd driven the hard packed dirt road more times than he cared to think about, but it felt different now. The shadows under carports and door eves seemed darker, and wind pushed against the Jeep like it was warning him away.

The parking apron in front of his parents' house was empty. That wasn't unusual. They only owned one vehicle, and his dad needed it to drive back and forth to work. Empty or not, he didn't feel right pulling onto the apron, so Kyle stopped on the street. Parking on the apron felt too...familiar.

When the Jeep stopped, he slipped it into PARK, turned off the engine, and allowed himself one solitary sigh to brace himself before he opened the door. When his feet hit the walkway leading to the front door, he felt like gongs should have sounded. He almost felt the vibrations in his feet, the chipped and dirty concrete path trying to reject him before he could take another step.

"You don't have to like it any more than I do," he told the walkway, then continued on. The rain lightened, but that didn't make his journey any easier. When he finally arrived at the front door, he felt like he'd walked a mile. That was nothing to the weight that pressed down on him as he raised his right hand and rang the doorbell.

The woman who opened the door wasn't his mother. She had the same vague shape, the same penciled-on eyebrows and beauty mark above the right side of her frowning mouth, but it wasn't her. Rita Mason was a smiler, a woman who carried sunshine on her face even when the darkest clouds gathered. The woman at the door was pallid and stooped, while his mom had been a proud woman, maybe too proud, who always stood straight and square shouldered. The woman standing behind the screen door looked something like what he remembered, but with none of the life, the light. This wasn't the mother he'd driven away from six years ago, and her first words confirmed it.

"Well hell, look what the rain washed in. What do you want?"

The breath Kyle hadn't realized he'd held whooshed out of him. "Wow. Love you too, Mom."

Instead of replying, she dug around in the pockets of her apron, the one she always wore when she cleaned house, and dragged out a pack of Royal Flush cigarettes and a yellow plastic lighter. Kyle felt another punch hit his middle. His dad had been a smoker since before Kyle was born, but his mom had never touched them, not once. Yet here she was, her thin fingers pulling out a smoke and jamming it between her pale lips like she'd done it all her life. The lighter took a few flicks before a flame caught and turned the end of the cigarette bright red. She blew a few puffs of smoke from the left side of her closed lips and pocketed the lighter. Kyle's stomach turned, and not just because of the cigarette's stench.

"When did you start smoking?"

"About ten minutes after you drove off," she replied without missing a beat.

He felt like a boxer getting worked across the ribcage. "So you smoking is my fault?"

"You can take the blame, or you can leave it on the porch." She took the cigarette from her lips and filling the air between them with a foul blue-gray cloud. "Don't much matter to me either way."

The sense of disconnection Kyle felt as he drove into town was nothing compared to what he felt standing before the woman who had once patched up his skinned knees and took all the pain away with a wink and a kiss. Now was just a shadow in the darkness of the doorway. His childhood suddenly seemed like a dream of someone else's life.

"I'm not here to fight." He tucked his hands into his pants pockets. "Can I come in?"

His mother stared at him, her eyes still and unblinking for several long seconds, but then she shrugged, turned from the door, and shuffled away. "Suit yourself."

The screen door opened with a rusty grown, and he held it as it closed behind him so that the spring connecting the door to the doorframe didn't slam it shut. The inside of the house was dark and smelled musty. There were a few new pictures here and there on the walls – all of them of Taylor – and a decoration or two he didn't recall being there, but all in all the hallway leading away from the front door looked more or less the way he remembered, as did the small square living room. It was the same, yet like his mother and the rest of the town, it wasn't. Everything, from the wobbly ceiling fan to the brown shag carpeting, seemed dusted in a thin layer of grim. Wide dark stains soiled the prehistoric couch cushions like bruises.

"Don't bother looking in your old room." His mom flopped down on the left side of the couch. It was the closest place to sit next to his dad's worn out green recliner. "Your dad stores all his crap in there now."

Between the two pieces of furniture stood an end table, on which sat a glass of tea and two ashtrays, each one spilling over with crinkled butts. He noticed the tea didn't have any ice in it, and the glass wasn't sweating. *First the smoking, and now lukewarm tea. This has to be a pod person*, he thought with a sad chuckle. *Has to be.*

"I didn't come to see my room." He considered taking a seat on the other end of the couch, but the dark stain on the cushion kept him on his feet. "I came to talk to Dad. Where is he? It's after five. He get a second job or something?"

His mother snorted harshly. "Yeah, right. He's probably still at the mine. They got him workin' later and later every day. He goes in at the same time he's always done, but every night I stand around wondering when he'll finally show. I better see a bump in his paycheck, or there'll be hell to pay, I tell ya that right now."

"Working late?" Mine work was nothing if not predictable, at least as far as the hours went. But if it wasn't work, what could it be? Alternatives were limited, and none of them good. "You don't think he'd...?" He couldn't bear to finish the question.

"What, cheat?" His mother's graying lips broke into a sneer. "Your daddy ain't exactly a man of great passion. He sure as hell ain't gonna be out there chasing around what I can barely give away."

Bile burned Kyle's throat at hearing his mother talk about their sex life. It was another sign of how much she'd changed since he left. The woman he'd known wouldn't have said *shit* if she'd had a mouth full of it.

"Wow, Mom, that's way more than I needed to know."

She puffed on her cigarette. "You asked."

"Fine. Is Taylor here then?"

He tried to ask the question as nonchalantly as he could, but the sentence had barely left his lips before his mother squinted her eyes and stared into the back of his head, her hands as still as an ice sculpture with the cigarette halfway between the ashtray and her mouth. Like a dog sniffing out rats, she'd clued to his intentions directly.

"So that's it." She stamped out the cigarette in the ashtray and rose from the couch. "What, did she call you? Say that life here was gettin' too hard? That we wasn't lettin' her go out there and sin herself straight to hell? Is that it? 'Cause if it is, you can just climb back into that shiny Jeep you got out there and get the hell outta here. She may be a dyke, but she's *still* my daughter, and if anyone is gonna make her right with the Lord, it's gonna be *me*."

Feeling like a roundhouse punch socked him straight in the jaw, Kyle staggered back a step and shook his head.

"Dyke? What are you talking about?"

A dark light lit up his mother's eyes, and the smile spreading across her face disturbed him. "Oh, she didn't tell you? And here I thought you two was so tight, just thick as thieves. Surprise, surprise."

The sickness that rolled around in Kyle's stomach started burning, and the anger felt better, felt easier, so he latched onto it for strength. "Maybe you could stop being a bitch for two seconds and tell me what the hell is going on."

His mother either didn't understand what he'd said, or it didn't bother her, because she kept on smiling that sick smile. "Your sister's a dyke, son. A lesbo, a...what do they call it...carpetmuncher. She's gay as a rainbow, and apparently she don't care who knows it, 'cept you maybe. Funny about that."

"Just shut the fuck up." Kyle shook his head and held up his hands. He'd had enough, and he wasn't going to listen to one more second of his mother's haranguing. "Taylor hasn't said a word to me about being gay, but even if she is, so what? She's still my sister, and I'm not going to have you talk that way about her."

"Oh, now that's funny." His mom laughed and put her hands on her hips. "I'd have thought a big bad Army boy like you would be more horrified than we were. Don't they keep faggots out of the military, condition all you boys to kill 'em on sight or somethin'?"

Kyle snorted and rolled his eyes. "No."

"Well hell, then we should probably just roll out the welcome mat for those commie chinks then." His mother pulled out another cigarette and lit it. "Or, is that why you joined up? You and your sister more alike than we thought?"

The fire in Kyle's stomach exploded, and he took two thunderous steps toward his mother. Instead of cowering or showing fear, she laughed, her pallid face like a gargoyle's. That stopped him in his tracks. She looked so small and petty to him, so unlike the woman he remembered, and it sickened him to see what had been lost.

"Mom, I don't know what happened to you. If it was me leaving that turned you into this, then I'm really sorry. But whatever the fuck is going on, the only thing I care about is seeing how Taylor is. Either you tell me, right now, or I'll go drive around until I find her. Cut the shit and try being a decent human being for a minute, if that's possible."

For a fleeting moment Kyle saw pain and a hint of the person she'd once been filter through his mother's eyes. It was there, like a break in the clouds, but vanished just as quickly, and in her darkness she puffed on her cigarette and tucked her left arm under her apron covered breasts.

"Hell fire, I sent her over to Cubby's to get a carton of cigarettes. Happy now?"

Cubby's Convenience Store was a couple miles away on the other end of King Street. Not the cleanest place in the world, but back in the day it'd had a Street Fighter cabinet in it, and he'd dropped more than his fair share of allowance into its mechanical guts. The idea that his mother had sent a minor over there to get cigarettes, though, was nearly enough to make him blow his top.

"What the fuck were you thinking? She's not eighteen yet! They won't sell her shit. They might even call the cops and have you arrested for having her try. Not that that sounds like a bad thing."

His mother rolled her eyes. "She's been gettin' us smokes for years now, so you can stop with the drama. 'Sides, Cubby's son Beau runs the register now after work, and he's sweet on her, so he cuts her a few extra packs. Stupid sombitch thinks she wants what he's got." She laughed until it turned into coughs and her face turned red as she got control of herself again. "That dumb nut didn't roll far from the tree, let me tell you."

Knowing there wasn't any further reason to be there, Kyle shook his head and turned to leave. Over his shoulder he said, "Tell Taylor I'll be by later to see her."

He opened the front door with a hard twist and a yank, then threw the screen door wide open. His mother followed him down the hallway, and he hoped the screen door would slam in her face. He half turned as he stepped off the small concrete porch, then frowned as his mother caught the door.

"Don't bother." She waved the cigarette around, leaving zig-zagging smoke trails in the air. "She may be your sister, but I'm her mother, and I say what goes on so far as she's concerned. You been out of our lives for six years, and we don't need you back in it, so get gone. We won't open our door to you again."

Kyle opened his mouth to tell her what he thought of that bullshit, but the rattling of bike tires over cracked asphalt caught his attention. When he turned toward the sound he saw a familiar young woman rolling toward him on a bike too small for her, a carton of cigarettes in the front basket and a plastic bottle of soda in her left hand.

"Oh my god!" Taylor coasted into the yard. "Kyle? Is that you?"

Just as his mother was someone he barely recognized, so was his sister, but with Taylor it was completely different. He'd left a chubby little girl behind, her hair usually a rat's nest of curls and her hands always covered in dirt from playing outside, but the young lady she'd grown into was nothing like that. Even seated on the bike he could tell she was nearly as tall as he was, and a bit too thin. Her reddish blond hair was still curly, but she'd learned how to wear it so that it framed her round, pretty face. Gone were the Osh Kosh B'Gosh overalls, and instead she wore faded jeans that rode too low on her hips and a t-shirt with a picture of Lady Gaga covering the front of it. Her hands were long-fingered, and her dirty nails were replaced by alternating pink and black polish. She was as precious to look at as a baby bug, but the best part was her eyes. They were clear and blue and clean, everything their mother's weren't. She still had light in her, still had life. It was a relief.

"Hey, baby sister." He opened his arms.

Taylor stopped the bike five feet from him, jumped off it, and ran into his hug. When he held her, he felt some of the darkness of Stillwater lift from him. She smelled wonderfully of vanilla and sweat. A bit of his heart broke when they eventually parted, but it healed again when he saw her smiling up at him.

"You came." A wry smirk curved her lips. "You really came. That's awesome."

Behind her Kyle saw their mother stomp across the yard and bend over the front of the ditched bike. When she stood back up she had a carton and several loose packs of cigarettes in her hands.

"Enjoy this little family reunion, 'cause it's gonna be the last one you get for awhile. Kyle was just leavin'."

Panic blossomed in Taylor's eyes, and she clutched her bottled cola tightly in her hands. "What? But...but you just got here. I—"

"You've got homework that needs doin'." Their mother broke in. "That's what you got. And then you got school tomorrow, and then more homework, and I know there's plenty you need to tend to around the house. You ain't got time for your brother or nothin' else. Now get inside and get to studyin'."

Taylor barely opened her mouth before her mother grabbed her by the arm and pulled her toward the front door. Kyle was furious, but there was little he could do. He wasn't her guardian or had any legal right to stop them. Instead he caught Taylor's attention and held his hand up to his head in a I'll-call-you-later gesture and then crossed his heart when their mother turned away to open the screen door. Taylor nodded as her mother pushed her inside.

"And I'll only say this one more time." His mother stood in the doorway, her apron heaving from her sudden exertions. "Leave. You're not wanted here. The town doesn't want you!"

Her feelings made perfectly clear, she stepped into the house and slammed the front door closed. The screen door clattered in the doorframe.

Part of Kyle wanted to laugh at her strange pronouncement – *The town doesn't want me?* – but it was crushed beneath the part that wanted to cry over how wrong everything had turned out. He'd left Stillwater because he wanted a better future than what the mines had in store for him, thinking that whatever ills their father's apathy delivered to Taylor would be made up by their mother's love. Instead, both of his parents had spiraled out of control, and Taylor had been left to find a way to survive them both. Kyle felt torn to his soul, and he hated what his selfishness had wrought. The only thing he could do now was make right what little he could, and if that meant petitioning the courts for Taylor's custody, he'd do it. Oh yes he would.

This isn't over by a damn sight, he thought.

Since he had nothing else to do at the moment, Kyle walked to the Jeep and started it up. If he was going to be in Stillwater for a while, he needed a place to stay. Since Stillwater only had one motel, the choice of where to go was fairly easy. He hit the gas and steered toward Tazwell Street and the Smoky Mountain Motel.

CHAPTER THREE

As Maya crested a hill overlooking Stillwater, she pulled over to the side of the road, making sure she didn't run over any glass or sharp pieces of metal. Below her, Stillwater looked like a decaying fish in a green sea of basswood and white ash trees. Along the western edge of the town ran a narrow river that once upon a time – according to everything she'd read before starting this little adventure – had been much wider, with half the town sitting where it used to flow. That had been before the dam was built, which she could just barely see several miles north of town. Beyond the dam lay the Stillwater Reservoir surrounded by deep forest that blanketed mountain after mountain for as far as the eye could see. It was a breathtaking sight, even with the heavily overcast sky and spattering of rain.

Hidden somewhere in those mountains, though, concealed behind the beauty of trees and waters, was a secret. Even if weeks of internet searching and phone calls hadn't told her things were wrong in Stillwater, being this close to the town she felt the malevolence of it in her bones. It felt like a song played out of tune, the hum of it vibrating inside her, making her sick to her stomach. Something was very much wrong with this town, and she planned on finding out just what it was. Discovering secrets was her mission; not just for Stillwater, but her life.

Now that she had a basic lay of the land she put the car back in DRIVE and continued north. The closer she got to town, the more she sensed the darkness beneath it. Far away it sounded like a distant hum, but quickly it became more than that, more than she'd ever experienced before. She could practically smell it, a sickly sour scent that made her think of animal carcasses covered in fungus. After a few minutes the smell was nearly forgotten, as a bad scent often was when a person smelled it long enough, but the hum in her bones remained.

Rain turned the town into a ruined painting in her windshield as she crossed a set of railroad tracks and turned onto Tazwell Street. Before Maya drove too far she parked in front of a closed down store, HURLEY'S HARDWARE barely legible on the cracked sign resting above the storefront, and pulled out a Google Map of the town she'd stuffed in her purse. On it she'd marked places she wanted to visit, among them the library, the town hall, and the cemetery – they were the usual locations a person could get local area information from.

She checked her cell phone – she had one tiny bar of service – and saw it was almost five in the evening. That took the town hall and library off the list since both of them closed at 4PM according to the people she'd spoken with before making the drive to Stillwater. That narrowed her options considerably. But, when you wanted to know the history of a place beyond what you could find online, there were other ways to get it.

Maya looked up from the map to scan the street. A couple blocks down she spied half a dozen rusting vehicles parked in front of a brick building. WOODY'S DINER was painted on the windows in flaking broad strokes. It was just the place she needed.

Finding a parking space wasn't hard, so she slid into the first available spot. Before getting out of the car she reached into the backseat and grabbed a digital recorder. According to its display she had plenty of battery life and enough memory for twenty-six hours of recording. She slipped the device in her purse, careful to make sure it stayed powered on and that the microphone was pointing up, and then opened her car door. The metal squealed sharply, setting her teeth on edge. With her car locked and secured, she drew her purse strap over her shoulder and walked the short length of cracked sidewalk to the diner.

When she opened the diner's door, a cloud of anger and hatred billowed over her like smoke from a burning building. She nearly fell over from it, but she managed to hold herself up long enough to see what had caused it. Inside the diner were eight white people – four split into two booths to the left, and the other four seated at the counter running along the diner's right side. All of them turned to look at her as she stepped over the threshold, and for a fleeting moment she swore their eyes were black empty sockets surrounded by deathly gray faces. To hide her fright she closed her eyes and shook her head. When she reopened them the diner patrons had eyes once again, but their skin had a nauseating pastiness, and the storm cloud of animosity still whirled in the air of the diner. She wasn't entirely sure what caused the negative atmosphere, but she figured she might have an idea about part of it.

Back home in Memphis her red skirt and black blouse would have been perfectly normal, but in Stillwater the skirt's hem being above her knees was probably scandalous, as was the open neck of the blouse and the fair amount of cleavage it showed. Her black sandals were sensible, though, and for that small mercy she was grateful. She figured the small West Virginia town didn't see too many black people. The fact that her father was white probably wouldn't have raised her stock any. Her skin was darker than theirs, and that was all that mattered.

Still, racism aside – though it wasn't ever – that couldn't account for the things she felt clawing at her mind as she walked to the nearby counter and took a seat. The atmosphere was too charged for that, too…she searched for the right word…*imbedded*. Everything was coated with it, like the counter around a cooktop slimy with grease and congealed bacon fat. As her hands settled on the counter she felt darkness in the chipped Formica, sensed it in the vinyl seat beneath her. There was evil in this place, and it was more than human. Much more. She bet if she dug down into the soil she'd find more of it, straight down to the bedrock. The evil in Stillwater was far worse than she'd imagined, and she'd only just arrived.

Maya, what in the hell have you gotten yourself into? she wondered, not for the first time.

The waitress shuffling toward her from behind the counter didn't look like she was the head of the town's welcome wagon. Her bare lips were set in a slanted smirk, and eyes the color of used dishwater peered out at Maya from beneath bottle blond hair, dark roots splitting her scalp like a hatchet wound. She had the same dull tone to her skin as the rest of the people in the diner had. A greasy white apron struggled to cover her gut and heavy, sagging breasts. Frayed jeans rode low on her hips, exposing a roll of fat riddled with stretch marks like a road map of poor choices. The name badge pinned to her chest read DOLORES.

"What do you want?" Dolores didn't bother getting her order pad out.

Maya wasn't sure, all thoughts of eating now gone. Between the horrible vibes and the sullen diner, she didn't imagine she'd eat anything until she was back home. But, she still had a job to do, so she plastered on a smile, checked her bag to make sure the recorder was on, and got on with it. "This place looks amazing, and I'm really hungry. How are your burgers?"

Dolores pursed her lips and snorted. "Like everything else we got – greasy."

Maya's fake grin widened. "That sounds...great."

"I bet," Dolores replied with a smile that stayed far away from her eyes. "You want fries with that?"

Fries were the last thing Maya wanted. She thought of the digital recorder in her purse and wished like hell it was a gun instead. "No, Ma'am, just the burger."

Dolores nodded, the fat in her neck squishing together like a dog's chew toy, then turned to shout at the kitchen. "Dean, order up! One burger!" When that was done she looked back at Maya, and again Maya saw a flash of black eyes leading down to darkness so old it seemed outside of time. Delores ran thick fingers through her oily hair, and as her hand moved across her face, the image vanished. It took every ounce of Maya's courage to not leap up from the chair and run. "That'll be three dollars."

Reaching into her purse blindly, Maya's fingers found her

wallet. The bills were in her hand as quickly as she could get them, and when she put the money on the counter her hands were shaking. Being afraid was bad enough, but to show it mortified her even more.

When the waitress picked the bills off the counter, she used the tips of her chipped nails to do it, then stuffed them in her apron like she was putting away something unseemly. After that she turned and shuffled away, her job done.

The man on Maya's left leaned toward her, his breath a heady mix of tobacco and whiskey. "We don't get many of your kind around here."

Maya leaned away to get clean air, but she put on a smile when she turned toward him. His half-closed eyes floated in the same whiskey coating his breath, and the salty beard circling his mouth was stained brown and yellow beneath his pockmarked nose. His plaid work shirt and jeans were stained with dirt. Maya figured him for a farmer, though he probably had a bottle in his hand more often than a hoe.

"My kind?" Maya pretended she hadn't heard the undercurrent of his words. "You mean out-of-towners?"

The woman on the other side of him snorted with laughter. She was much younger than he was, but she had the same rheumy eyes and unpleasant nose. She was also dressed like him, though a lot more dirt was worn into the cuffs of her shirt and on her knees. "No." The woman barely turned her head Maya's direction. "He meant niggers."

Maya's gasp was inaudible over the laughter that rumbled from the people in the diner. When Maya had been called that word in the past, it was usually said so no one else could hear, or when no one else was around, but these people had no such discretion. She looked from one sallow face to another, hoping she'd find someone as insulted as she was. In the back booth were a couple of teenagers, both of them probably fresh from a long day in school, and their eyes were wide open in shock, but when she looked at them they ducked their heads and tried to disappear. Everyone else, though, stared at her bold as brass. Their open hostility held her spellbound.

"Here's yer burger." Dolores dropped a grease-stained

brown bag on the countertop. The sound of the paper slapping against plastic snapped Maya out of her momentary daze. Dolores snorted again before turning away to wipe down the serving counter behind her. "I made that to go, so you should do that. Now."

Maya's shock at being openly treated like a worthless animal quickly turned into fury mixed with fear. She knew, though, that standing her ground or saying something would only make things worse, so she grabbed her bagged burger, got up, and walked out of the diner with her shoulders straight and her head high. As soon as the door closed behind her, she threw the bag in a nearby garbage can and hurried to her car. The engine barely turned over before she reversed out of the parking space and headed back the way she'd come. Her hands shook so hard that she had to grip the steering wheel extra tight to hold onto it. When Hurley's Hardware slid by on her left, she stopped in front of it again.

"No!" Her voice boomed in the car's interior. "You are not going to let those assholes bother you. You're *not*. You're better than that, better than them. You came here to do a job, and that's exactly what you're going to do. Fuck those small-minded bigots. The only person who runs your life is you, so get it together girl and move on."

She knew she looked stupid sitting in her car talking to herself, but she didn't care. Each word took away some of her fear, until eventually her hands relaxed their death grip. After several cleansing breaths, she squared her shoulders again and picked up the Google Map. She'd told herself she still had work to do, and that was true, so she pushed the diner from her mind as best she could and looked over her options. With the hour being what it was, there really was only one.

Turning the car around, Maya drove past the diner, went down two more blocks, and then turned right. Next to the road was a small brown sign. On it was printed the name of her destination – STILLWATER CEMETERY.

Maya was special. Most parents say that about their kids, but with her it was true. For as long as she could remember she'd heard things no one else heard, saw things most others were blind to – cold spots, groaning walls, strange breezes. For her, weirdness was just a fact of life. So, when she'd visited her first cemetery at the age of twelve, she'd been filled with dread. The dead were already too much a part of her life.

Her father's sister, Teresa, had been married to a Memphis businessman with deep roots in the community, so when she passed away from breast cancer she was buried in Elmwood Cemetery. Maya barely knew her aunt before she died, so the church funeral had bothered her only so far as it had meant a great deal of grief for her dad, whom she loved dearly.

Maya had worried her head would explode when she crossed over the white bridge that led into Elmwood. But, to her amazement, she'd felt nothing. As far as her sixth sense or mind's eye or whatever she had in her was concerned, Elmwood Cemetery was as free a place of supernatural spookery as she could have wanted. Her sigh of relief had been long and satisfying.

Since that day she'd gone to many other cemeteries, some for work and some not, and all of them had been just as free, just as clear. It wasn't until she heard a comedian joke about how having a prison near your town wasn't a bad thing because anyone who broke out wasn't likely to stick around and check out the housing market that she understood why cemeteries were so psychically blank. In all the world, what could be more unappealing to a spirit than a place no one wanted to stay for long? Spirits, both kindly and not, sought out the one thing they didn't have - life.

Standing beneath a ratty umbrella that barely kept the rain off, Maya knew Stillwater Cemetery was no different. The wrought iron text that arched over the entrance gate said it had been established in 1906, and judging from the number of tombstones and grave markers littering the land beyond the tall black fencing she believed it. It was a reaper's garden that had been well tended and fruitfully planted. In the distance, graves continued up the side of a mountain that rose up at the rear of the cemetery, as though the dead were being led to

Heaven.

Cemeteries said a lot about a community. It wasn't just in how well they were maintained, but also in how many graves had flowers or other tokens left by loved ones, and in what had been inscribed on the tombstones. But, what she liked even more, were the grave markers themselves, especially the ornate ones. She'd stood before more towering spires and life-sized weeping angels than she could count. The biggest and boldest one she'd ever seen was a ninety-foot tall granite pyramid in Richmond, Virginia's Hollywood Cemetery that had been erected to honor the tens of thousands of enlisted Confederate soldiers buried nearby. That marker had humbled her more than any other.

The cemetery in Stillwater fell a bit short in Maya's estimation. The grass was halfway up to her knees, and long dead flowers wilted in soggy arrangements over several gravesites. It wasn't terribly neglected, but if someone didn't come out soon it would be. After her recent trip in town, she didn't know why she'd hoped for better.

The gravestones nearest the gate looked old, their engraved faces weathered and faded, with some of the words and dates on them unreadable. She walked slowly through the wet grass from stone to stone, getting a feel for the area, seeing who had died, when, and perhaps even how. Life had been hard back near the turn of the twentieth century, especially for miners, and the graves were a testament to that. Most of the people were lucky if they lived longer than forty years, though from the epitaphs it looked like the love of those left behind was powerful, sometimes even poetic. The grave of Mozell Watkins, 1872 - 1913, read, "Mother's love was as the sun, and it warms us even after it has set." It was a beautiful sentiment, especially given the black clouds that never seemed to stop pouring down.

The further Maya walked from the gate, the newer the graves were, and the easier it was to trace family lines. Some families were even grouped together in large plots bordered by stones or poured concrete borders. The Conways were energetic breeders judging by the number of tombstones clustered beneath a red mulberry tree, as were the Harrods grouped close by. The largest collection of graves, though, belonged to the Tazwells. They were also the only family in the cemetery with a mausoleum.

The grave markers continued up the mountain a ways, and she turned to continue her tour, but a stone marker sitting far off to itself near the base of the rise caught her attention. She walked over to it, careful not to slip on the wet grass. She hadn't realized how far it sat from the rest of the cemetery until she'd walked the distance, but it was easily twenty yards. A distance like that wasn't accidental.

Sure enough, as she rounded the tombstone, the situation became clearer. The marker, a standard granite gravestone without any frills or familial touches, memorialized someone named Stanley Wellen, born September 3rd, 1980, died March 15th, 2008. Beneath the dates was etched, "May he find the peace in death he could not find in life." It was a rather unremarkable headstone, but words spray-painted in white across it gave the marker a special touch - "ROT IN HELL U FUKER!"

That wasn't the only bit of vandalism the headstone had suffered – various swear words, renditions of middle fingers, and chisel marks were arranged artfully across its face – but the white spray paint was by far the largest. It was also the most recent judging by the condition of the paint.

The grass around the grave lay wilted and brown, probably from someone pouring chemicals on it, while beer cans, bottles of whiskey, and cigarette butts littered the ground. Whoever Stanley Wellen was, he hadn't been well loved.

Something about the name struck a bell in Maya's head, so, using the hand not holding the umbrella, she patted her pockets for her phone to try a quick internet search, found only her small Nikon digital camera; her phone was back in the car, charging. With a well-practiced hand she took out the camera and snapped off a few pictures of the desecrated headstone. The grave itself probably wouldn't have any bearing on her research, but the pictures would remind her to look up Stanley and see why people took such delight in defiling his grave.

As she tucked the camera back in her pocket a sudden shiver ran up her spine, and her entire body shook as a deep chill closed around her like a corpse's embrace. She stumbled backward, her breath fogging the air, and instantly realized her earlier presumption was wrong.

The cemetery wasn't empty.

A hand erupted from the earth at her feet, skeletal fingers clawing through dirt and withered grass. Maya jumped backward and squealed in shock. Another bony hand tore through the ground, strips of flesh stretching over joints and blood oozing across the mangled turf as the hand reached out and pulled its way upward.

This isn't real, she told herself as she closed her eyes and slowly backed away. *This isn't real. It's just a spirit too stupid to move on trying to scare you. They feed on that. Don't give in. Deny it. Don't be afraid.*

"It's coming, Maya," a voice said, the words sliding over her like clouds slipping across the moon. "And it will devour you whole."

She knew keeping her eyes closed would only make her more afraid, and therefore more vulnerable to the spirit's hunger, so Maya forced her eyelids open. Slime covered bones and ragged bits of bloody skin filled her vision, but it was the gaping black maw of Stanley Wellen's skull that made her clutch her umbrella like a bat and shuffle away. Pale white orbs rested in the skull's eye sockets, and ratty hunks of stringy blond hair hung from the cracked dome, but it was the mouth – the impossibly moving mouth – that filled her with horror. Beyond the broken teeth and clacking jawbones was a darkness unlike anything she'd ever seen before. Bottomless. Eternal. Devoid of light, and joy, and life. It was a black from before the creation of the universe, and through it spoke the dead. It terrified her, yet drew her in like a riptide swirling around her feet.

"What's coming?" Maya asked the question before she knew the words were leaving her lips.

Stanley's vile spirit dragged its blackened ribcage up from the spreading muck of its grave and laughed. "Fire, you stupid half-breed bitch. And blood. And death. It's coming, and there's nothing you can do to stop it." Chunks of putrefied organs slithered between his ribs and plopped onto the mud.

"You're lying." She spoke the words with all the conviction she could muster, but even as she did she knew the lie was hers.

Heaving upward, the rotted body of Stanley Wellen nearly came free. Only its lower legs remained buried in the grave. "Look at you, a frightened little black bird thinkin' your tiny wings will carry you away from the evil that's comin'. Sorry to tell ya, but it's too late. It's already here, all around you, and soon the world will suffer. Won't that be grand?!"

Stanley tossed back his skull and cackled like shards of glass being jammed in Maya's ears, but then it lunged forward in the muck and grabbed her ankles. The bones of his hands were ice cold and hard as stone where they gripped her flesh, and she felt the burn of his deathly touch creep up her legs. Her mind panicked, her heart leapt into her throat, and all she could think to do was close her eyes and swing her umbrella. It was a convenience store piece of shit, little more than thin strips of metal, pink plastic, and waterproof fabric, but in her terror she wielded it like a flaming sword. Her arms rose and fell, rose and fell, and her voice cried out, "No! No! Let me go! Get away from me! No!" Stanley's laughter pounded against her. She beat the ground, screamed, kicked, flailed, fought for life with all she had. It wasn't until she fell down and the umbrella slipped from her hands that she dared look at the grasping skeleton again.

Other than a few gouges in the earth, Stanley Wellen's grave was unmarked. *Of course it is*, she thought, her pulse beating so hard she felt it in her temples. *It was either his damn spirit playing with me, or it was...something else. Hell, maybe it was neither. Or both. Shit.*

Regretting she'd ever heard of the town of Stillwater, Maya calmed her breathing as best she could, then picked herself up and grabbed her umbrella, which was now useless.

Tufts of dead grass and yellowish mud clung to the bent tines and torn fabric. She didn't give the grave another look as she turned toward the cemetery's entrance. She wanted to run back to her car, but she'd already given into her fear enough, so she kept to a slow jog.

"I think we've had enough excitement for one day," she said as the cemetery gates slid past. "Alan will be here tomorrow, and together we'll find out what is really going on around here. Yep, that's what will happen. Yes indeedy."

Worried that if she started laughing she'd never stop, Maya exhaled a warm gust of air from her nose, opened the car, and got in. Her next stop was a motel room and a very long, hot shower. As she drove away, part of her wished she'd had her EM detector and video recorder with her at Stanley Wellen's grave. He might have scared the crap out of her, but actual evidence she could post on her site would have almost made the experience worth it. Not enough, though, for her to turn around and try her luck again.

INTERLUDE
DREAMS IN THE DARK

The mountain cavern was vast. So much so that after Ash and his crew first broke through to it they'd had to setup lighting rigs to begin their work. But, as powerful as the lights were, the far end of the rocky chamber was beyond their reach, lost in darkness. It was as though someone had punched a hole in the world that went so deep it tore through the universe into something far older and cosmic. But now, a month later, the lights had been turned off and removed. The men no longer needed them to see in the dark. Ash was thankful for that. Light was an abomination in this place, this…cathedral, and a blight against the Holy Darkness that slumbered deep within it.

Ash stood at the very edge of the cavern, the toes of his work boots peeking over a sheer drop that would end his life if he took one more step, and stared. His eyes, once as green as a freshly mowed lawn, were now pitch black orbs that swept over the rocky walls around him, and then down at the water that gently lapped at the cavern walls two-hundred feet below. It was a peaceful setting, the calmness of it broken only by the distant sound of a pump. He was used to that, though. The pump operated around the clock, and the unending monotony of it turned it into background noise that scarcely registered anymore.

Beyond that, though, another sound permeated the cavern. It wasn't something you perceived with your ears, that could be recorded or amplified. It was a vibration in the bones, a slow throb felt more than heard, and fangs glittered as Ash smiled in the darkness. It was the heart of his god beating a rhythm older than the mountain that surrounded them, and with every hour the beat increased little by little. His god slept, buried in the underground lake at the bottom of the cavern, slept and dreamed, but as the water level lowered, his god stirred. Soon he would awaken, and when he did his dreams would change the world. When that happened

Ash would be by his side, reborn as his first Acolyte of Shadows. It would be a glorious day.

Hard rubber scuffed over rocks, disturbing the stillness behind him, but Ash didn't turn. He didn't need to. He knew who approached by the way the man grunted as he walked.

"What is it, Gus?" Ash asked, his eyes locked on the black water below.

Gus Mason coughed and stopped several feet back. "Boss, Tyler and Wil finished setting up that room you asked for, and some of the guys already have their kids here. You want they should...you know...start loading them in?"

Ash wanted to laugh. Over time his crew's bodies had changed because of the holy water that cascaded over them after the cavern was breached, but so far the signs of their rebirth were small, barely noticeable. A darkened iris here, a lengthened canine tooth there. Ash's body had gone through more extensive changes, and it amused him that his crew could work in service of the ancient god and yet still feel fear in his presence. But perhaps that was only as it should be. Within the mountain Ash had found new purpose, and in embracing that he'd been elevated above all others. If his men's admiration and love also contained fear, so be it.

"Yes, lock them up as soon as possible. When our god rises he'll be mighty hungry, and I want a fitting meal ready for him."

Gus nodded so quickly the fat beneath his chin bounced like a turkey's wattle. "So does that mean I should bring my daughter in too?"

"Would that bother you?" Ash's black eyes flashed in the darkness.

"Oh, no, sir. No, not at all. She uh...she's been getting mouthier by the day, and it'd be good for her to finally get put to a good use."

Gus was as solid as the mountain that pressed down on them. Ash respected that. "That's good, Gus. Anything else?"

Gus's chins bounced again as he nodded. "Yes, sir. We're all set to start up the second pump. Are you ready?"

"The better question, Gus, is if the world is ready," Ash

replied, squaring his shoulders as he kept his back to the rest of the mine. "And the answer to that is no, the world isn't ready. It will be soon, though, and when it is, you and I and the others will stand first amongst the new order. We are his chosen." Ash turned his head and graced Gus with a glance. "But to do that we must finish awakening our god, so yes, turn on the second pump."

Gus went back the way he'd come. He shouted orders and directed the crew while Ash turned his attention back to the cavern. The affairs of the small were best left to the small.

With the interruption over, he stared down at the water, envisioned the glorious being that slept far beneath it, and wondered what dreams filled his mind. Sometimes those dreams rose up and touched Ash, filling him with a sense of power and majesty so great he fell to his knees and wept. As his god slowly awoke, the dreams came to him less and less, but it was a sacrifice he was only too happy to make. The dreams would be real soon enough.

As he sought out the dreams of the ancient god, the second pump kicked into life, and the increased noise filled the mountain tunnels with a growl. Moving without thought, Ash reached up and scratched at his right ear as though he were shooing off a fly. When the claws that had replaced the fingernails of his hand scraped against his skin, the ear tore loose and dropped onto the ground with a moist *plop*. Only a small nub of gray flesh remained, black veins pulsing beneath it. He glanced down at the torn ear next to his feet, but he wasn't bothered. He was being reborn, his body the clay of his god's dreams, and the ears of his old skin meant nothing. His crew would come to know the same glory soon.

CHAPTER FOUR

The musty smell billowing up from the bed after Kyle tossed his duffel bag onto it was enough to push him back a step. The motel room appeared to have been cleaned, but how long ago that had been was anyone's guess. He was just glad there wasn't a dead body stashed in the closet or decaying in the bathtub. Kyle hadn't recognized the guy manning the motel's front desk, but he'd looked sketchy enough that the idea wasn't unbelievable. A little mustiness he could deal with. In the Army he'd dealt with worse.

As he unpacked what few articles of clothing he'd brought with him, Kyle pulled out his phone and checked to see if Taylor had called or texted him. No new messages appeared, so he pulled up their text thread and typed, YOU FREE YET?

No answer immediately appeared, so he kept the phone in one hand and moved clothes from his duffel bag to the room's cheap particleboard dresser. As the last pair of pants settled in the bottom drawer, his phone let loose a brief electronic dance beat.

NO. MOM IS WATCHING ME LIKE A HAWK. (O.O)

After their less than pleasant exchange, that didn't surprise Kyle. I BET. LATER?

AFTER 8. WILL SNEAK OUT AND CALL YOU.

He didn't want to encourage bad behavior, but he had little choice. He'd snuck out of the house by her age, and for lot less savory reasons. OKAY. DON'T KEEP ME WAITING.

I WON'T. PROBABLY. ;) LOVE YOU.

He sighed. Kids. LOVE YOU TOO.

:) x

Their digital conversation over, Kyle pocketed his phone, turned to the TV on the squat dresser opposite the bed, and looked for the power button. Like the pumpkin orange curtains and green wallpaper that made the room seem like a relic from the 70's, the television could have come from a museum. It was an old 21" tube TV, made long before high definition was even a glimmer of an idea. When he finally found the ON/OFF knob and turned it, the screen took a good half a minute to warm up, and even then the image was fuzzy. He snorted and turned it back off.

"I'll take that as a sign" He pulled on his leather jacket, then patted his pockets, making sure he had his wallet, car keys, and the room key (an actual metal key, not the plastic cardkeys that most modern hotels and motels used). Satisfied that all was in order, he unlatched the door and opened it. Wet air billowed into the room, adding to the musty feel. He wondered if he would ever be dry again.

The Smokey Mountain Motel was laid out in a horseshoe shape, with parking slots in front of each room and a vinyl-covered pool in the middle surrounded by a waist-high chain-link fence. When he'd first pulled in, the parking lot had been empty save for a dented beige Ford Bronco sitting in a space marked MOTEL EMPLOYEES ONLY. Now, in addition to the Bronco and his rented Jeep, he saw a red Honda Civic two slots to his right that seemed oddly familiar. When he noted the tiny spare tire on the front passenger wheel well, he realized why. Loud cursing rolled out from the car's other side.

Kyle stepped around the car from the front and saw a woman bent over and struggling with something in the backseat. He instinctively opened his mouth to ask if she needed help, but the shape of her body stopped him cold. She had curvaceous hips and a cushiony behind – what some of his Army buddies would have reverently called a badonkadonk – and while the red skirt she wore didn't look painted on, it might as well have. Shapely light brown legs extended down from the skirt to small feet in black leather sandals. He couldn't see her from the waist up, but from memory he recalled the black blouse. All in all it was a very pleasant view, but he considered himself too much a gentleman to enjoy it for more than a moment.

Hoping not to startle her, he stepped back, coughed, and asked, "Can I help you, Ma'am?"

"What the huh?" Her body jerked as she pushed herself out of the car.

Yep, it was definitely the woman he'd seen on the side of the road. Her pretty face and bouncing curls were easy enough to remember, but it was her eyes that captured his attention again. They were pale blue, almost gray, and the way they looked out from her creamy brown face made them seem lighter in color. She was gorgeous, easily one of the prettiest women he'd ever seen in person.

"Who are you?" she asked quickly, looking at him and then looking around for anyone else close by. She was probably used to being stared at, but *used to it* and *liked it* were two different things.

Hoping he wasn't blushing like a schoolboy developing his first crush, Kyle put on his warmest smile. "Sorry if I startled you. I...uh... It sounded like you were having a hard time with something, and I thought I'd lend a hand."

To emphasize the point and show he wasn't holding anything, he extended his arms and held his hands out. Her eyes flicked down then back up to his face. After a moment the skin between her brows crinkled and she tilted her head slightly.

"Do I know you?"

"Kinda." He pulled his hands back. "I saw you this afternoon. You were on the side of the road in your car. I pulled up next to you to help, but you were on the phone and waved me off."

Her eyes lit up and her lower jaw hung open for a second. "Ohhhh... Right! I remember now. Yeah...um, thanks for stopping, it was just..."

"You don't have to explain." He shook head. "I understand. The side of the road in the backwater of West Virginia probably isn't the safest place, especially for someone on their own who doesn't know the area. From the look of it you got things all sorted out. I won't insult you by assuming a boyfriend or something came along and changed it for you."

The last comment was a bit of fishing on his part. He hoped she didn't notice it. She blushed and rolled her eyes, but to his relief the gesture seemed directed at herself.

"Oh, insult away. I'm a modern woman, but changing tires isn't something I ever got around to learning. My insurance company has roadside service. That's who I was talking to when you pulled up."

The smile he wore made his cheeks hurt, but he didn't want to lower it until he was sure she felt comfortable. "It seemed like an intense conversation."

"Have you ever had a conversation with an insurance company that *wasn't?*"

He laughed, hitched up the right side of his mouth in a *we're just folks* smirk, and extended his right hand again. "Good point. My name's Kyle."

Her eyes went from his hand to his face just like she'd done before, but this time she returned his smile and shook hands. Her strong grip stood at odds with her soft, warm skin, and his fingers tingled with electricity.

"I'm Maya. It's good to know I'm not the only newbie in town."

When she let go of his hand, part of him sighed in regret, but to make sure he didn't seem too eager he leaned back on his heels and put his hands in his pockets with his thumbs sticking out. "No, you're the only new person around. I was born and raised here. I left to join the Army a while ago, and now I'm back visiting. No room at home, you know how it is. But uh... At the risk of putting my nose where it doesn't belong, do you need some help? When I came by it seemed like you were having a time of it back there." He pointed at the backseat to make himself clear.

Maya glanced over her shoulder and scowled. "Oh, yeah. To get my tire changed I had to move some stuff from the hatchback to the backseat. I guess I didn't do a good job of it, 'cause now it's scattered all over the place."

Kyle had dealt with his fair share of messes, so he felt qualified to help. "Well, if you don't mind, I'd be more than happy to help. If not, just say the word and I'm outta your hair."

"I..." Maya stopped, frowning as she tossed her options around in her head. He would take any excuse to share more time with her, but he wouldn't blame her a bit if she told him to scram. "Okay, sure, I'd appreciate it. You can go over to the other side and gather up whatever slid over there."

Forcing himself to not smile so wide he'd split his face in half, Kyle nodded and jogged over to the passenger side backseat door. It squealed like a pig getting butchered when he pulled it open. Crumpled paper and fast food bags littered the floorboard, but he forgot about those when he got an eyeful of her cleavage as she ducked down and started gathering things. Her upper body was just as sexy as her lower half, and it took every ounce of his restraint to swivel his eyes away. To occupy his mind he gathered things and made a pile. It wasn't until he grabbed something familiar that his brain slid back into gear.

"Whoa." He hadn't expected to find a pair of night vision binoculars. He'd seen a lot of them as an Army supply grunt, but finding a pair out in the wild, especially in the backseat of a woman's car, gave them an alien feel. "What exactly is it that you do for a living, Maya?"

The woman across from him looked up quickly. When she registered what he held in his hand she closed her eyes and sighed. "It's...complicated."

"Hey, yeah, none of my business." He shook his hands at her. "If you're some sort of investigator or journalist, the last thing I'd want to do is get in your way or screw things up. Forget I asked."

Maya made a *hmm* sound as she opened a canvas bag and stuffed a bundle of notepads into it. Kyle couldn't help but notice the SLR camera, digital camcorder, full spectrum lens attachment, and IR camera light the notepads were settled against. If he'd seen that sort of gear in a place like Manhattan or Paris, his immediate assumption would have been she was a Langley spook, but in a nothing town like Stillwater, West Virginia? The idea was laughable. And Maya didn't seem anything like a spy, though he figured a good spy wouldn't. The one thing he *was* certain of was that she was a mystery he'd like to solve.

"I tell you what." She zipped the bag closed and stood up. He grabbed the binoculars and a half-empty leather satchel, then stood up as well. "It was really nice of you to stop earlier on the road, and just now, so let me say thanks with a meal. I can't afford much, but I figure there has to be a McDonald's around here somewhere, right? It's, like, the law or something. While we eat I'll tell you what's brought me to town. Since you're a local you might even be able to help."

He wasn't sure what she meant, but if it came with a free meal plus more time in her company, he had no problem with that. "Sounds like a plan, thanks. It's been awhile since I was last here, but I know a place called Woody's Diner just down the street that has amazing burgers."

Maya's light brown face turned gray and she shook her head while staring straight at him. "No! I...uh... I went by there already. I don't think it's the same as you... Is there anywhere else?"

"Sure." Maya looked scared silly, and he had no idea what had brought it on, but he wanted to do whatever he could to calm her down. "Across the road is The Basement. It's a bar, but they serve food too. Would that work?"

The relief that washed over Maya's face eased his mind but made him wonder what had happened at Woody's. It was one more mystery to add to her collection.

"Yeah, that sounds fine."

"All right, then let's get this stuff unloaded, and we'll go."

With a nod, Maya hefted several bag straps over her shoulder, then turned and walked to the room next door to his. She had a time getting the key for it from her purse without dropping everything, but eventually she made it and had the room open. He stayed outside while she unloaded her bags and then came out for what he had. A brief peek told him her room was identical to his, but laid out in reverse. Once all the bags were set down, she shut the door and tested it to make sure it was locked.

"We good to go?" he asked.

Maya smiled and pulled her purse over her shoulder. "Lead the way."

CHAPTER FIVE

The sign for The Basement stood on the side of the road displaying a stream of foaming beer cascading down a set of wooden steps. Kyle and Maya waited for a truck to blow by and then crossed from the motel. In the bar's parking lot were two motorcycles, a yellow construction truck loaded with dirty tools, and a shiny new Cadillac plastered in bright red Republican bumper stickers. After sidestepping a series of puddles, they reached the front door and Kyle opened it. A bell rang overhead.

Kyle, even though he'd grown up in Stillwater, had only been in The Basement twice, and always with his dad. Because of that his memory of the place was dim at best, but he couldn't imagine it had looked as rundown as it did now. Half the light-up signs on the wall were dark, and those that did work seemed weak and hazy. Even the flatscreen HDTV above the bar looked less than high-def. In a day that had seen Kyle's estimation of the town plummet further than ever before, this was one more weight pulling it down.

"You two here to drink?" a woman asked from the hostess station to the right of the door. Kyle thought he recognized her, but her stained apron, badly applied makeup over ashen face, and stringy hair dulled her appearance. By the lack of recognition in her own eyes, she didn't seem to know him either.

"Uh, no, we'd like to get something to eat if the kitchen's open." Kyle slapped on a smile and crammed all the positive energy he could into his face.

The waitress glanced at the ceiling and sighed as she grabbed two menus. "Follow me then."

Without waiting to see if they were ready, the waitress crossed in front of them and walked to a booth sitting against the front wall to the left of the door. The next booth over was occupied, but he couldn't see by whom or how many. All he saw were muddy work boots and a faded denim pant leg. The rest of the dining area was barren save for a man and woman in biker leathers at one table and a man in a suit eating by himself at the bar, his slimy hands holding onto a rib bone as he gnashed his way back and forth across it, picking it clean.

After they were seated, the waitress pulled a pencil from above her right ear and withdrew an order pad. "Okay, what do you want?" The tone of her voice said she really didn't give a shit.

Maya raised her left eyebrow. "A few minutes to look over the menu, for starters." She paused to look at the waitress's greasy nametag. "Helen."

Helen's nostrils flared as she shoved her pencil back into her limp hair and pocketed her pad. "Two waters it is then." She turned and walked away without another word.

"Wow." Kyle laughed. "She's a real tip go-getter."

Maya tapped her fingernails against the booth's tabletop and shrugged. "She's a delight compared to the Klan folk I met earlier."

"Really?" Kyle had little love for his hometown, but one thing he'd never have called it was racist. Then again, the first time he'd met an African-American in the flesh was after he'd left town and joined the Army, so the lack of non-whites in the area had probably dampened whatever latent bigotry the people of Stillwater harbored. "What happened?"

"I'm...sorry. I shouldn't have brought it up." Her eyes stared at the menu with a gaze as flat as her tone.

Kyle didn't want to press the point, so he let it lie and picked up his own menu. The sheet of laminated paper was as greasy as the offerings printed on it. The Basement wasn't a place you wanted to go to if you were a vegetarian or didn't want everything deep-fried. His mouth watered while his stomach flip-flopped in revulsion.

"Only in the south does something like fried pickles sound reasonable," he said. "And I haven't had fried green tomatoes in years."

Shaking her head, Maya looked up and offered a tiny smile. "I refuse to eat friend green tomatoes that didn't come from my Aunty Elle's kitchen. It would just be a letdown."

"Seems reasonable," he replied, grinning back at her. She lit up the room when she smiled, and he wanted to encourage it as much as possible. "Is there anything on the menu that isn't reserved for family meals then?"

Dimples formed in Maya's cheeks as she blushed and gazed intently at the menu. "There might be. Let me give it a good look."

They sat in silence for a minute as they looked over their options and settled on what they wanted. By the time they'd lowered the menus back to the table, they were ready to order. Their waitress, though, was nowhere to be seen, nor was their water. Kyle didn't want the silence to turn awkward, so he coughed into his hand and reached for the first topic of conversation that sprang to mind.

"So, what's brought you to this shithole of a town?"

Maya picked at her nails for a moment, then looked at him with eyes that were as guarded as they were blue. "I'm a writer. A journalist, really. Well, to be more specific, a blogger. I'm here to uh...well, write." Her light brown cheeks turned to roses in her awkwardness.

"Huh." Blogger hadn't been the first thing he'd thought she would say, but it made as much sense as most everything else that had tumbled through his head. "Blogger. Interesting. That was some odd gear in your backseat for a blogger though. No offense."

"I guess that depends on what you're blogging about," she replied with a short laugh. "Have you ever watched one of those shows on cable where people go ghost hunting?"

Out of all the things the attractive young woman could have asked, that would have been the last question he'd have imagined. It left him flat-footed. "Umm... Not really. I think I've seen bits of 'em while walking through post rec rooms, but – ya know – that's it. I'm more a General Hospital kinda guy."

A smile turned Maya's lips into a bow, and inwardly Kyle pumped a fist in victory.

"So was my grandmother, smart aleck. But, seriously,

what those people do is what I do. Sort of. My site is called spookyamerica.com. I started it a couple of years ago as a part time thing, a way of indulging a...passion of mine, but now I do it full-time. I'm hoping if I can find a juicy enough investigation then I'll be able to get a book deal. Then on to obvious fame and fortune."

Questions popped up in Kyle's mind like plastic heads in a game of Whack-A-Mole, and he didn't know where to start. After a couple of seconds he went with what to him was the most obvious question. "What on Earth could there be in this town that would interest a person who writes for a site called Spookyamerica?"

"My website is populated with stories about famous places that are haunted or have a mysterious past, but if I want to make a name for myself I have to find places that *aren't* so well known. Places off the beaten track. So, a friend of mine wrote me a program that would search the internet for certain keywords and correlate data in the hopes of finding somewhere that had the markers of a haunting but didn't also match up with previously known locations. Stillwater is the first place it spit out."

He didn't believe a word she said, but the tone of her voice and the look on her face said she did, so for the moment he was willing to put aside his personal beliefs. "So you're saying that the town I grew up in is haunted?"

She raised her eyebrow and nodded slowly. " Very. Do you know anything about the number of people who've died here?"

"No, can't say I ever thought about it." It was the truth. He'd been a kid while living in Stillwater, and to a kid death was something old people had to worry about.

"Death is the only real constant in the universe." The way her head tilted to the side as she schooled him made him giggle inside. "Not life, not time, not light. All things end. All things die. But, because death is a moment when this world and the world beyond touch, it's also a catalyst for supernatural activity."

"You say that you've actually seen a ghost." Kyle wanted

the remark to come off as a joke, but the look in her eyes told him she took it very seriously.

"I know it sounds strange to you. Ghosts and hauntings aren't something that most people come across in their lives. I'm not most people though."

Her words intrigued him even if he had a hard time taking them sincerely. "Other than being beautiful, what makes you so darn special?"

Maya blushed, but her eyes never left his, and her expression was completely earnest. "I get...feelings...from time to time. If a spirit is near I can normally sense it. Sometimes I know what someone else is thinking. My Aunt Mozell called it a gift. She had it too. I grew up with it, and now I use it to help with the blog and investigations. If you want to laugh, now would be the time."

He knew he should laugh, and had it been anyone else who said those things he probably would have, but the stillness of her eyes and the way she presented it as just a part of her life, stopped him. He didn't know if he believed it, but she did, and there wasn't any reason for him to make an issue of it. Perhaps – if things continued on and they saw each other again – she might even get a chance to prove it.

"No, I'm not going to laugh. I'm a man of little faith in anything, but I always try to leave my mind open for surprises. Now, you were talking about death?"

Maya smiled and nodded. "From a pure numbers point of view, Stillwater is brimming with death. Compare the rates of murders and suicides in Stillwater to the rest of West Virginia and the percentages are off the charts. We're talking several orders of magnitude higher. I was shocked the FBI hadn't opened a field office out here just to see what the fuck is going on. The numbers are ridiculous, yet it's like no one's noticed."

A shiver trickled down Kyle's back. "I knew I never liked this town, but now you're giving me all new reasons to be glad I left."

"There is something very peculiar going on here, and I plan on figuring out what it is."

As glad as he was that Maya was warming up to him, what she said had him puzzled. But, before he could ask her to tell him more, the waitress returned, two glasses filled with water in her hands. A single cube of ice floated in each one.

"You two ready to order or not?" she asked, drawing out her order pad like she was lifting the weight of the world. When she pulled her pen from above her ear, part of it caught in her hair, but she didn't seem to care as the strands tore loose from her skull. Kyle watched them bounce in the bar's weak light, the cap holding them against the pen like soggy bits of hay.

Maya stared up at Helen with narrow eyes, but whatever verbal jabs she created in her head died before they reached her mouth. Kyle was more inclined to make an issue of the waitress's attitude, but the indifferent way she looked at them stole his thunder. He would have been shouting at a wall. Early on in life he'd learned to pick his battles carefully, and this one wasn't worth the fight.

"Yes, we're ready," Maya said. "I'd like your catfish plate. Can I get corn instead of coleslaw?"

Helen barely nodded. "Whatever floats your boat. What do ya wanna drink?"

"Diet Coke."

The waitress grunted as she scribbled on her pad, then shifted watery eyes over to Kyle. "And you?"

"I want a burger, medium rare, with pickles and some red onion if you have it. If not, no onion at all. No lettuce or tomatoes either. Add ketchup and mustard to it though. Oh, and for the fries I want a thing of mayo on the side."

"Christ on a stick." The corner of Helen's mouth arched up, revealing yellowed teeth that hadn't seen a dentist in a good long while. "And to drink?"

Kyle looked over the waitress's shoulder and saw a neon sign for Coors Light. It wasn't his favorite brand, but it would do in a pinch. "Coors light in a bottle."

Helen made another series of notes, then shoved her hairy pen back over her ear. "I'll be back with your drinks."

Helen left with the same irritated air she'd arrived with,

leaving Kyle and Maya to roll their eyes and laugh.

"Sorry about that," he said, genuinely embarrassed for the town he'd once called home.

Maya shook her head and tapped her fingers against the glass of water sitting before her. "Not your fault people in this town are weird."

"Speaking of weird," Kyle said, hoping to steer the conversation back where it had been headed a moment ago, "so you're a ghostbuster or something?"

She laughed, then opened her lips to reply, but her unsaid words hung in her throat as her eyes shifted from Kyle to something over his shoulder. He felt a shadow fall over him as someone came around from the neighboring booth, and then a voice dropped down on him like a ghost of school years past.

"You got a lot of guts showing your face around here, Mason."

When Maya saw a guy with a thick beard stand up from his booth and hover over Kyle's shoulder like a raven settling on a gravestone, the bottom of her stomach dropped out. *Is this town full of crazies or what?* she asked herself as a chill spread across her limbs.

From the look in Kyle's eyes, a similar thought ran through his own mind, but as soon as the man spoke, a smile broke across Kyle's face and he jumped up from the booth like his seat was spring-loaded.

"Dirk, you son of a bitch! Oh my god."

Maya expected the two men to greet each other in a bro-hug. It was the usual way for guys to embrace, with one arm around the back and the other held between them, affectionate without being *too* affectionate, but Kyle and Dirk went for a full-on hug. That impressed her. Most men she'd met were too afraid to show emotion out of fear of being called names she didn't care to repeat, so to see two men ignore all that and really embrace was a strange treat.

"You are a sight for sore eyes, man," Dirk said as they parted. "I can't believe you're here."

Dirk's beard was the sort usually seen on lumberjacks and swamp folk, but his dark brown eyes were kind and genuine. He was a big guy, several inches taller than Kyle and broader across the chest, but the grin on his face turned him into a teddy bear. He was dressed in dirty jeans and a plaid flannel shirt unbuttoned to reveal a Big Head Todd And The Monsters t-shirt. The work boots on his feet were scuffed and caked in mud. He looked like a man who worked hard and played harder.

"I can't believe it either, man. Family stuff, you know."

Dirk nodded like he understood without needing to hear another word. He then turned and looked down at Maya. She clasped her hands together beneath the table, hoping there wouldn't be a reenactment of the diner scene from earlier in the day. When he smiled and tilted his head, her fingers relaxed their death grip on each other.

"Please tell me you're not really here with this asshole." A laugh twitched the corners of Dirk's lips as he extended a hand. "You have to be available, or I'll die."

Maya laughed as she reached out and shook his hand. "I'm Maya."

"And I'm enchanted." Dirk winked.

"You're full of shit is what you are." Kyle gave his friend a hard pat on the back.. "Wanna join us?"

Dirk nodded and stepped aside to let Kyle sit down first. He then leaned back into the booth he'd just been in and grabbed his bottle of Bud Light. "Just leave the check, man," he said to whomever was still in the booth. "I'll take care of it. Oh, and remind dad I'll be getting those extra detonators in the morning, so I'll be late to the job. Okay?"

"Yeah, whatever," the hidden person replied.

Raising an eyebrow, Dirk nodded and turned to sit down next to Kyle. Once seated, he shrugged his shoulders and grimaced. "What an asshole."

"Speaking of which," Kyle said, "how are *you* doing, man?"

Dirk laughed hard and opened his eyes wide, exaggerating how funny he thought Kyle's joke was. "Ah hah! I see what you did there. Nice. You haven't changed a bit."

"True classics never do." Kyle wore a smug smile. "But no, seriously, how have you been?"

Taking a sip of his beer, Dirk shrugged and pushed back into the booth's seat cushion. "Eh, been better, been worse."

Helen approached the table like a troll weary from its work. After dropping napkins on the table she put Maya's glass of Diet Coke and Kyle's Coors Light bottle in front of them. "You're food'll be out in a minute." She hardly looked at them before shuffling off again.

"Is it just me," Kyle asked, "or is she a complete bitch?"

"It's ain't just you." Dirk sipped from his bottle and stared down at the table. "I moved back into town a month ago, and since then shit has gotten bad, not that Stillwater was ever a shining example of southern hospitality. People treat each other like shit, fights have broken out at work, and even my folks are acting like they've been replaced with bitter, angry versions of themselves. That'd be bad enough, but lately everyone looks like plague victims with all the pasty grey skin and dark eyes. I know it sounds crazy, but…something ain't right here. Not right at all. I've half a mind to skip town again."

A chill settled across Maya's shoulders. She'd been in town less than a day and sensed the very same thing. She hadn't thought she'd been crazy – she'd wrestled with her own strangeness too long for that – but it was nice to have confirmation.

Kyle closed his eyes as he took his first pull on the beer bottle, the oddness of Dirk's words rolling off his unaware back. "I must have started a trend when I took off."

"Hardly." Dirk chuckled. "Unlike you, I didn't run out of town right after graduation like my feet were on fire and my ass was catching. I waited at least *a week* for the ink on my diploma to dry before I left to become a rock god."

Kyle laughed and rolled his beer between his palms. "You never did dream small. So what happened? Why aren't you on MTV or whatever the fuck?"

By way of answer, Dirk held up his left hand. A nasty scar

ran across his palm from thumb to pinky. Maya and Kyle hissed in unison. He flexed the fingers into a loose fist and grimaced. "A couple of months ago I got into a bar fight out in Buttfuck, Kentucky. A drunk asshole stumbled into me, I tried to help him back onto his stool, and he cut me for my trouble. Fists start flyin', and the next thing I know a doctor's telling me I'll never play a guitar worth a shit again. The guys in the band tried to talk me into working through it and staying, but...I'm no pity fuck. So I came home and started working for my dad. He always told me that so long as I could swing a hammer I'd always have a job with him, but I never imagined I'd actually have to take him up on it."

"That sucks, man." Kyle tipped his bottle in Dirk's direction. "You were a damn good guitar player."

The right half of Dirk's lips curled up in a smile. "Thanks."

Maya felt bad for Dirk. He tried to downplay the pain his lost dream cost him, but she could see it in his aura like a fractured light around his body.

"But that's enough about me and my tale of sorrow." Dirk finished off his beer and slouched. "What about you two? You an item? If so, Kyle, you better offer up a prayer of thanks, 'cause she is waaaay too good-looking for your sorry ass."

Maya choked on her Diet Coke. Dirk and Kyle were nothing like the people she'd met at the diner, and through them the town rose a tiny bit in her esteem.

"No, we're not together." Kyle stared into her eyes and gave her a sly grin that made her stomach flutter. "It's not for lack of trying though. I was just getting ready to put my moves on her when you stood up and went all Lurch over my shoulder."

"Ah shit," Dirk replied with a smirk. "I know how to take a hint."

Dirk moved to exit the booth, but Kyle grabbed his shoulder and laughed. Maya blushed so fiercely she felt like her face was on fire. She would have been lying though if she'd said she wouldn't have liked to see Kyle's moves.

A series of electronic notes blasted from Kyle's pants. He reached down, dug for a moment, and then came up with a battered flip phone. After flicking it open he pressed it to his ear and said, "Hello? Taylor? Is everything... Yeah, I can come over... Do mom and dad... All right, sure. I'll be right there... Love you too... Bye."

"Baby sister need her big brother?" Dirk asked as Kyle pressed the END button on his phone.

"Yeah. She's the whole reason I'm here. I–"

Helen shuffled over to the booth before he could finish speaking and laid plates down. "Here's your food." Her eyes passed over the booth without a hint of real interest.

"I need a to-go bag," Kyle said.

Deciding she didn't want to eat in the bar if Kyle wasn't there, Maya said the same thing.

Helen sighed and closed her eyes. "Jesus wept. I'll be right back then."

An electric jolt of anger ran up Maya's spine. "That bitch is on my last nerve."

Kyle nodded while handing his phone to his friend. "Sorry I have to split, but put your phone number in there and I'll call you tomorrow. We'll reminisce more then."

"Only if you bring this pretty lady with you," Dirk replied as he took the phone and started pressing buttons. Once he was done he flipped it closed and handed it back. "Man, you need a smart phone. Get in the twenty-first century with the rest of us. These old things kill my thumbs."

"Yeah, yeah, yeah." Kyle took the phone and slipped it back in his pants pocket. He then looked at Maya and said, "As for the pretty lady, that's up to her. What do you say, Maya? We didn't get to finish our conversation, and I'd like to see you again. Will you have some free time tomorrow?"

Considering how much work she had to do the next day she didn't know how to answer him. But, she knew that she liked him, and that the idea of spending more time in his company was greatly appealing, so after a few seconds she nodded. "Yeah, I'd like that. Give me a call."

Maya opened her purse and withdrew one of her cards.

Kyle took it from her hand like it was precious and fragile, and then slipped it into his pocket. A moment later Helen returned with two Styrofoam containers and plastic bags. As she transferred the food from the plates to the containers, Maya took out her wallet and withdrew a twenty-dollar bill.

"Enjoy that," she said to the waitress as she handed her the money. "It'll be the last you get from me."

Helen took the money with fingers that looked like rotten sausages and slipped it into her bra, the turned and walked away. "I'll try not to cry myself to sleep."

Maya looked at both men, aghast.

Dirk shook his head and shifted out of the booth. "Like I said, I can't understand it either. Makes me glad I have a place far enough out of town that I rarely have to deal with these people."

Following his example, Maya and Kyle stood up and grabbed their bagged food. Kyle used his free arm to hug his friend again, and Maya shook his hand.

"I'm glad we ran into each other, man," Kyle said.

"Yeah, me too." Dirk turned to Maya and nodded his head in a slight bow. "It was a pleasure to meet you, Maya. I hope I get to see you again."

Maya returned his nod, feeling much the same way. "I'm sure we will."

Their farewells made, Kyle and Maya left The Basement as Dirk handled his bill. The sun was a distant memory, and only a few lights lit up the road that separated the bar from the motel. They crossed it in silence, both content to tend to their own thoughts until Kyle reached his rented Jeep and deactivated the alarm.

"You sure it's okay to call you tomorrow?" he asked. The vulnerable look on his face made her want to laugh, but she knew that was the wrong thing to do. Men liked to act tough, but inside they were fragile, and experience had taught her that even a friendly laugh could be killer when their hearts were on their sleeves.

"I'll be mad if you don't."

A smile broke across his face, making his brown eyes

glitter in the light of the parking lot. "Excellent. Tomorrow then."

Maya was filled with the sudden urge to step close and kiss Kyle's cheek, but her mother had raised her better than that, so she stayed put. Deep down, though, she hoped Kyle would be less mannerly and do it for her. When he instead waved and got into the Jeep, a pang of disappointment vibrated through her.

She was surprised by how much she was attracted to him. He was handsome, most definitely, and despite her preconceived ideas about what someone from a place like Stillwater would be like he was also intelligent and sure of himself without being arrogant. The fact that his little sister meant so much to him appealed to her love of family. And while his gentlemanly wave frustrated her, it also spoke well of his character. He was definitely dating material. What more he might be remained to be seen.

As he engage the Jeep's engine and backed out of the parking lot, she waved back. She then reached into her pocket for her room key, hoping the bar's food was better than its service.

It wasn't.

CHAPTER SIX

The dark of night should have hidden how rundown Stillwater had become, but to Kyle's surprise it only made it worse. Grime seemed grimier, holes were bigger, everything was falling into shadows. It was depressing. When he pulled onto King Street, his headlights swept the decrepit neighborhood like cleansing fire, but as soon as they shifted away the darkness rushed in to bring ruin to everything again. He saw his father's brown Ford pickup sitting in the driveway like a beast of rust and regret.

A shiny face appeared in his headlights, and all thoughts of his parents fled his mind to make room for spine-chilling panic. He hit the brake pedal so hard he nearly pushed it through the Jeep's floorboard and into asphalt. Once he was stopped he reached to open his door, but the face appeared again, this time next to his window. It took him a moment to recognize it as Taylor's. His dread quickly turned into anger.

"Hey, big bro!" She tapped against the glass. "Nice ride!"

He felt around for the window crank before remembering the Jeep had power windows. He stabbed the button with his finger and moist, chilly air flowed in.. "Jesus H. Christ! I damn near ran you over!"

Taylor shook her head and laughed. "Naw, not even close. I'm agile. Like a cat. Rawr."

"You still scared the shit out of me." His heart slowly climbed down his throat as she grinned at him. "Now get in the car before you catch a cold, Piglet."

"Oh, God, you know I hate that name." Rolling her eyes, Taylor ran around the front of the Jeep and opened the passenger door. She still wore the jeans and Lady Gaga t-shirt from earlier, but she'd added a few lengths of brightly colored feathers to her hair like she was heading to a rave.

"You're all dressed up," he said as she pulled her seatbelt across and clicked it into place.

"A girl needs to look good, bro. Always."

"Is there anywhere in particular you want to go?"

Taylor thought about it for a moment, then shook her head. "No. Just drive around awhile."

"Okay." He shifted into reverse and backed down the street. "Your wish is my command."

Once they were out of their parents' neighborhood Kyle thought Taylor would erupt into typical teenage girl babble, but she didn't. Instead she pulled her knees up until they were resting on the dash and looked out the window beside her. His instinct was to reach out, talk, catch up on things, engage her in some way, but the air around her had a fragile feel to it, so he let her be and just drove.

His hands moved purely on muscle memory as he steered down the back roads of Stillwater. Ten minutes later, as they crossed a set of railroad tracks, Taylor sighed and turned to look out the front windshield. "So, I guess Mom told you I'm gay."

"She…uh…mentioned it, yeah." He wished like hell he'd given some forethought on what to say about the topic. "Want to talk about it?"

"Not if you're gonna get all condemny on me I don't." She looked up when a set of bright lamp poles and a Joe-D's Gas & Sip sign came into view through a strand of trees. "Stop there. I'm crazy thirsty."

The convenience store was set off to the right of the road. Gravel crunched under the tires as he pulled in and parked next to the building. He then handed her a ten dollar bill. "Get me a coffee. Two creams, two sugars. And some chips. I don't care what, but no pork rinds. Get yourself whatever you want."

Taylor leaned over, kissed him on the cheek, and then snatched the money and bounced out of the Jeep. Through the rain-smeared windows he watched her go to the back and pour coffee into a dark brown Styrofoam cup, then measure out the cream and sugar. The store clerk sat behind his counter, his head down but his eyes raised and staring at his sister's ass like a hawk eyeing a field mouse. The twerp tracked her as she went to get a bottle of Diet Coke and then grabbed an armful of chip snack bags. Kyle put his hand on the door handle, ready to leap out if the clerk decided staring wasn't enough. Instead the two of them laughed like old friends as she paid for the food and drink. When she came out she looked like she had no idea she'd been mentally raped. He hoped he never looked at women with that same level of naked hunger.

"What's wrong?" she asked as she opened the Jeep door.

He thought about telling her what he'd observed, but then shook his head. After years of not being the big brother she needed, he didn't want to come off now like an overprotective jerk. Complimentary would be the better tact to take.

"I just can't believe how beautiful you've become, that's all."

Taylor blushed and handed him his coffee. Once the chip bags were stashed in the open space between their seats, she got back in and buckled up. "You're not so bad yourself, mister soldier man. Looks like the Army's made you into a lean, mean, lady killing machine."

The hot coffee burned his lips as the Jeep bucked across the bumpy parking lot, but it tasted sweet enough to be drinkable. After setting it into a cup holder he steered them down Old Mine Road.

"I can't believe you'd think I was capable of condemning you. You're my sister."

Taylor took a quick swallow of her soda. "After the things Mom's said I don't give blood the benefit of the doubt. Besides, aren't you military types supposed to be all 'no fags in this man's army' and all that?"

Kyle coughed to cover a laugh. "First off, I'd never say that, so fuck off. Second, there are gay people in this man's army that I know personally, and I trust them with my life. And lastly, I gotta be honest – knowing I'll never have to sweat about you being out on a date with some douche bag dude-bro makes me kinda happy."

Taylor leaned over and gave him a quick hug around the shoulders. "Aw, I'm glad we're both in the 'We Like Girls' club."

"Mom said you were actually dating a girl. Is she someone you really like, or is it more of a limited option thing?"

She reached down and grabbed a bag of Bugles, then pulled it open and shoved one of the small tornado shaped treats into her mouth. "You'd be surprised. Stillwater might be backwoods, but there's a fair number of gay kids if you know where to look. And I do."

"What's her name?"

"Morgan, though she likes to be called Morgana. Don't ask. It's a goth thing."

The way Taylor rolled her eyes made Kyle laugh. "And is she your little mistress of the night?"

"Mmm hmm," she replied around a swallow of Diet Coke. "She avoids the sun like crazy. Cramped my style over the summer, but that creamy skin of hers is worth it. And don't even get me started on her tits."

The Jeep nearly went off the road when Kyle tried to laugh and shout in outrage all at the same time. Taylor pointed and laughed, obviously pleased that she'd gotten the reaction she wanted. Once his hands were back under control, Kyle took a long drink of coffee and focused on the heat of it sliding down his throat.

"You're so easy." She giggled around her soda bottle.

"Whatever. You're not the little girl I once carried around like a stuffed animal."

She turned toward him and tilted her head. "And is that a good thing, or a bad?"

"A good," he told her, not hesitating for a moment. "Definitely a good."

Taylor's face lit up in a smile. "I'm glad to hear that."

It was nice to have his sister beside him after so many years away, and if all they had to talk about were boobs and the latest pop bands, he'd have been as happy as a pig in shit. But he'd returned to Stillwater for a reason, and he figured now was as good a time to get into it as any.

"So… What's going on at home?"

From the corner of his eye he saw her chewing on her

lower lip. It was almost a minute later before she replied.

"Something's wrong with Mom and Dad."

"You think?" Kyle wanted to laugh at her statement of the obvious.

"No," Taylor replied, shaking her colorful head. "I'm serious. They're both a couple of weirdos, sure, but lately they've been taking it up a notch. Lots of notches. It's... It scares me."

Taylor had used the word 'scared' in her messages, but in text it had felt like over exaggerated young girl drama. Hearing her say it, with her voice soft and fearful, the word took on a new level of importance.

"How do you mean? Why scared?"

"It's like..." She paused and ran her left hand through her hair, played with the beads and feathers she'd braided in. "It's like they're not the same people anymore. It started with Dad. He's always been closed off, ya know? Hard to read? But about a month ago he started opening up in a bad way. If I or Mom did something that pissed him off, he'd yell at us. At first it was once or twice a day, but then it became more and more. When I still had Mom I could deal with it, but then she started getting weird too. Instead of yelling, she got condescending, walked around like someone put a crown on her head and made her Queen Bitch of the world."

"Hey now." Kyle interrupted her. "As bad as she seems, that's still Mo—"

Taylor twisted around in her seat and pointed a black-lacquered fingernail at him. "No, Kyle. You don't get to play that card. You left. I could have hated you for that, maybe sometimes I even did, but I understood why you did it. Hell, you were an inspiration. But when you left me here with them, you lost the right to tell me how I should talk about our parents. And I'm telling you, those people aren't my parents anymore."

"What, you mean like pod people or something?" he asked, unable to keep a small laugh out of his voice.

"No, not... I don't know. I mean, no, I don't think aliens have fallen from the sky and replaced Mom and Dad so they can take over the world. 'Cause, if so, epic fail on that plan. But there *is* something wrong with them. When I look in their eyes, I don't see any love there. No love, no joy, no happiness. Every day they get a little more angry, a little more...dark. I don't know how else to say it. I don't even recognize them anymore."

Kyle was a man used to dealing with facts, statistics, black and white info. He didn't understand what Taylor was trying to say, and that frustrated him, because he wanted to understand. He wanted to help. "By dark, what do you mean?"

Taylor chewed on her lip again and looked down at her knees. "The other day I got up and went into the kitchen to get breakfast before leaving for school. When I went past the living room I saw them sitting on the couch. The only light was what came from my bedroom, so they were just sitting there, in the dark, dressed in the same clothes they'd had on the day before, staring at nothing. I swear to god I just about screamed. It was the creepiest thing I'd ever seen."

"Did they say anything?"

She gave her head a slight shake. "Not at first. They just sat there. I stood there watching them breathe and stare. I didn't know what to do or say. It was almost... It was like they were in church, just sitting and listening to Pastor Lucas preach. After half a minute of me building up a good freak-out, Dad turned and looked at me with eyes that...I can't believe I'm saying it...with eyes that weren't there. I swear, they were just black holes in his face. And then, just as I'm ready to scream, he said, 'You better get your ass to school, girl, or I'll take you to work with me, and we'll see how you do in the deep dark.' His voice sounded like it was coming out of the ground, Kyle, like...like he was talking from that goddam mine. I was so scared I didn't even go back to my room to get my book bag. I just grabbed a breakfast bar and ran out. It was awful."

"Sounds it," Kyle replied, choking on the understatement. "Have they done it again, or anything like that?"

"The sitting in the dark thing? Not really. Dad's barely

home anymore. They've got him working the mine practically around the clock. Mom's way of dealing with it is to smoke more and call me a dyke every chance she gets. I've been staying at friends' houses to get away from it, but it's not just Mom and Dad."

"What do you mean?"

Taylor sipped on her drink and stared into the darkness outside the windshield. "It's the whole town. Fights have been breaking out in school more and more, some of them so bad ambulances had to be called. I've seen people who used to be friends yell at each other like they were born enemies. And…I know this sounds stupid, like I'm a doctor or something…but everyone looks sick. I know Fall isn't the best time to get a tan in these mountains, but people are walking around looking almost like corpses. It's crazy. It's all around here, and I'm scared."

The words his little sister used bothered him. What she'd said so far was awful, but surely her mind had exaggerated things. As bad as Mother had been to talk to, she hadn't been possessed or anything. Taylor's worries were likely a reaction to their disapproval of her sexual orientation.

Speaking of disapproval, he thought as his headlights swept across a street sign reading ELMWOOD WAY, *if they catch her out with me she's going to get in a world of trouble. Me too. I better get her home.*

"That sounds weird, no doubt about that. Tomorrow I'm going to talk to Mom and Dad both. We'll get this situation figured out, one way or another. Okay."

Taylor nodded, then shrugged her shoulders. "If you say so."

"I do. Now I better get you back."

"You're taking me home?" The skin between her eyes wrinkled. "Already? Why? What did I do wrong?"

He brought the Jeep to a stop in the middle of the dark country road and turned to face her. "You didn't do anything wrong. This isn't a punishment. It's just that it's getting late, and if Mom and Dad haven't found out that you slipped away, they will soon. The last thing either of us needs is them getting all in an uproar or calling the cops."

He let off the brake and continued their drive, but Taylor crossed her arms and glared forward. "I don't want to go back there, Kyle. Didn't you hear what I said? It's goddam scary in that house. Something is *wrong* with them."

"Mom seemed off, yeah," he replied, trying to calm her down, "but don't you think you're exagger-"

"Don't you do that! Don't put this off as some stupid girl shit! You don't live in that house! You don't know!"

He knew that everything she said she believed, that to her none of it was exaggeration. And, with everything he had he wished he could believe her, because then he could whisk her off and never have to worry about the consequences. But he didn't live in a world where he could do that. In his world people didn't get possessed or replaced by aliens. In his world people had to follow the law, had to do what was right, even if it sucked ass doing it. If Taylor wasn't strong enough to realize that, he'd have to be strong enough for the both of them.

"I don't like making you do what you don't want to do, believe me, but if we want to have a chance of making this situation better, we have to be careful, and we have to handle it the right way."

She laughed, the burst of sound anything but joyful. "Oh, right, sure. 'The right way.' There's nothing right about any of this. Stick around long enough, and you'll see that too."

He dimmed the lights as they rolled to a stop two homes from their parents' house. "I'm *going* to stick around. We'll see this through. I promise."

Taylor's fingers held her arms in a white-knuckled grip as she stared forward. He watched her nostrils flare, wondering what he could say that would help, but after a moment she opened her door and slid out.

"Yeah," she said without turning around. "We'll see. Thanks for nothing."

She closed the Jeep's door, careful not to slam it even though she was angry, and jogged off into the night. The shadows of the surrounding houses and the trees that bordered them quickly swallowed her up, removing all trace of her as though she'd never existed.

"Well that went well," Kyle said to himself. "Good job, dumb ass. Real good job."

Kyle put the Jeep back into drive and rolled on, scratching his head and wondering how he could have handled it better. The drive back to the motel felt like it took forever as a million better word choices poured through his brain.

Taylor ground her teeth together as she walked past the Nichols house, her feet trampling through mud patches in loud plops. This wasn't how things were supposed to go. After weeks of dealing with her parents' gradual slide into total freakdom, her brother had finally arrived to make it all better. But instead of listening to her and understanding just how strange things were, he'd blown her off like some kid crying wolf. How could he do that? How could he not get it? Frustration rolled through her chest like a ball of flame, making her blood boil.

As she rounded the Nichols place her parents' house slid out of the darkness, the front door and driveway lit by a scarcely functional streetlamp. The back of the house where her bedroom was located was lost in shadows. She'd snuck out of her room lots of times, though, so she knew exactly where to go even though she could barely see.

Beneath her window, standing amid a riot of daylilies and begonias, were two gnarly cement garden gnomes. She'd picked them up the year before at a small craft shop halfway between Stillwater and Williamson, and over the course of several weeks she'd painted them to look like little gnomy vampires named Drago and The Count. As an ironic touch she'd even glued plastic rhinestones to their faces and hands so they glittered when the sun hit them. At first they'd been meant as whimsical touches to decorate the flower garden she tended beneath her window – she loved the smell of them in the spring when the rain and sun drove them into a frenzy of growth – but it hadn't take long for her to figure out they also made for great step stools. All she had to do was make sure not to leave any tell-tale shoe prints on their stony black hats, and no one would be the wiser. That was the idea, anyway.

Careful to not crush her flowers, Taylor wiped her feet off on the grass and then put her left foot on the Count's head to hoist herself up. Her window was shut, but not locked, and she shoved it up with the palms of her hands. Wood scraped against wood, but the window made little sound. Once it was open, she leaned over and pushed herself over the sill, making sure Lady Gaga's face didn't catch on anything and tear. It was her favorite shirt, and the last thing she needed after the night's massive disappointment was to ruin it.

Once inside her room she turned to close the window, but then paused. Just because her stupid brother had dumped her here didn't mean she had to stay. She hadn't been exaggerating one bit when she'd said staying in the house scared her. When the lights went out and the house was quiet, all she could think about were her parents sitting on the couch, staring into space. Telling Kyle about that had been hard, because it was a memory she didn't enjoy recalling, but there were other things she hadn't told him, things she kept to the furthest reaches of her mind. She didn't tell him about the whispers she heard coming from the bathroom when her dad went in there, or the way he sometimes cocked his head as if he was listening to something no one else could hear. She didn't tell him about the blackened fingernail she found in the bathtub the other day that was too large to belong to anyone else but her dad, and she certainly hadn't mentioned the way his eyes sometimes seemed to darken when he got really mad, like the light inside him was buried by something. Every night she spent under her parents' roof was a test of her resolve and love-- a test she was slowly failing. Now she felt like an end to it might be in sight, and that possibility made the prospect of another night in her room seem unbearable.

The decision to leave made, Taylor stooped down next to her bed and pulled out a green duffel bag. Other girls would have preferred a Hello Kitty backpack or some other lame shit, but not Taylor. Her mom had gotten the duffel bag for her years ago from an Army/Navy store, and when she'd said it was probably like the one Kyle used, the bag quickly became her favorite possession. The wear and tear it had developed over the years only made her love it more.

If she left now and peddled hard she could get to Morgan's in twenty minutes so long as the rain hadn't washed out Gosselin Road. Morgan knew how Taylor's family life had been going and had begged her repeatedly to stay over. Now was as good a time as any to take her up on it. Then they could even ride to school together tomorrow.

As Taylor walked to her dresser to get some clean clothes, a hand reached out from the darkness of her closet and grabbed her arm. She opened her mouth to scream, but another hand came up to smother it. She stumbled backward, pulling the figure with her, and in the weak light spilling through her window she saw her father. His skin looked as gray as storm clouds, but it was his eyes that sent her heart quaking in her chest. They were black and bottomless.

"You are such a disappointment," he said, the words dropping from his mouth like chunks of ice. "At least now you'll be of good use."

The grip on her arm tightened painfully, and when she looked down she saw that none of her father's fingers had nails on them anymore. The soft grim skin that remained pulsed sickeningly, and the dark veins layered over it like webbing bulged and pushed outward. When several vessels burst and sent black tendrils twisting around her wrist like thin shadowy snakes, her mind broke and she fell into an unconscious heap. In the darkness the thing that had once been her father picked her up like she weighed next to nothing, hoisted her over a lumpy shoulder, and carried her into the night.

CHAPTER SEVEN

Water fell on Maya all day, but the warm spray of her motel room's shower banished the memory of cold rain. The little bathroom was grimy, and the towels were rough, but the water flowed hot and strong. Every muscle kink and awkward moment the day had given her spiraled down the drain. It was a wonderful sensation.

Washed and toweled off, Maya walked to the bed. Her suitcase lay open on top of it, and after a few seconds of rooting around she came up with a navy blue Tennessee Titans t-shirt and a pair of red panties. After both garments were slipped on, she looked to the other side of the bed. Her cell phone lay dark on the nightstand.

She flopped on the bed and picked up her phone, figuring a quick email and Facebook check would be a good way to wind down before sleeping. As her fingers slid across the phone's glass face she saw Alan had called and left a voice mail while she was in the shower.

He probably called to say he'll be late, she thought as she opened the voice mail app. *Typical.*

"Hey, Maya, it's me." Alan's slow, gloomy voice set off an alarm bell in her belly. "Listen, I…yeah…I can't make it to the investigation in Stillwater. A last minute wedding videography job got booked, and my boss is still out of town, so I have to do it. I tried like hell to get one of the other guys to cover for me, but I work with a bunch of useless assholes, so I'm stuck with it. I'm really sorry."

Maya knew he was sorry. Alan was a good guy, and most of the time really dependable. For him to beg off an investigation, especially one that appeared as juicy as this, it had to hurt. But, as the consequences of this change of plans played out in her mind, she realized she would end up being the sorriest of them all.

"So, as I'm sure you've surmised by now, that means I

had to ask Darius to help you in my place. I know, I know, your ex-boyfriend is the last person you want to see right now. He wasn't all that happy about it either. If there was someone else I could send, I would, but the three of us are it – for now at least. If things go south in a hurry and you two absolutely cannot work together, just cut the trip short and come home. You and I will investigate it another time. It's not like the town's going anywhere, right? Anyway, I really am sorry. I'll make it up to you somehow. Try not to kill him. Talk to you when you get back. Bye."

It took all her willpower to not hurl her phone against a wall. Of everyone she didn't want to see, Darius topped the list. She didn't need the stress of him being around adding to what was already proving to be a tough investigation. But shit, what was done was done. Darius was probably already on his way. The only thing she could do now was grin and bear it.

All thoughts of sleep now banished from her head, Maya closed the voice mail app and started a game of Sweet Smash. The game was addictive, but when she imagined Darius's face in place of the small sweet treats she destroyed with a touch of her finger it became all the more pleasurable. She didn't look up from her phone when a pair of headlights swung past her window accompanied by a growling engine, but a knock at her door jerked her back to reality.

Instinctively she looked at the deadbolt and chain lock – both were secured – then checked the time on her phone. 10:34 PM. Her purse sat next to her, and she reached inside it. When her fingers circled the hard plastic handle of her taser she felt a tiny bit better. Getting out of bed as quietly as she could, she crossed to the door and took a look through the peephole. Kyle stood outside. As much as she looked forward to seeing him again, this seemed a bit soon.

"Kyle?" she asked through the door. "Everything okay?"

Even though the peephole's lens distorted his face, his red eyes and disheveled hair told her he wasn't okay. Her heart thudded with an extra beat.

"Not really," he replied, his voice muffled by wood and wall. "If you don't want any company, though, I understand. I just... I just needed to talk with someone."

If Maya had a weakness, other than peanut butter cups and the smell of cigars, it was sad guys. And even though she knew that about herself, she was powerless to do anything about it. Wanting to mend broken men was just part of her DNA.

"No, it's fine. Umm...give me a second." Maya put her taser on the dresser, then opened a drawer and grabbed a set of pajama bottoms. They were faded green and didn't go with her shirt, but at the moment beggars couldn't be choosers. After they were on she did one last check of the room to make sure nothing was out that shouldn't be. With her heart hammering in her chest like a caged animal, she went to the door, unbolted the lock, and opened it.

Kyle felt stupid as hell. Here he was, knocking on the door of a woman he barely knew, and all because his little sister had copped an attitude with him.

No, it's more than that, and you know it. You don't want to admit it, but every crazy thing she said, you believe it. You've got no evidence but one bad conversation with your mother, but even so, Taylor's not lying. So what does that mean? What are you gonna do? Maybe you should run away again. That's at least something you're good at.

Those were the thoughts plaguing him on the drive back to the motel, and no matter how reasonable he tried to be with himself, they just wouldn't leave him. He felt worse and less sure with every mile he drove, but when he pulled into the motel's parking lot and saw Maya's car he knew he had to see her. If anything could lift his spirits it was her beautiful blue eyes and bright smile.

She proved him right the moment she opened the door. She was a vision, even in old green pajama pants and a Titans t-shirt. A breath of cool air blew through his head, clearing away some of the angst-ridden dust. "Wow."

A blush spread across Maya's face like an early sunrise, and she tugged at the hem of her shirt as she backed away from the door. "Shut up and come in already."

The air inside her room was damp, and a towel hanging

from the bathroom door said why. Once through the threshold he turned left and settled into an empty chair next to the cheap table located between the bed and window. Behind him Maya locked the door, then followed him and sat facing him on the bed.

"So, you wanted to talk?" The question was direct, but her tone was soft.

Kyle nodded, yet as he soaked in her warmth all the tangles in his head loosened, deflating his anxiety. "I do. Or, at least, I did. I don't know. My head and my heart are struggling to understand each other."

"I can understand that." Maya leaned against her headboard. "Is it your sister? You worried about her?"

"She's part of it. Like I said, I don't... I knew coming back to this damn town would be a mistake."

"If your sister's in trouble, then it's not a mistake."

He knew that. In his heart he knew she was right. In his head, though, he felt like David up against a Goliath made up of the entire town. It felt like too much, or he felt like too little. Or maybe it was both. Either way, he didn't fell ready for what was coming.

"I just feel so damn guilty." A warm tear fell down his face. "I never should have left her here. I was selfish, and stupid, and arrogant. I graduated, left town, joined the Army, and not once did I consider what might happen back home. How could I do that to my baby sister?"

With each word his tears fell harder.

Great, now I look as pathetic as I feel. I am such a loser.

"You're not a loser," she replied as she leaned toward him, the caring quality of her voice sweeping his mind away and caressing his heart. "You were a kid. You couldn't know. We all do dumb things we later regret. You shouldn't beat yourself up about it. You're here now, right? Better late than never."

"Is it?" He reached for a handkerchief in his front pocket, but Maya reached out and wiped his tears away before he could get it. Her skin was warm and smooth against his, and just like when he'd first shaken her hand a jolt of electricity coursed through him. Under her touch he felt naked, exposed, and in a strange way completely at home. The swirl of sudden emotions made him dizzy.

"It is." Maya's eyes locked onto his, giving him a center to hold to. "Bad people don't cry about what they've done or have regrets. You didn't know what would happen, you did what you thought was right at the time, and now you're back to try and make a difference. Your sister is lucky to have you as her big brother."

Kyle wanted to believe her so much. "You don't know that."

"I do." Shifting her legs around to hang off the side of the bed, she reached out and took both his hands in hers. "Believe it or not, I know more than you think. You're a good man. You care. You have your doubts, but your love for your sister shines through that. You're a remarkable guy, Kyle."

Her words were healing, reaching into him and making right so many of the things that were wrong. Yet, as good as they felt, they also shined a light on fears and worries he normally kept in the dark.

"Remarkable. Right." He sniffed back tears and rubbed at his wet eyes. "If I'm so remarkable, then why do I feel so helpless and alone?"

Using a hand under his chin to draw him close, she whispered, "You're not alone," and then kissed him. His instinct was to pull away – he barely knew Maya – but the feel of her hands as they held the sides of his face kept him right where he was. She leaned forward, pressing closer to him, the heat of her body washing against him in waves. After a few moments they both stood up and wrapped their arms around each other, giving and taking comfort.

Her lips were warm and smooth against his. The way their tongues tentatively explored each other made him think of eating a sun-warmed peach. She tasted sweet in his mouth, and her breath gave him new life. He worried his desire to drink her in made him too aggressive, but she gave as good as she got. Her fingers slid into his hair and her chin rubbed against his urgently. It was the longest kiss he'd ever experienced in his life, and without doubt the hottest. When they eventually parted it was with deep regret.

"I want you," she said, her eyes half closed. "Now."

He hated looking a miracle in the mouth, but he didn't want to feel like he was taking advantage of anyone. "Are you sure? I—"

She shushed him with a quick kiss and started pulling off her clothes. First went the sweatpants, and then went the red panties underneath. He felt like a little boy peeking at his birthday present as he gazed at the light brown cleft between her legs and the trimmed thatch of hair above it. When she removed her shirt and revealed her breasts he wanted to faint. They looked ripe and full, the right breast just slightly larger than the left, and his hands ached to hold them.

Giving himself over, his hands shook as he pulled off his shirt. As he tugged it over his head he got caught up and had to struggle to clear the neck hole. Embarrassment made his face feel like it was on fire, but Maya only smiled.

"Let me." She pressed against him.

Her nipples were like hard chocolate candies, and the feel of them made his head swim. He barely knew what was happening as she took his shoes and socks off, and it wasn't until he felt cold air blow past his groin that he realized he was naked as a jay bird. When she took him in her hand, he trembled.

Within seconds they were on the bed, their hands ranging over each other's bodies, their mouths consuming everything they could reach. She felt like velvet in his hands, her body soft and warm and endlessly curved. She was a bundle of desire, both to give and receive, and he did everything he could to match her, though she didn't make it easy. When she eventually pulled away, the space between their bodies felt cavernous.

"Do you have any protection?" she asked, her voice breathy and deep.

A sinking sensation hit his stomach. "No, I don't. I...uh...wasn't planning on this."

The corners of her lips turned down in a frown, but then

she got up from the bed and walked to her collection of bags. He loved watching her move, seeing her body from every angle possible. Her hands moved quickly as she opened one of the bags and rooted through it. Several seconds later she pulled out a box of condoms. The scuffed, bent cardboard container looked like it had been there awhile, but when she shook it three small plastic wrappers fell into her hand.

"I got it." He reached for one of the wrappers, but she shook her head and tore one open with her teeth as she tossed the other two on the nightstand. Just watching and feeling her hands on him made him want to climax there and then, but he bit his lower lip and held on. The true test came when she straddled his hips and guided him inside her.

His brain slipped into a place without language as he entered her. She rode him in long, slow motions, and all either of them could utter were grunts and half words. Her hands were on his chest, and he held her hips, holding her right where she was. He couldn't say how long they lasted – it could have been seconds or hours – but eventually his eyes rolled up in his head and he crested the mountain.

Maya lowered her head and rested it beneath his chin. He slid his hands from her hips to encircle her back. Her skin was slick with sweat. Her chest moved in the same frantic motions as his.

"That was...that was perfect," she said with barely enough breath to voice the words.

He kissed the top of head and hugged her close. "Yeah, I'd say that just about describes it."

She looked up at him, her gray eyes and brown face so strange and yet so perfect. When she smiled, he smiled too.

"Do it again," she said, sliding her hand down to take hold of him.

And so they made love again. He knew little more than her name, yet when he looked at her he saw something he recognized, something that pulled at him and made him feel like she had always been there. He'd never felt anything like it, not with any other girl he'd been with, and the feeling gave the act of loving her body that much more meaning and passion.

By the time they were both spent and the sheets were a sweaty tangle, he felt a connection to her that seemed almost magical, even if it scared him.

"Sleep here tonight." She spooned against him and drew his arm around her. "If that's okay, I mean."

"There's nowhere else I'd rather be," he told her, pulling her close and kissing the back of her neck.

She murmured something in return, but he didn't hear it, and that was okay. He stayed right where he was, holding Maya close and letting the warmth of her lull him into a deep sleep. He barely felt it when Maya grumbled and shifted her body around as dark dreams slipped inside her head. His sleep was deep and unbroken.

Interlude
Children Of Shadows

Standing in the lightless cavern, Ash dreamed of an ancient world. It was the dark world of those who came first, colossal beasts of great power rising from the muck of a planet just beginning to cool, when raw magic and power were free for the taking. And take it, they did. With strength that made mountains crumble and appetites that drained oceans, the First Ones ravaged the world and each other, created armies from dust, sired foul children out of the ooze. There were no stars in that world, just a black sky and a moon that looked down on it like a blood-filled eye. For millions of years they warred and tortured and killed. But then came the light, and then the rain.

Ash saw only darkness in his dreams after that. He wanted more blood, wanted to see the ancients tremble the world and shape it to all the dark purposes that boiled in their minds like burning pitch, wanted to see them drunk on their power, but he didn't. He saw only what became of his god after the water fell. It was tragic for a being as mighty as he that slept in the flooded cavern below, but it wasn't the end of the story. The sound of rumbling pumps and the increased stirring in his head promised more was to come, and Ash would be there when the greatest of the First rose again, returning the world to what it should have been.

Rocks scattered in the tunnel behind him, followed by the sound of several beating hearts. One was calm, its pulses slow and steady, but the other was frantic, like a rabbit caught in a snare. The erratic beat of it stirred Ash's appetite, and jagged teeth pushed through his gums, ruining the pink meat and dislodging old teeth to fall useless to the ground in a spatter of bloody gore.

"Sir, we've got a problem," Gus said as he stopped outside the cavern's entrance.

Casting a glance over his bony left shoulder, Ash looked at his underling and was amused by the way he held his hat in his hands and twisted it. There wasn't a single ray of light to be had in the mine, but Ash saw everything as though in the brightness of day. It was just one of the many gifts his god had bestowed upon him. Gus couldn't see as well, but even so when he looked at Ash he flinched and looked away quickly.

"We're standing at the dawn of a new age for humanity," Ash said, his voice deeper than ever before, with a rumble in it like the earth grinding against itself. "How can there be a problem with that?"

Gus wrung his hat and kicked at small stones next to his boots. "It's my son. He's...uh...come back to town. Could be trouble."

Laughing, Ash ran his tongue over the new fangs populating his mouth. The sharp teeth cut his tongue and sent small steams of brackish blood running into his throat. The taste was wonderful, but the cuts closed a moment later, staunching the flow.

"You're son's no trouble to the darkness that rises below us. Nothing can stop what's coming."

It was Gus's turn to laugh, the sound of it mirthless and pitiful. "No, and praise be."

Ash sighed and ground his teeth together so hard they shredded the insides of his gray cheeks. Gouts of blood and torn meat poured down his throat before the wounds healed, and the taste of it hit his body like a drug, sending his blackened heart into a gallop.

"Indeed. Praise be. Soon our Lord will be risen, and all the sons and daughters of Stillwater will meet the fate that has been written for them. Our Lord's will cannot be denied."

Gus nodded and put it through another round of twists.

Ash's patience with those who were among the first of the awoken was great, but Gus's hemming and hawing stretched it. "Now what plagues your mind?"

"Kyle ain't the only new face in town," the old man finally said. "Some bitch rolled in 'round the same time. People think she might be a reporter or something. All she done so far is ask a few questions, but I don't like it."

"Do you think she and your son came together for some

purpose?"

Gus shook his head and crushed the bill of his hat in his hands. "Naw, don't seem to. They came in different vehicles, and they're staying in different rooms over at the motel."

Sighing, Ash turned and looked back down at the lowering waters. There lay his future, his destiny. "It don't matter. The time of awakening is at hand, and in another day or so the whole world is gonna change. Hallelujah."

"Oh, yes, sir," Gus replied, a light shining from his eyes and a smile on his face. "I also wanted to let you know I brung my girl like I said I would."

Stepping to the side, Gus cleared the passageway to reveal his daughter. A piece of thick black tape covered her mouth, and one of the night crew held her in place, his grip so tight on her arms the skin around his fingers bruised. The young girl's cheeks puffed in and out, and tears streamed from her eyes as she cried into a darkness so deep it blinded her.

"She's pretty," Ash said, his teeth aching at the thought of tearing her head off and eating the bloody stump until all that was left was to suck the marrow out of her spine.

"She's trouble is what she is. Never been anything but. Least now she'll do something worthwhile."

Ash pushed his lust to kill and feed to the back of his mind. His god would be hungry when he rose, and it would be a sin to deny him such a tasty treat as Gus's daughter. He would feed when all of civilization lay in ruin, and the cattle of humanity lain at his feet.

"Go put her with the others, then." Ash licked the gray flaps of skin that were his lips, he noted a small change in the noise rolling off of the equipment outside the cavern. "And get someone to take a look at the pumps. I don't want anything delaying the glory to come."

"Will do, sir." Gus shoved his hat into his pocket and turned away. His daughter stumbled after him, her muted cries and sniffling filling Ash's body with so much pleasure that what remained of his cock hardened in his pants.

There was great glory to come, oh yes, and when his god awoke the whole world would fall to their knees. Ash ached to see that day come as quickly as possible. Blood and spit oozed down his gleaming teeth, coating his chin in gore.

In the darkness below, the water stirred.

CHAPTER EIGHT

A loud thump and violent vibrations yanked Darius from the pull of sleep hours of night driving had induced. His hands shook as he clamped down on the steering wheel of his car and pulled off the gravel shoulder he'd drifted onto. His eyes felt gummy, and after eating nothing but chips and microwave burritos his mouth could have easily been mistaken for the floor of a convenience store. To wake himself up and clear some of the gunk from his mouth he lifted a bottle of water and sucked out what little remained. He glanced around for another bottle, but a quick glance around the interior of his Ford Taurus came up fruitless.

A flash of white and green in his headlights caught his eye. When he looked up, a sign reading ENTERING STILLWATER went by on the right. A few hours ago he wouldn't have thought he'd be relieved to see a sign like that, but now he was ecstatic. He'd been driving for ten hours, and playlists full of Jay-Z or Flo Rida pumping through his speakers hadn't made it easy or fun.

His cell phone was clipped to his dash, and he glanced at it with an angry eye. He knew Alan had told Maya he was coming, yet she hadn't bothered calling or texting to let him know where she was staying, where to meet, anything. He was up and driving deep into the asshole of night, and she was ignoring him. Typical.

Reason 1, he thought, *for why I dumped your ass. Reason 2? You're scary as hell.*

For both those reasons Darius was glad this was his last job to work with Maya. Whenever any sort of spookiness reared its head she lost sight of everything and everyone else, which might not have been the worst thing in the world, but with her, spookiness was never just some strange knocking sounds and the occasional cold spot. No, with her it was always screaming and running and swearing the next day he'd never do it again. She said she had a gift, but to him it was more like a curse. He'd managed to escape relatively unscathed, and he planned on keeping it that way once this investigation was done and she was finally out of his life. He felt bad for the next guy who got caught up in her weird wake

The LOW FUEL alarm dinged, shocking him back to the real world rolling by.

"Ah fuck. Great. Just great. And what do you wanna bet there ain't a gas station for miles."

The universe surprised him when a lit-up sign rose into view as he crested a hill. It read VANCE'S GAS-N-GO, and beneath it were prices for different grades of gas. Darius exhaled a thankful gust of wind.

The gas station was small, comprised of a tiny cashier's station flanked by four sets of pumps. As Darius pulled in he saw the pump closest to the entrance was being used by three big guys fueling a beat-up old Dodge pickup. Judging by the dark stains on their plaid shirts and the dirty baseball caps on their heads, he felt safe in profiling them as rednecks. Something about them didn't look right though. Maybe it was the fluorescent lights, or maybe they were just tired from a long night of working, but all three of them looked sick. They were each hunched over, their movements sluggish, and their skin was the sickly gray color of dirty snow. Not wanting any trouble, he stopped at the pump on the opposite side of the station.

As he stepped out of his car, the moist, crisp air slapped him in the face. From the corner of his eyes he saw the ashen rednecks turn and look at his car. A shiny purple Taurus was probably something these backwoods hicks didn't see every day. In any other time or place he would have stared back and given them a "What the fuck you looking at?" but this wasn't any other time or place, so he ignored them and pulled his wallet from his back pocket. His credit card slipped into his fingers as he saw a sign on the pump's card reader. "Card Machine Down."

"Shit." He looked around at the other pumps, and all of them had the same sign. He then looked in the cash pocket of his wallet, but he already knew what he'd find there – nothing. "Shit."

Hoping the attendant might be able to help, he walked over to the booth. Inside the small cinderblock building sat a kid so dreadful looking the three hicks down the way seemed fresh as daisies. Pasty flesh stretched across bones so sharp they stuck out in odd angles, and lesions covered his greasy face like a shotgun blast. He sat on a stool reading a magazine behind a Plexiglas window, oblivious to the world. On the magazine's cover were two naked Asian women kissing and grabbing each other's tits. The kid licked his cracked lips with a thick, dark, dry tongue.

When the kid didn't acknowledge his presence, Darius reached up to tap the clear plastic window, but something held him back. He couldn't explain it, couldn't understand it, but a tingle in the back of his mind told him to stop. Stop and run.

"You're gonna die, coon." the kid sounded as if he were commenting on the weather, his eyes still glued to the magazine.

A chill hit Darius's chest like an icy spike plunging through his heart. "Um, what did you say?"

The kid, still without glancing up, licked his chapped lips and flipped to the next page. "I think ya heard me just fine."

"Listen, I don't want any trouble." And that was the truth. Darius was no coward, but nothing about this situation felt right. "I just need–"

The kid finally put his porn down and looked up at Darius. His eyes were dead fish staring out from an ashen face, and pockmarks on his cheeks oozed blood and pus. "You don't want trouble, coon, but you're about to get a heaping fuckin' load of it."

Fury rose up in Darius's chest, and he hammered the Plexiglas with both fists. "You better shut the fuck up or I'll get a tire iron and beat the shit out of you with it!"

The kid wiped his leaking face with his right hand. Reddish ooze smeared his fingers, but then he licked them clean with his swollen black tongue. In spite of his anger,

Darius wanted to vomit.

"Bye now." The kid cast his eyes back down at his porn.

Angry and sickened and frightened all at the same time, Darius didn't understand how the early morning had gone so wrong so quickly. Fearing what was coming, he tried to run back to his car. When he turned he found the three rednecks surrounding him like gray Neanderthal statues.

"Hey." The fires of his emotion dampened at the sight of their wide, hunched bodies. "Like I said, I don't want any trouble."

The redneck directly in front of him sneered with the lips of a drowning victim, puffy and almost black, and rolled his shoulders. Thick ropes of muscle bunched against his filthy work shirt. In the harsh lights hanging overhead Darius noticed the redneck's hands were stained with dark powder. His fingernails were black crescent moons.

"You shouldn't have come here, nigger," the redneck said in a voice created by decades of cigarettes and hard drinking.

In a flash, Darius's fury rose up again, and before he knew what he was doing he punched the redneck square in the jaw. A loud, meaty pop filled the air, followed by Darius swearing loudly as he yanked his bruised hand back and cradled it next to his chest. He felt like he busted one of his knuckles, maybe two, but he was okay with that when he saw the redneck's jaw hang at a broken angle. His victory was short lived, though, when the redneck didn't react or cry out. The guy looked like he didn't even realize he'd been hurt. Darius panicked, thinking the men around him might be high on drugs as well as sick, but then a shadow pass over the redneck's eyes, turning them black as midnight. Darius looked at the men on either side of him, and their eyes were the same pitiless voids.

"You got spirit," the redneck to Darius's right said.

"The ancient one will enjoy eating it," the one to his left finished.

Darius barely had time to fear for his life before all three men moved in and pounded on him. The rednecks were strong, and within the first few swings they'd pummeled him to the ground with punches so powerful they sent shockwaves of anguish through his mind. He swung back instinctively, but his movements were wild and frantic. What few hits he landed meant nothing. The rednecks tightened their circle, punching and kicking in an endless stream of punishment. His arms broke in meaty snaps, sending bile up his throat from the searing pain, and then they smashed his leg to dust. The agony soon became overwhelming, and in the small part of his mind that he still had control of he wished like hell he would just black out. At least then he wouldn't feel pain anymore.

With detached cruelty the three men pounded him to mush, their hits and kicks delivered with a terrible rhythm. By the time they finished Darius was little more than a bleeding bag of broken bones barely clinging to consciousness.

As though hearing things from another world, Darius noted the stool in the attendant booth creak as the kid stood up. "You gonna take him to the mine?"

"Yup," the first redneck replied, his jaw popping as he spoke. "Ash will want him before he bleeds out."

Darius could only watch through eyes nearly swollen closed and fear what new terror was coming as the redneck grabbed him by his shirt collar and dragged him to the Dodge pickup. Picking him up like a ragdoll, the redneck lifted him and tossed him into the truck bed. Darius's head smashed against rusted metal, and a groan of pain gurgled past his broken lips. It was the last sound he ever made. When the world went dark and his heart squeezed its last beat, he was thankful.

CHAPTER NINE

When Kyle heard the door next to his room open and close, he turned off the ugly television – nothing but stupid morning talk shows were on anyway – gathered up his keys, put a light jacket on, and left. Outside he found Maya standing next to his rented Jeep. To his disappointment she wore jeans and a thin green sweater over a white t-shirt instead of the skirt and revealing blouse from the day before. But, with a figure like hers, even a burlap sack would have been sexy. The leather hiking shoes laced to her feet and lumpy bag of equipment slung over her shoulder said that today she was all business.

"So where are we off to first?" he asked as he unlocked the passenger door and opened it for her. He pulled his jacket collar up to keep the rain from falling down his back.

Maya smiled as she leaned in and took the offered seat. "Let's go to the town library."

It had been a long time since he'd been out there, but the drive was easy enough to remember. "That I can do." He closed the door and walked around the vehicle. After getting in next to her, he buckled his seatbelt and started the engine. But, before he disengaged the break, he pulled out his phone and said, "Give me one second. Need to call Taylor." He then opened his contacts list and pressed the line for Taylor's cell phone. Ring tones chirped against his ear, but eventually he was dumped to voice mail.

"No answer?" Maya asked.

Kyle shook his head and redialed. When he got her voice mail again, he hung up. "That's odd. Kids these days might as well have their phones surgically implanted on them."

"Maybe her school doesn't allow cell phones. It *is* almost nine in the morning on a school day, don't forget. She probably has it turned off, or it's on vibrate and she can't answer it right now."

Kyle felt like a dumbass as he opened his text message

app and started typing. Of course Maya was right. On his phone he wrote, "HEY SIS, BE BY AT 11 TO TAKE YOU TO LUNCH. LOVE YA." When he hit the SEND button he felt better.

"Okay, you have me all to yourself for the next several hours." He turned his head and backed out of the parking slot.

Rain splattered the Jeep as they left the motel and headed toward what passed for downtown Stillwater. Even though it was morning on a week day, the roads were nearly empty save for the occasional truck wheeling from one unknown location to another, their tires spraying watery tails behind them. It was a dying town, but its demise seemed to be coming sooner rather than later.

"I guess if you aren't one for hustle and bustle, this is the town for you." Maya stared at the vacant asphalt around them.

"No kidding. Just add that to the list of weird shit goin on."

As disconcerting as the lack of life was, it did make the drive to the Stillwater Public Library a quick one. When they pulled up the sad looking brick building, the parking lot was just as empty as the roads.

Maya rifled through her purse, mumbling as she pulled out and then redeposited a moleskin notepad, pens of various colors, her cell phone, and an audio recorder. "It looks like I have everything I need. I've done this sort of research before so let me handle things. You can just sit back and watch the magic."

Chuckling, Kyle nodded at her before opening his door and getting out. She followed him into the rain seconds later. Together they walked up the three concrete steps leading to the library's front door. Raised to be a gentleman, he opened the door and waited for her to go through first.

The inside of the library reflected the town around it — dark, dingy, and dying. Wooden shelves stood around the walls laden with dusty books, while racks held limp magazines, bent and ready to fall. A green Formica counter stood on the right, its top chipped and faded. No one stood behind it, but noises came through a doorway beyond it. On the pebbled glass was stenciled LIBRARIAN'S OFFICE. A small bell sat on the middle of the counter.

"Allow me." Kyle headed to the counter, hoping he wasn't walking into another nasty encounter. "This is my town, after all." He rang the bell when he stood before it. The *clang* that echoed through the library was louder than he'd anticipated, the sharp sound making his teeth ache.

The sound of shuffling papers in the office stopped, and all fell silent for several long seconds, but then plodding steps clomped toward them. Kyle felt an irrational fear build in his chest, and he stared at the doorway. Maya stepped close behind him and took one of his hands in hers with a grip so tight it was painful. A second later a shadow slid through the doorway, a dark and twisted thing of darkness. What followed it struck Kyle like a hard slap across the cheeks.

Ms. Kirkland had been old when he was a boy, her face a craggy moon above him as he borrowed his first book, but she'd always had a smile and a kind word for everyone who passed through her library. To kids old people seemed scary, with their wrinkled skin and angry words, but not Ms. Kirkland. Never Ms. Kirkland.

The bent old woman who walked through the office seemed a bit like her – the same gray hair, the same blue and white gingham blouse – but that was where the similarities ended. Gone was Ms. Kirkland's powered face and broad smile. Now her skin was nearly the same color as her hair, which hung from her head like a wet mop, and her thin lips were pressed into a scowl. Gone was her pleasant plumpness, the old bows and bends shaved off so much that her bones seemed to press against her skin like twigs waiting to rip through a burlap sack. She looked sick and frail, ready to fall apart at the seams, but when she leveled her pale eyes on Kyle and Maya it was with a gaze they could feel press down on them.

"What in hell do you want?" Ms. Kirkland asked, her lips falling backward over toothless gums that turned her mouth into a murky cave.

Kyle cleared his throat and tried to find a smile to ease the moment. It took a few seconds to locate it. "Ms. Kirkland, I doubt you remember me, but I'm Kyle Mason. I used to come here when I was a boy."

"Mason, huh?" The old woman looked him up and down like she was sizing up a side of beef. "Ain't but one family in this town with that name. You must be Gus's boy; the one that run off like he was too good for this place."

"That's not exactly it." Part of him wanted to correct her, to tell her his side of the story, but most of him wanted to turn and flee the library with all the speed he could muster. Ms. Kirkland's deterioration was plainly evident, but as he stood before her he felt that it went far beyond the flesh. Something had changed her, and as much as he hated giving credence to all the spiritual mumbo jumbo he'd heard recently he couldn't help but sense that her rottenness went straight to the soul. This wasn't the woman he'd known. This was someone else, a creature of hate and spite walking in her skin, draining her dry of all the goodness she'd once had. It sickened him, and he wished he could get back in the rented Jeep and leave West Virginia far in his rearview once more.

But he couldn't.

"Don't split hairs with me, boy. And frankly, I don't give two craps." Her scowl impossibly deepened. "Now like I said, what the hell you want?"

Kyle decided to let the pleasantries go – Stillwater and its residents seemed beyond niceties now –and got to the point. "We need to look at whatever archives you have for the town. Old newspapers, books written about it, that sort of thing."

A gray eyebrow rose on Ms. Kirkland's forehead like a storm cloud. "And do you or your half-breed girlfriend there have a library card? Don't bother answering. You don't. You ain't residents of this town, so you won't be getting one neither. Now why don't you two get the hell out of here and go back where you came from before I call the sheriff for harassment?"

When the librarian insulted Maya, Kyle's instinct was to snatch the old woman up by her collar and shake her until her hair fell out – which, given its thinness, it probably already was – but Maya didn't rise to the slur or show any sort of anger. He admired her for that.

"Do you offer a temporary card?" she asked, her tone smooth. "Most libraries do."

"Well we ain't most libraries." The scowl she gave Maya could have withered a tree.

"Couldn't we at least look…" Kyle began.

"You ain't wanted, so get out of here. Now!"

Blood boiled in Kyle's chest and his hands curled into fists, but Maya placed a hand on his arm before he could take a step or say anything.

"We understand. Sorry to have bothered you."

Maya tugged at Kyle's arm, and when he looked her way her expression was sincere and apologetic.

What the fuck? What's she got to be sorry for? That old bitch is the one who should be sorry.

"Save it." Ms. Kirkland gave a dismissive wave of her liver-spotted hand. "And don't come back."

Kyle let himself be pulled away from the library counter, but he made sure he didn't leave without saying something. "At least I'm not going to die alone in this shithole town."

Gray lips curled like a dog growling as the librarian grimaced at them. As the door opened and he was pulled into wet outside air, the old woman got the last word. "Don't be so sure."

"What was that about?" he asked as the door closed. "I thought we needed information."

Maya glanced around the building, then up and down the street. "We do. But there's more than one way to skin this particular cat. Come on."

When she grabbed his arm again and pulled him toward the far end of the building, Kyle gave up trying to understand. She looked like she had an idea, which made her one up on him. They walked around the library and came to a rear door. An ancient Ford Galaxy sat rusting down toward the other end. Maya took the doorknob in hand and gave it a gentle twist. It was locked.

"Was that the sort of cat skinning you meant?" He wanted to laugh, but his mood was far too dark for it.

Maya gave him a bemused look, then lowered her purse to the ground and reached into it. After a few seconds she came up with a small leather case. He'd seen enough movies to know what it was even as she unzipped it, but when she opened it and laid it flat next to her purse he still couldn't believe it.

"No, this is," she replied as she nodded at her set of lock picks.

Maya looked around, checking for prying eyes, before she lowered her knees down on wet concrete. A door, metal with reddish-brown paint flaking off it and rusting, stood before them. The doorknob and deadbolt were made by Schlage, and if she had to guess, she figured them for five-pin standard locks. Nothing she hadn't handled before.

Thank God for cheap people and small town trust.

"Why in the hell do you have lock picks?" Kyle leaned over her like a mother hen trying to scold an errant chick. "Better yet, how do you even know how to use them?"

She picked up her tension wrench, which was really just a small L-shaped piece of metal, and set it inside the keyhole at the top. "I went through a long period of dating bad boys, and I picked up a few things along the way." Applying a slight bit of pressure on the tension wrench to turn the lock ever so slightly, she then grabbed a small pick and inserted it beneath the wrench. With a practiced motion she raked the pick across the pins while adding more pressure to the wrench.

The lock didn't turn.

"I think I hear a car coming." Kyle stood up and walked a few feet away.

Focusing all her senses, she raked the pins again. Then again, this time more slowly. Nothing.

"Shit, they're getting closer. If you're really going to do that, then do it faster!"

She didn't need the pressure, so she tuned him out, but not before she heard engine noise. In spite of the cool air and ever-present rain, beads of sweat broke out on her forehead. After taking a deep breath, she pushed the pick to the back of the lock and put her ear just above the knob.

"Maya, they're practically parked back here!" He came back to stand behind her again.

Gently she wiggled the pick up and down. *Tick!* Keeping the tension wrench turned, she hastily moved to the second pin and wiggled the pick again. *Tick!*

"We have to go, Maya! I can see headlights!"

She pulled back to the third pin. Wiggle. Wiggle. Wiggle. Sweat dropped into her eyes, but she ignored it. Wiggle. *Tick!* Her hands started to shake, but she gritted her teeth and pushed away all her emotions. Her pick moved to the fourth pin. Wiggle. Wiggle. *Tick!*

"Let's go! Let's go!"

Exhaling sharply, Maya pulled the pick to the final pin. The tension wrench moved ever so slightly with each pin, and she knew she was close to turning it, so she wiggled the pick as if scraping away the gray stuff from a scratch off lottery card. Wigglewigglewigglewiggle! *Tick!*

"Oh shit, it's a sheriff's car! He's gonna see us!"

As if by magic the pick slipped from the keyhole and the wrench twisted 180 degrees. The door opened into the building so quickly she almost fell forward. She reached blindly behind her while gathering up her purse and lock picks, grabbed Kyle's arm, and jerked him as she threw herself inside the library. They both fell into a heap past the threshold. The door closed behind them with a pneumatic hiss.

"Holy shit." Kyle's voice shook. "That was close."

Putting the picks back in their leather holder, Maya nodded. "Closer than you think. There was also a deadbolt. Thankfully no one locked it."

Kyle stared at her with wide eyes. "You mean… Oh man. We could have still been out there, plain for God and everyone else to see."

"Could have, but we're not." The leather case went back to the bottom of her purse. "Let's be happy for small favors and do what we came here to do."

"Do?" He looked around, unsure what she meant. After a couple of seconds he realized where they were and stared at her again. "How did you know?"

Maya stood up and set her purse next to a microfiche machine. "Because I saw a sign for the archives room on the back wall of the library. Above it was an EXIT sign, letting me know there was a back way in. Now here we are."

Laughter came from Kyle's mouth in shallow huffs. "Can you also hack into the CSI, or Walmart?"

"I can barely upgrade my website, so no. Picking locks is about the extent of my criminal repertoire."

Kyle walked to a chair and settled into it with a sigh. "Hey, don't count yourself short. Breaking and entering ain't small potatoes. If we get caught I'm sure you'll be quite popular at the women's prison. Maybe you'll even be able to pick up a few more skills."

Scarcely holding in her own laughter, Maya rifled through her purse again, looking for her notebook. When she had it she opened it to the first page with a folded over corner. TOWN KILLERS was written along the top. "Maybe you're right, but while we wait to get caught why don't you just sit there and look pretty while I do some research, m'kay?"

Kyle didn't look thrilled, but at the moment she wasn't too concerned. She had a lot of information to look up, and a stopwatch ticked loudly in her head. The old bitch librarian could come back there at any moment, and that would end their field trip right quick. Maya had no plans on being passed around a women's prison like a pack of smokes.

As pretty as Maya was, there was only so much looking at her he could do in the glow of a microfiche machine before he grew bored. After what felt like forever he got up and looked around. Dozens of newspapers hung from wooden rods, stacks of magazines sat on shelves, and various microfiche drawers were pulled out from their cabinet in varying lengths. After a few seconds a shelf labeled LOCAL HISTORY drew his attention. Most of the books on it looked fairly new, but mixed among them were tomes with splitting spines and cracked leather bindings. Those drew his interest first.

STILLWATER: A DARK HISTORY OF COAL AND HEARTS by Stephen Lumley, PhD, caught his eye as soon as he stood before the bookshelf. The book wasn't in terrible condition, but even so he pulled it from the shelf as gently as he could, then went back to his seat. Once the book lay cradled securely in his lap, Kyle opened the cover and slowly turned yellowed pages.

The book, published in August of 1962 by the West Virginia University Press, was hefty, and Kyle only skimmed the first few pages. When he came to the table of contents he glanced at the chapter titles hoping something would pop out at him. But, instead of finding one or two titles that might be interesting, nearly all of them begged to be read.

"I hate to burst your bubble, Maya, but I think this Lumley guy was way ahead of you."

Maya's head popped up from the microfiche reader and turned his direction. "What do you mean?"

He held up the book, careful to not let the pages hang loose. "It's a history of this whole area, even going back before the town was here. He's got lots of chapters about murders, people going crazy, mining problems, the whole thing. The first chapter is about Native American legends."

"Huh, so I'm not the only one who clued in to this place. Whatever conclusions he drew must not have caused too much of a fuss though. Unlucky for him, but maybe lucky for me. I don't recall finding any ancient legends about this place though in my internet searches. Why not give that a read and let me know why you find."

Kyle was glad to have something to do that might contribute, so he set to reading immediately. Two pages in and he wished there was a movie about it to watch instead. He just wasn't much of a reader, and the dry style Stephen Lumley, PhD, wrote in only made it worse. Listening to a lecture was bad enough, but reading one… It was just too much. To save himself from falling asleep, he skimmed pages again, his eyes like fishing hooks dragging across the page in hope of catching something interesting. After ten minutes he'd only written down one actual note.

Well that wasn't the fun sort of researching I'd hoped for.

Suddenly the sound of heavy footsteps broke Kyle and Maya from their work.

"Oh shit." Maya's eyes glowed blue from the screen in front of her. "I think the librarian is coming."

Kyle set the book down on the table next to him, gingerly walked to the door, and put his ear to it. Sure enough the steps grew louder with each slow footfall. "I think you're right. We've pressed our luck long enough. You got everything you need?"

Looking around at her notes, Maya nodded. "I'd love to dig deeper, but yeah, I think I've found enough to continue my investigation. There's some spooky shit here."

"I don't doubt it. Now come on, let's get out of here."

Maya gathered up her notebook, pen, stray sheets of paper, and phone, then shoved them in her purse and turned off the microfiche machine. She stood up and walked toward the exit door, but then turned back. "Crap, I forgot to take out the fiche and put it back in the drawer."

"There's no time for that." Kyle grabbed her shoulder and steered her back around.

Maya resisted for a moment, but eventually nodded and opened the door she'd unlocked barely an hour ago. As soon as she was back outside he followed after, making sure to set the lock as he went. He made sure the door closed securely behind him, and as the last half-inch of space disappeared he thought the inner door opened and Ms. Kirkland's face stared into the archive room. Whether or not she saw him or the door close, he didn't know.

CHAPTER TEN

Leaving the library parking lot as quickly as they could without drawing attention, Kyle turned onto Reservoir Road and gave the Jeep plenty of gas. A large dump truck roared past them, sending a spray of dark, filthy water in the air like a speedboat. Kyle had to flick his wipers into high to clear off the drenched windshield.

"That truck was going kinda fast." Maya whipped her head up to follow it. Her bag lay on the floorboard behind her feet. She pushed her heels against it to keep it from spilling over.

"You get used to it. Back when a lot of mines were open they were probably a real menace, but now with just the one...not so much."

As though to emphasize his point, a closed metal gate with the words "MINE CLOSED. STAY OUT!" passed by on their right, followed by another in quick succession. A larger gate with rusted chains lashed around it stood like a muzzled mouth between a pair of tall trees with a sign secured across it, but graffiti and time had made it unreadable. The point was clear though – yet another mine had closed its doors.

"What do you know about the mines?" Maya pulled out her notebook and leafed through it.

Kyle glanced at her for a moment before returning his focus to the wet road ahead of him. "As little as possible. My dad has worked in them his entire life, just like *his* dad did, but I tried to steer as clear of them as I could."

"You're probably better off than you realize," Maya replied as she settled on a page of notes. "According to what I found, over the past hundred years there have been over a dozen mines opened within twenty miles of the town of Stillwater. Do you know how many of those closed down?"

"All of them." For a kid who grew up in the lengthening

shadow of the mountains, that was an easy one.

Maya gave him half a chuckle. "Yes, but do you know how many closed down because the coal seam actually ran dry?"

Kyle powered up his memory banks and raked through them, seeing if that bit of information had ever filtered through the many layers he'd put between himself and the future that had been expected of him. After a few seconds he shook his head. "No idea. I'd guess all of them. If the coal was still there, why close?"

"Good answer. Wrong, but good. Half the mines closed due to no more coal. The other half because the companies that owned them went bankrupt."

"Bankrupt?" That didn't make sense to Kyle. If there was still coal to be dug, then there was still money to be made.

"Uh huh. Several went belly up because insurance claims went too high from people being hurt in the mines. Others were sued into extinction because of claims of unsafe working conditions. One of them was dissolved when the owners *disappeared*. One day they were at the mine, working in the office, and the next..." Maya whistled like a wind blowing through a graveyard. "But not everyone who was hurt in the mines was wounded physically though. Some of them were committed to psychiatric hospitals. The diagnosis, you ask? What a great question. Sudden onset paranoid schizophrenia."

"All of them?" A chill crept up Kyle's spine.

Maya nodded slowly. "Uh huh. All them talked about hearing voices in the dark, seeing visions of demons burning the world, claiming they were being hunted in the tunnels by creatures they couldn't see. Pretty nasty stuff. I'm sure that spending too much time in the dark of the mines, working beneath millions of tons of rock, snaps a brain every now and again, but the number of cases for this area is *way* out of the norm. And that's not even getting into the higher than average number of suicides among miners."

"Huh." Kyle was a loss to say anything else. Growing up he'd heard tell of someone going off the rails every now and again, but hearing her lay things out like that put a sinister spin

on it. It also sparked a memory – a recent one by the feel of it
– but when he tried to grab for it, it fluttered away.

To the left, the Stillwater River came into view, poking
along under the rain. The river ran next to the road, matching
it curve for curve. The Jeep handled itself well on the slick
road, and after a wide bow curve they passed the entrance to
the Badger Mine, the only coal mine in operation in the area.
The large truck they'd seen earlier was parked near a
bulldozer. Kyle didn't get a chance to see much as they
rounded the curve, but it looked like a group of men were
having a less than friendly conversation near the truck.

"If things are so bad for mines here," he said once the
Badger parking lot was lost to view, "why did a company
come in and give it a go?"

"I tried to find out the same thing. The company that
owns Badger is in Canada. I called their corporate office, but
was never able to make it past their public relations office who
simply said, and I quote, 'Stillwater, West Virginia, is still a
viable coal producing area. We at Badger are working hard to
keep that coal flowing, and the people of Stillwater working.'
End quote."

Kyle snorted again. "They might as well have just told you
to fuck off."

"I've been brushed off worse. When you ask the kind of
questions I ask, most people just look at you like you're crazy.
The rest get openly hostile. It's the rare few that actually want
to help, and usually they're the ones contacting *me*."

As they rounded a wide curve, the Stillwater Dam came
into view. A hundred feet high and three hundred feet across,
the dam sat in a small valley between two mountains, its
vertical surface broken by half a dozen sluice gates that
maintained water levels for both the river and the reservoir.
During the spring and summer months, the reservoir covered
an area just over three square miles, and the surrounding
forest made the place a genuinely pretty site from a distance,
but for the life of him Kyle couldn't remember a single family
outing to the lake during his youth, or one weekend spent
fishing or swimming or camping by the water. Nor could he

remember any of his friends doing it either. If it hadn't been for the occasional high school party thrown on one of the beaches around the reservoir, and therefore far from the eyes of lame parents and authorities, he doubted he would ever have gone out there at all. It only now struck him how odd that was.

"Wow, it's so beautiful." Maya sat up straight in her seat and gazed out the rain-splattered windshield.

Kyle glanced at her for a moment, wondering if she was staring at the trees, or the shadows. "And I bet you're about to tell me hundreds of people died out there." The look she gave him made him wish he hadn't said anything.

"Don't joke. You're not far off the mark."

His hands grew cold as they held the steering wheel and turned them onto the road that led across the top of the dam. Maya didn't say anything else, but shook her head and settled back into her seat. When they reached the middle of the dam, he parked on the right shoulder. "It's raining out, but I think the view's worth it."

It was. After a few moments they were standing side by side in the drizzle and looking out over the reservoir that stretched like a vast piece of smooth, wet shale from one mountain to another. The water was far too dark to see through despite how still the surface was, with the few ripples caused by raindrops. As Kyle stared down at it, he wondered how far it went, how far he would fall before light became a forgotten memory, and what would greet him when he hit the bottom. In his mind, none of it was good.

"There are a lot of deep dark places here." Maya echoed his thoughts as she stared down at the same stretch of placid water.

Kyle shifted his eyes back to the trees that ringed the reservoir like a giant verdant collar. "And apparently a lot of dead bodies."

"That too," Maya replied, leaning on the railing and taking the scenery in.

"Speaking of dark places." Kyle pulled out a sheet of paper with his one research note. "According to that book I found, over the centuries a lot of tribes came through this area, and the name Stillwater was originally used by the Seneca for the river behind us. There was also a reference to these mountains in an old Cherokee story. It seems they avoided this place like the plague. They called it *gv-ni-ge-a-da-nv-do.*" He contorted his mouth and tongue to get the pronunciation out properly. "That's as close as I can get it anyway."

"And what does it mean?" Maya asked.

"*Black heart.* Comforting, huh?"

"Not really."

As though on cue, a bolt of lightning cracked down over a mountain to their right, a wall of thunder swept past them. The patter of rain increased with it, fat drops hitting the them like tiny, wet hammers.

"Something is definitely going on here in Stillwater," Maya said, "but we're not going to get any closer to it standing here getting wet." She stepped back and pulled him toward the Jeep.

Kyle let himself be pulled, and he opened her door. "You don't want to take any pictures with that fancy camera of yours?"

"Not in this weather," she replied as she got in the vehicle. "Besides, this stuff is for catching ghosts, not Instagram."

He closed her door and hustled around to the driver's side. Once seated he said, "Taylor should be getting close to the lunch bell, so let's head back. After we're done I'll take you wherever else you want to go."

"Are you sure you want me coming along and meeting your sister?"

He looked at her and screwed up his lips in a scowl. "Why? Because you're black, or because we just met?"

Maya mirrored his face back at him, adding her own bit of 'tude to go with it. "Either. Both. Take your pick."

"Trust me, Taylor is the *last* person who would ever judge anybody."

"I've heard that before." Maya settled back in her seat and winked as she pulled out her phone. "And by the way, my dad was white, so watch how you label people, cracker."

Feeling properly rebuked, Kyle let his muscles steer them toward Stillwater High School, home of the fighting Honey Badgers.

CHAPTER ELEVEN

Getting all of Maya's equipment loaded in the back of Kyle's Jeep didn't take much time, but it would have taken even less if he hadn't had to be extra careful with some of it. Night vision goggles and infrared camera lenses were fragile things, not to mention expensive. But soon enough they were on the road. While he drove, Maya checked her phone to see if Darius had called or sent a text. He hadn't. She then tried calling him but only got his voice mail. Anger poured through her body as she envisioned him looking at his phone and ignoring her out of spite, but along with it came a thin trickle of worry. As childish as Darius could be, the silent treatment wasn't his usual shtick. Unsure of what she could do about it, however, she closed her phone down and jammed it back into her pocket.

"Your phone piss you off?" Kyle asked.

"It's not my phone. It's Darius. He's the person I'm *supposed* to be out driving around with today. He's...like my mule. This stuff can get heavy."

Kyle sniffed and leaned his head over toward her. "It's none of my business, but you seem a bit more upset than an AWOL grunt should warrant."

Swirls of awkwardness tumbled around Maya, twisting her emotions up and causing her to blush. She had nothing to hide, but that didn't mean she felt comfortable airing her laundry either. And really, how appropriate was it to talk about an ex-boyfriend – one she still worked with, no less – with the guy she'd just slept with the night before? She felt like a character in a stupid romantic comedy, so she shook her head and pushed the awkwardness to the side.

You're a big girl. It is what it is. Fuck it.

"He's my ex." She hoped her eye-roll illustrated her feelings about the relationship. "We broke up a couple of weeks ago. My friend Alan was supposed to be out here helping me, but he got caught up with work, so he asked Darius to help instead. I wish he hadn't."

"And are you sure Darius knows you broke up?" It was a fair question, and he didn't ask it with any hint of jealousy.

Maya twisted her lips and gave him a deep nod. "Trust me, we are way over, and we're all more than fine with it. Helping me with Stillwater is the *last* interaction we'll ever have, and if I have my way it'll be over and done with A.S.A.P."

"Huh." Kyle increased the Jeep's windshield wiper speed to keep pace with the rain. "I didn't know you were in such a rush to leave town."

A new set of awkward waves rolled over her, but these had a different flavor. She hadn't meant to imply she wanted to flee or that the investigation was the only thing that interested her in town. Kyle sounded just the tiniest bit hurt, and she regretting her words. He was a really cool guy, insanely attractive, and scored nearly 100% on her checklist of things she liked in men, so of course she had a reason to linger. But Darius... Even when he wasn't around he somehow managed to screw with her life. Her frustration toward him, and her attraction to Kyle, made her head spin. Before she could say anything, Kyle turned left onto a small road and pointed with his right hand at a sinister looking building.

"There's the high school." Years of teenage angst weighed his words down.

Made of red brick that long turned black from dirt and coal dust, the squat building looked more like a prison than a school. The tall cyclone fence that surrounded it was missing only a roll of razor wire to complete the effect. An all-weather flag fluttered limply in the rainy breeze over a parking lot that had more potholes than cars. All the windows were fogged over and covered in what looked like chicken wire. It wasn't exactly heavy on the curb appeal.

As they pulled in, she saw kids milling about in the courtyard between the school and parking lot. Some were clustered in small groups, their eyes down and their heads hung low, like they were trying to stay off everyone's radar as they talked, while others just stood and stared at nothing, or sat in small, silent circles. It wasn't the loud and energized sort of scene she experienced when she'd been in school, that was for sure, and the rain couldn't be the only thing keeping them all down.

"So when did fun get outlawed?" she asked, her eyes roaming from one dour face to the next.

"No kidding. School wasn't exactly a party when I was here, but this is ridiculous."

He stopped the Jeep next to a blue STUDENT DROP OFF sign and craned his neck to look around. After a few seconds he dug in his pocket and brought out his cell phone. "Taylor's not out yet." He dialed her number, held the phone to his ear for a moment, and then pulled it away. "Voice mail." He then typed in a text message, his big man-thumbs working overtime on the small keypad.

While they waited for her to reply, Maya said, "No offense, but if I'd gone to school here, I'd have left town too. My parents were fortunate enough to afford private school."

"Must have been nice." Kyle's eyes never left his phone.

"Not really. I mean, yeah, it had smaller class sizes and the teachers were on top of their game, but...you know...being half black and half white can have its downsides."

Kyle spared her a quick glance. "I could see that, but you're hot though, so...you know, win." He flashed her a smile before turning his gaze back down.

"Thanks." Warmth flashed through her cheeks. "I'd like to think I'm fairly intelligent as well."

"I didn't mean to imply you weren't." He gave her an *I'm sorry* grin. "Hot and smart. Double win."

Seeing that Kyle's phone screen had yet to light up with a call or text, Maya gestured toward three kids sitting on a picnic table beneath a large plastic awning. They all had long black hair, wore black clothes that looked way too warm for the weather, and were deathly pale. They talked amongst themselves, but their mouths barely moved, and they watched the people around them with constant vigilance. As cloistered as they were, they were also the most approachable looking. "Maybe you should ask The Cure over there if they know where your sister is."

"Huh?" Kyle looked up at her like she'd just spoken gibberish.

"The goths," she replied, gesturing again. "They might know something."

Kyle followed her hand and saw the kids sitting on the table, then nodded. After rolling the window down he stuck his hand out and waved. "Hey! Can I talk to you for a minute?"

Jerking like they'd been tasered, the goth kids flicked their dark-rimmed eyes over at him and glared before leaning even closer together and shrugging their shoulders.

"I only need to ask a question," he shouted over to them, undeterred. "Come on, my baby sister was supposed to meet me, and I'm starting to get worried."

The person sitting closest to the Jeep — a girl judging by the fullness of her chest — stiffened and sat straight up, then turned to look at him again. After a couple of seconds to confer with her friends, she got up and walked over. Dressed as she was, and with all the heavy makeup on her face, it was hard to tell what she really looked like, but beneath it all Maya guessed she had a pretty face and a curvy figure to match. Most boys probably wouldn't know it from looking at her, and Maya figured that was the way she wanted it.

"Did you say your sister?" the girl asked once reached the Jeep. A mass of black dreads fell from her head like a nest of snakes. "Are you talking about Taylor?"

Kyle nodded quickly and his eyes opened wide. "Yeah, Taylor. How did you know?"

"She told me you might be coming into town." A blush set the girl's face on fire, even through the thick white foundation. "She was really excited about it."

Kyle stared for a moment, and but then closed his eyes and nodded as though a mystery of the universe had just been solved. "You must be Morgan. I mean, uh, Morgana."

"She mentioned me?" the girl asked, her face lighting up.

"Really? Then...she told you about...us?"

"Yes, she told me she was gay, and that you two were dating, if that's what you mean."

Morgana turned her head down, but her raccoon eyes stared at him, cataloging his every twitch. "And you're okay with that?"

"Sure, why wouldn't I be?" he answered. The lack of pretension or condescension in his voice won him points in Maya's heart.

Morgana turned her head and gave exaggerated looks to everything around her before leveling a weighty gaze on Kyle. "Pardon me if I don't give everyone the benefit of the doubt."

Maya stifled a laugh. She knew firsthand what the girl was implying, and hoped she hadn't experienced the same sort of treatment the people at the diner yesterday had given her. Persecution was blind to race, creed, and love.

"I understand what you mean," Kyle said. "And maybe we can talk about it more sometime, but right now I'm looking for Taylor. I saw her last night for a little while, and I told her we'd try and get together today. I've called her and sent her text messages, but she hasn't gotten back to me. Do you know what's going on?"

A dark look passed over Morgana's eyes, and her pale cheeks deflated. "No, I don't have any idea. She didn't come to school today. I've tried calling her too, but she hasn't tagged me back either. I'm worried."

"So you haven't seen her at all today?" Kyle asked

Morgana shook her head. "No. And she's not the only one either. It seems like half my damn class is gone."

A tone in the girl's voice set off an alarm in Maya's head. She reached into her bag, and after a couple of seconds brought out a digital recorder, clicked it on, and pointed it at the girl's face. "Half your class is gone? What do you mean by that?"

"Huh?" Morgana replied, pulling back. She glared at the mic and then at Maya before turning back to Kyle. "What the fuck is this? Who's she?"

Kyle huffed and pushed Maya's hand down, giving her an

angry look as he did it. "It's nothing. Sorry. I just need to know where my sister is, that's all."

The girl didn't look certain of anything, but after a moment she rolled her eyes. "Okay, whatever. All I can tell you is that she's not here. Give your mom a call. I'm sure that bitch will be more inclined to talk to you than she is to me."

"I wouldn't be so sure of that, but I'll try anyway. Thanks. When I hear from her I'll have her call you, okay?"

Morgana nodded, her lower lip curled inward as she chewed on it, and then walked back to her friends. Within seconds the small pale collective was off the table and shuffling into the school.

"Smooth move, Anderson Cooper." Kyle let her hand go. "They teach you that interview technique in private school?"

Maya opened her mouth to defend herself, but she closed it when she couldn't think of anything to say. He was right. In her eagerness to get some local input on what could be yet another example of something being off in Stillwater she'd let her journalistic drive outrun her good sense. In the process she'd not only recorded zilch, but she'd angered a guy she liked who was worried about his sister. Talk about epic fail.

"I'm sorry." She felt as lame as the words that came out of her mouth.

He shrugged and reached for his phone. After a quick search of his contact list he pressed a button and held the phone up to his head. Seconds later his eyes lit up.

"Hey, Mom, it's... Can we not? I called to talk to Taylor, is she... What do you mean, sick? She seemed fine last night. I..." He looked up at the Jeep's roof liner and sighed. "Well maybe if you weren't busy ostracizing your daughter she'd tell you a couple of things. If you'll put her on the phone I just want... Hey, she's my sister, and I've got a right to talk to her!" A shrill laugh echoed out of the phone loud enough for Maya to hear, and it made her skin crawl. Kyle's knuckles went white from gripping the phone, and he hit his steering wheel with his free hand. "That's bullshit! I'm coming ov... Yeah, that's what I said... Whatever, Mom, we'll talk about it when I get there, and... Hello? Hello?" Kyle pulled away from his phone and looked it like it had tried to bite his ear off. "She hung up on me. That goddam bitch. Oh, no, this isn't over. Not by a damn sight."

Maya slipped her digital recorder back into her bag and made sure her seatbelt was still secure. For a moment she considered asking him to drop her off at the motel, but if she did that meant she'd have to pick up where she'd left off with Darius, and she much preferred helping Kyle deal with his drama rather than dealing with her own. Still, that didn't mean she could just butt in, and she knew it.

"If you'd rather not have me around while you deal with whatever it is you need to deal with, you can drop me off at the motel. It won't hurt my feelings."

"Does that mean you don't mind sticking around?" he asked. "My parents' house is nearby, but the motel is on the other side of town, and I'd prefer to get this over with as quickly as possible."

Maya nodded and hunkered down in her seat. "No, that's fine. I'll just sit out here while you...you know, deal with it."

The trip took only a few minutes, but to her it felt like a lifetime as Kyle fumed and raged silently in his seat. He didn't need to say anything. She felt every ounce of his anger as his aura expanded like a star going nova.

CHAPTER TWELVE

Kyle walked up the cracked walkway leading to his parents' house hoping like hell his mother wouldn't cause a scene at the front door. He didn't know if he could handle another round of bullshit with her, especially with Maya in earshot. He barely knew Maya, but he found himself growing more and more attracted to her, and the last thing he needed was family drama making her want to run for the hills. If things went smoothly – at the front door at least – then it would be a very good thing for all concerned.

He wasn't holding his breath though.

After pulling open the screen door he curled his right hand into a fist and knocked. When no one answered after a count of ten, he knocked again, harder this time. He was halfway through another ten count when muted swearing built on the other side of the door. A cloud of rank smoke billowed out when it finally opened.

"Who in the fuck is pounding on my front door?" his mother asked with a cigarette dangling from her mouth, her eyes watery and dark. Though had hadn't imagined it possible, she looked even worse than yesterday. Her skin color rested somewhere between gray and yellow, like her entire body was one big bruise, and he could practically see her bones beneath it. "Jesus H, can't a person be left alone?"

"I told you I was coming, Mom." He waved smoke from his face.

Her eyes narrowed and she leaned forward to get a closer look, a scowl turning her face into wrinkled laundry. It only made her look worse. "And I told you not to." She stopped speaking and raised a hand to cover her mouth as a quick series of coughs flew out of her. The ash from her cigarette broke off and tumbled down her dirty apron. She brushed at herself, but it only smeared the ash into a long streak.

"I want to see Taylor." He chose to ignore her sarcasm

and terrible appearance.

"And what makes you think she wants to see you?" His mother took a drag on her cigarette and blew out a wall of fog to foul the air between them. "Just go! You're no son of mine!"

Kyle wanted to slap the snide look off his mother's face, but his hands remained at his sides. There were troubles enough without adding assault to the mix. "Mom, let's not get started, okay? Just let me see her, and then I'll be out of your hair."

"I should have slit your throat when I squeezed you outta me." Her dark eyes burrowed into Kyle like twin pickaxes, flaying him straight to the bone. Her eyes cast over the rented Jeep, where she stopped and took a long look. A sinking feeling hit Kyle's stomach.

Aw shit.

"It ain't bad enough that your sister has to be a goddamn dyke." His mother's head swiveled back around to him. "But now I got to see you riding around with some nigger? You ain't my son, you hear me?!"

Hoping like hell his mother's voice didn't carry far, Kyle crossed his arms and leaned forward. "Leave Maya alone. She's good people."

"She could be the goddamn queen of Sheba, that don't mean I want her around here."

"Then fucking look away," Kyle said, the urge to slap her greater than ever.

His mother fixed him with a flinty stare before shrugging and taking another drag on her smoke. "I already cast you from this family, so what do I care."

"You can disown me all you want, but I'm still Taylor's brother." He crossed his arms.

"No you ain't." His mother waved her hand at him, sending thin streamers of smoke in the air. "I told you yesterday, get in your vehicle and go. You've been gone, so just go and stay gone. Nothing here for you anymore."

Kyle uncrossed his arms and put his hands on his hips. It took every ounce of restraint he had to not take the woman by her shoulders and shake her until she puked. "Yeah, well, that's not gonna happen. Now let me see Taylor, or by God I'll walk through you."

Shaking her head, his mother dropped her cigarette on the cement outside her door and ground it out with a slippered foot. "You're sister ain't here, but even if she was, I still wouldn't let you in. Now get going before I call the cops."

"Not here?" Kyle replied. He hadn't been prepared for that. "What do you mean, not here?"

"Ain't here means ain't here."

Kyle didn't believe her for a moment, and when she started closing the screen door his anger and frustration boiled up in a flash of heat. Without thinking he grabbed the screen door and pulled it from her grip. She stumbled forward but righted herself quickly when he stepped into the house. He barely waited for her to flatten against a wall before barreling forward. Every step he took into the dank hallway was an effort. It only took a few seconds for the oppressive atmosphere to press down on him and fill his lungs. He wondered how Taylor had lived with it for so long.

"You get outta my house!" his mother yelled behind him. "I'm gonna call the police!"

Once past the living room, he turned to the right and approached the closed door to his sister's room. It had a taped up poster of the band Paramour on it. He knocked, careful not to wrinkle the poster.

"Taylor? You okay?"

There wasn't a reply, nor did he hear any stirring.

"I'm coming in, so if you're...whatever, just cover up. I want to make sure you're okay."

His mother punched him on the arm as he reached for the doorknob. She wasn't a big woman, but she had surprising strength in her. Her bony knuckles left four small red dents on his skin. "I'm not gonna tell you again, boy! Get outta my house this second, or there'll be hell to pay!"

He ignored her threats and opened the door. Inside he saw the prototypical teenage girl's room. Posters for various bands and movies covered the walls, but instead of images of guys like Justin Bieber and Ryan Gosling, he saw lots of Amy Lee, Megan Fox, and more women he didn't recognize but who invariably had dark hair and dark eyes. Taylor definitely had a type, that was for sure. The white carpet of her floor looked like it hadn't seen a vacuum in years, and various gloomily colored clothing lay scattered across it. A wooden desk buried under magazines and long, gauzy scarves sat on the left, a beat-up recliner occupied by half a dozen stuffed animals was next to it, and an empty bed covered in a tangle of black sheets was on the right. The window across from the door stood half opened.

"I told you she wasn't here." Her words were knives thrown at the back of his neck.

Kyle pulled back from the door and turned toward her. "Then where is she?"

For a split second his mother flinched and leaned away, but then darkness crossed her eyes and she screwed her mouth into a sneer. "Your daddy took her."

"Took her? Took her where?"

His mother shrugged as though she neither knew nor cared. "The doctor I guess. God only knows what bugs she's got up in her since she became a dyke."

Kyle had to grab his leg to stop from lashing out. "Your daughter is gone, and you don't where the fuck to? Jesus Christ, what happened to you?"

Darkness returned to her eyes, this time so heavy is was like they disappeared into a void, and he took an unconscious half step back, which was all that saved him from a savage slap aimed for his face.

"You don't talk to me like that, you bastard!" Her anger added new color to her skin, deepening the bruised appearance. She pulled back from Taylor's room, and shadows fell across her face. "I wish you'd never been born, and soon...soon you will too. Oh yes. Now get the fuck outta my house and don't ever come back. If I see you again, I swear I'll kill you. You hear me? Go!"

As bad as everything had been since he'd returned to town, nothing had shocked him as much as what she'd just said. Worse, he knew she meant every word of it. Her thin muscles quivered and her hands curled into claws. Whoever his mother had once been, she was long gone, and what had replaced her felt…evil. Now, more than ever, he wanted to find Taylor.

"Fine, I'm going," he told her as he raised a finger and aimed it squarely at her face. "Threaten me all you want. But when I find Taylor – and I will – I'm going to take her with me. You're not fit to be a mother to anyone."

A vicious rebuttal twisted his mother's face into a hellish mask, but before she could unleash it he pushed past her and stormed out of the house. He was in the Jeep and starting the engine before she made it to the front door. From the corner of his eye he saw her standing half out of the house and shouting something, but the engine noise drowned out whatever it was.

"Your sister okay?" Maya asked, purposefully not looking out her window to see the mad woman raving on the porch.

Kyle shook his head. "I don't know. Supposedly Dad has her with him."

"So that means…?"

Knowing he was the only one who could finish the hanging thought, Kyle backed out of the driveway and steered them toward town. "It means we're going to the mine."

INTERLUDE
RIPPLES IN THE SHADOWS

If a mirror had been put before Ash, he wouldn't have recognized the face staring back at him. Gone was his dark hair, his cleft jaw, and the nose that tilted slightly to the left thanks to his years of high school football. Now his skin was a rancid shade of gray and hairless, the bones of his face were knives slowly pushing outward in sharp lumps, and his nose was a knob of flesh rotting on the ground at his feet, which were themselves growing and ready to burst through the leather laced around them. He felt himself changing more quickly as the water lowered and the ancient power increased, touching everyone for miles and miles, transforming them as well.

Using the two gaping holes in the middle of his face, Ash sniffed the air. Oil and exhaust mixed with the sweat of his workers and the fear of the children in a nearby chamber, and mingled with the omnipresent scent of broken earth and coal, but beneath all that lay a new odor. Or, rather, an old one. Very old.

Standing on the edge, Ash looked down, and his black eyes saw bodies laying across boulders that hadn't been exposed to the air in hundreds of millions of years. That the bodies even existed at all was a testament to the power they'd once had and to the strength that had made them the terrors they'd once been. Down in the wet reaches were figures like spiders, but with twice as many legs and fangs as large as cars. Some had the vague shape of humans, but were twenty feet tall and had too many eyes and arms. Some looked like animals, their dead bodies as big as a bus and covered in razor sharp needles long enough to impale a man on. In the ancient graveyard he saw claw, wing, tentacle, and fang, all of them as massive as they were monstrous. The worst, though, were those he didn't have words for, that compared to nothing he'd ever known. They were beings as alien to him as he was to an amoeba, and he shook as he tried to take in their magnificence.

I am becoming them, he thought, his anticipation marred by the faintest amount of apprehension. *These beings once lived, and through me they will live again. The old ones will rise again... in us.*

A strange sensation struck Ash in the chest and sent ripples through his body, dropping him to his bony knees. Looking down he saw the distant surface of the water rippling in echo. Far below, at the bottom of the mountain chamber, his dark god stirred. Long tendrils swished slowly in the murky depths, stretching after untold millennia of slumber.

"Sir?" a voice called from the black behind him. "Everything okay? I...thought I..."

"It's almost time." Ash pushed himself back to his feet. As he stood up, black claws erupted from the ends of his fingers, flipping up his nails so violently they tore off and fluttered to the floor. "Yes, nearly time."

The scent of fear blossomed in the tunnels under the mountain, this time not just from the children, but from his men too. That was okay, though. It was right that they should fear. He feared what was to come too, but he also lusted for it, yearned deep down for it to begin. His god was rising, and in the terror he would find his place. He would find his glory in the horror to come.

Inside the mountain and beyond, the dark god's influence increased, and in the dark reaches of Stillwater monsters stirred beneath the flesh of saints and sinners alike.

CHAPTER THIRTEEN

Kyle felt like he was driving over an alien landscape as he turned onto the gravel road leading the mine his father worked in. He'd been there before a few times as a kid, but his dad had driven then, and the occasions hadn't been filled with fear and anger. And it didn't help that the rain – the goddamn rain that didn't want to stop falling! – had turned the world into a soggy, gloomy mess.

"I… I don't feel good." Maya leaned forward in the passenger seat and put her arms around her stomach.

One eye stayed on the road while Kyle glanced at her out of the corner of his other eye. "Are you hungry? Shit, I completely forgot about lunch."

Maya shook her head. "No, it's something else. I feel it…out there."

"Feel what?"

She shook her head again, but then she reached for her door handle and jerked it open. Kyle slammed on the breaks, sliding the Jeep across gravel. It stopped just as she leaned out and vomited. He reached to unlatch his seatbelt, but she reached behind her and put a hand out to stop him. After a few more wet retches she pulled back inside and fell against her seat back with a gasp.

She took a deep breath. "Oh my God. I've never felt anything like this. Can't you feel it?"

Kyle had no idea what she was talking about. All he felt were his boiling emotions. "No."

"I don't know how to describe it. The best is…" She wiped her mouth with the back of her hand, then took another deep breath. "It's like I'm falling into some bottomless hole while someone screams in my head. It's crazy."

That's one way to put it.

"Is this one of those…psychic things like what you were

talking about last night?"

Maya nodded slowly before combing her hands through her wet, curly hair. "Yeah, but I've never felt anything this intense before. Ever. And whatever is causing it is getting closer."

Never in his life had Kyle experienced anything that led him to believe what Maya said, but he couldn't deny the things she'd told him about the town's history, couldn't deny what he'd experienced with the people he'd interacted with since arriving, not to mention what was happening to his mother. Even if he didn't know how or why, he knew something bad was going on. Did that mean he believed Maya could see ghosts and sense evil?

I can't believe I'm admitting it, but yeah, I kinda do. This town is too fucked up not to.

"Do you think you can hold on for a little bit longer? The mine is just around the bend up ahead. I promise, we won't stay long. You won't need to get out of the Jeep either."

Maya's face was the color of coffee with too much cream in it, but she nodded. "This is for your sister, so I'll hold it together."

Kyle's affection for her grew, warming his heart. "Thanks. Now let's get this done."

Gravel flew into the air as Kyle pressed on the gas. Seconds later the mine's parking lot came into view. To his surprise, it was packed with cars, some having to make do with muddy spaces beyond the gravel. Every miner employed by Badger Coal had to be there. Kyle added another odd checkmark to his mental list of Stillwater weirdness.

"It's getting worse, Kyle." Maya rocked in her seat and held her clenched fists in her lap.

It's the mine, he though. *That has to be it. It's something about the mine.*

He pulled over to the side of the road at the edge of the parking lot and set the emergency break as he put the transmission in PARK. He didn't turn the Jeep off though.

"Hopefully I'll only be a few minutes. I'll find out where Taylor is, I'll get her, and then..." He wasn't sure how to finish that line of thought. Nothing he did after that would be good, or at least legal, but he knew deep down in his gut that not getting her would be far worse.

"We'll burn that bridge when we come to it," Maya told him, her eyes closed and her arms around her stomach again. "Just go and find her."

He leaned over and kissed her cheek. "Thank you." A tiny smile touched the corners of her quivering lips. He then exited the Jeep and made his way toward the mine.

Maya was drowning. That was how she felt as she sat in the Jeep. Rain pelted the roof, each drop adding to her misery. In her mind she flailed and fought, but it surrounded her, consumed her.

But what is IT?

That was the real question, and one she didn't have an answer for. Whatever plagued the town wasn't a simple angry spirit. Those she knew, had dealt with before. No, this was something altogether different. It felt vast, alien, unknowable. More than that, it felt ancient. She stood closer to it than ever before, yet it already surrounded her, choking her from all sides. How that was possible, she didn't know.

She did know, however, that she wanted to leave. Now. Fuck the blog, fuck the book, fuck everything. Leave and not look back.

Come on, Kyle. Get your sister and let's go, before it's too late.

Too late for what? Another question she couldn't answer, yet one she knew her life depended on. All their lives did.

"Dad!" Kyle's voice carried through the parking lot like thunder. "Come out here!"

The entrance to the mine was a swamp of mud and dead grass, and a hunk of smashed metal vaguely resembling a mine cart sat off to the side in a useless heap. He looked into the mine itself to see if anything stirred, but all he saw was endless black. The sign-in board and manager trailers were to the right, so he headed that way.

"Come on, Dad, we need to talk!"

As he passed the sign-in board he stopped to see if his Dad had even checked in, but the date written on the board was more than two weeks ago.

That doesn't make any sense. Guys are obviously here working, and have been. What the hell is going on?

"Hey! Is anyone fucking here?!"

He turned toward the trailers, shivering as rain slid down his spine. The gravel was so soaked it barely made a sound when he walked. Beyond the trailers stood the mine's generator, smoke chugging from the exhaust pipe of the monstrous beast. He opened his mouth to call out again, but the door to the manager's trailer open in a squeal of rusted hinges. He hardly recognized the man who stepped out.

"Stop yer squallin', boy."

As much as Kyle hated his father, he didn't want to admit that the man coming toward him was Gus Mason. His dad had never been the most robust man, and years of mine work had bent his back until he always appeared hunched, but the man with his father's voice belonged in a hospital.

Or a morgue. Jesus, look at him!

Kyle thought he'd gotten over the sickly look everyone in town seemed to have, but they were nothing – not even his mom – compared to what approached. His dad's dirty blond hair was gone save for a few sad strands, his blue eyes sunken and dark, his skin corpse-like, and he leaned to the left as he shuffled forward on bowed legs. It was a terrible sight, not one he'd ever wished on his dad even at his most angry. But, he wasn't here for his dad. He was here for Taylor. He kept her face in his mind as a guiding light.

"Where's my sister?" He put all the steel he could into his voice.

His father sneered, teeth missing as his lips parted at the corner of his mouth. "Your sister? What the fuck you care?"

"I care a lot, so answer the question."

His father shook his ugly head. "You seem to have forgotten your place in the order of things, boy. I don't answer to you."

For the first time in his life, Kyle curled his hands into

fists and got ready to hit his dad. "You'll answer to me today, goddamn it."

"Is that so?" His father stopped just a foot away from him. A sweetly sour smell wafted off of his body, nearly making Kyle puke. "Well then go on, boy. Take your swing. Let's see what happens. Let's see how much you really love that faggot cunt of a sister."

Kyle's fist flew at his dad's head before he knew he was going to do it. He put all his strength behind the punch, rocketing it forward. His dad didn't even blink. But, instead of hitting him, Kyle's hand stopped when his dad grabbed him by the forearm and stopped the punch inches from his face. His dad's grip was tight, but the coldness of his skin shocked Kyle more. It was like his fingers were made of ice, and the chill slowly spread up Kyle's arm.

"Good try, boy." His dad smirked and tightened his grip, forcing the cold further up Kyle's arm. "I didn't think you had the balls. Too bad you ran off. You'd have made an excellent servant."

Between his dad's freezing hands and strange words Kyle didn't know what to think. All the anger in his heart evaporated, and in its place fear curled up like a snake. His dad's touch hurt, but the pain went past the skin. He heard voices in his head, saw visions of falling stone walls and water, felt his heart flutter as an outside pulse pressed against it. In his dad's grip he felt like he was falling…or drowning.

"That's it, boy. Ssshhhh. Let it happen. You'll be with your sister soon enough."

Hearing Taylor mentioned snapped Kyle's mind back into focus, and with all the strength he could muster he yanked away from his dad's grip. After taking several hurried backward steps he rubbed at his numb arm. "Don't ever touch me again, you son of a bitch. I'm gonna find Taylor, and when I do I'm taking her with me. You and Mom can die here together for all I care, but not her."

"Oh, I think this ought to be a family occasion." His dad lunged forward.

Kyle was shocked that his dad could move so fast, but his

adrenaline was pumping and all his senses were buzzing, so he saw the old man moving in time to scramble backwards. His dad's face twisted into a mask of savage glee as he tried again, pushing Kyle back further. He knew he'd have to find his sister another way. His dad was beyond reasoning.

"We're not family," he said. "Not anymore."

Spinning on his heels, Kyle ran back to the Jeep. As he neared the vehicle he looked over his shoulder, sure his dad would be hot on his heels, but instead he was nowhere to be seen. Kyle wasn't sure if that was a good thing, or a bad. Not stopping to ponder it, he dashed to the Jeep and jumped in.

"Did he tell you anything?" Maya asked. She was still pale, but she seemed to be handling things as well as she could.

Kyle put the Jeep in REVERSE and hit the gas. The Jeep lurched but didn't roll backward. He gunned the engine, and it lurched again, but that was all. He looked down to make sure he had it in the right gear and noticed the emergency brake was still set. Growling at himself, he let the brake go and hit the gas again. He just missed backing into a stand of trees before he hit the brakes, shifted into DRIVE, and took off.

"He said a lot," Kyle replied as he stopped at the main road. "Just nothing I needed to hear."

Maya nodded and finally let go of her stomach. After a few seconds she laid her hand on top of his leg. "Kyle, I think... I think your sister is back there. In the mines. I don't know why, but I do."

Hearing her words plunged a knife into his heart. Not because he didn't want to hear them, but because he'd already come to same conclusion.

It's the only thing that makes sense in this whole fucked up situation.

"I do too." He patted her hand.

"So then what do we do next?"

He paused, unsure himself. There hadn't been much time for thinking lately. "I still need to find Taylor, and I think I know how, but I can't drag you through this anymore. I'm taking you back to the motel. It's not your fight."

He grabbed the wheel and turned it to the left, but she

grabbed it and stopped him. "No you're not. I don't claim to understand everything that's going on, but what's happening to this town is tied up with your parents, Taylor…everything. Hell, I think Darius might have gotten wrapped up in it too somehow. It may not be my fight, but I came here for a reason, so I'm not leaving you. Um… I mean…"

"Thank you." He moved his right hand over and put it over hers on the wheel. Her skin felt warm and solid, healing him just by being there. "This shit is seriously fucked up, and God knows what's out there, but I know that meeting you was… I feel better having you with me. Thank you."

Without waiting for a reply, he turned the steering wheel to the right and pressed the gas. He had to get into the mine, and the front entrance wasn't the only way.

CHAPTER FOURTEEN

Half a mile down Geller Drive Kyle slowed the Jeep and scanned the trees lining the road. After a few seconds he saw a break in the wood, said, "Hold on," and turned left onto what could be considered a road in only the most charitable sense of the word. To most people it would have looked like little more than a wide strip of mud winding between tightly packed trees. Maya squealed in alarm as branches smacked at the windshield and roof of the Jeep, but Kyle didn't flinch. He'd driven down this road enough to know its limits.

"We're not going to fit through!" Maya said, her arms and legs stretched out to hold her in her seat.

Kyle tightened his grip on the wheel as one of the Jeep's tires caught on an exposed tree root and jarred the vehicle. "We'll make it, trust me."

They didn't speak another word until they finally came to a stop three jarring, tense minutes later. The road ended in a clearing just big enough for a large vehicle to turn around in. The mountain rose up on the left, and thick forest engulfed the area in gloom. The constant patter of rain falling on leaves only made the place feel more oppressive. In the distance the Stillwater River burbled.

"I don't even want to know what all you got up to out here when you were younger," Maya said as she got out. Once outside she opened the rear door and grabbed the night vision goggles. The high tech equipment looked strange and bulky in her slender hands.

Kyle joined her at the back of the Jeep. After digging around a bit in a tool bag he came away with a crowbar. He then led her around the front of the Jeep and down a narrow path into the woods. They walked for less than a minute when Maya cried out and stumbled toward a knobby oak tree on her right. She caught herself before her face smashed into the bark, but her arm was unsteady, and a moment later she was on her knees.

"I can feel it again." Her right hand clutched at her chest. Her face was pale and drawn. "But something's different. I think it's worse."

Kyle knelt down next to her and raised his hands to hold her steady, but as he moved his heart thumped heavily in his chest, as though someone had kicked him right on his sternum, and a wave of vertigo rushed over him. He managed to stay on his knees, but inside he felt like he was falling.

"The world is swallowing us," Maya said.

That was exactly how Kyle felt too.

After a few seconds, he took a gulp of cool, wet air, and as his lungs expanded he felt normal again aside from a few jitters in his stomach. Gone was the sense of falling, of being carried along helplessly by something he couldn't see or understand. His legs barely even shook as he got back to his feet.

Maya, though, looked like ten miles of bad country road. Crouched on her hands and knees, he could see only a little of her face, but what he saw wasn't good. Her skin had gone from soft brown to almost white, and her eyes were unfocused orbs that twitched aimlessly. Her back and chest rocked like the ocean from the heaviness of her breathing. Kyle stooped down and grabbed her shoulders, and heat radiated off her. When he shifted down to take her wrists and straighten her up, her pulse beat against his fingers in quick, powerful throbs. After a few seconds he got her settled on her heels, but she didn't seem to notice. She only gazed forward in a thousand-yard stare. It was then he noticed that, though he couldn't hear anything, her lips were moving. He leaned into her and put his ear toward her mouth.

"It's coming." she said, the words barely over a whisper and spoken in rapid succession. "It's coming, it's coming, it's coming."

"What's coming?" He pulled back. She didn't react to him, and instead kept up her urgent whispering. He grabbed her shoulders again and gave them a good shake. "Maya, snap out of it!"

She continued ignoring him, muttering all the while. He shook her harder, which made her head loll around, but her eyes remained glassy. Feeling like he had no choice, he pulled his right arm back to give her a hard smack across the face in hopes it would shock her back to consciousness, but before he could do it she sucked in a quick breath and looked around in sharp glances. He breathed a heavy sigh of relief.

"What happened?" she asked when her eyes settled on Kyle. "Why... Why am I on the ground? Are you about to hit me?"

Wondering what she meant, he looked down and realized his hand was still pulled back. He lowered his arm and grunted. "You were in a...I don't know how to describe it...like a seizure or something."

"A seizure?" Maya's light brown color returned, but worry etched her face in deep lines.

"I'm no doctor, but that's all I can think of. You shouted and stumbled, and then you started mumbling to yourself and breathing like you were running a marathon."

Maya checked her pulse at her neck for a few seconds "I remember feeling...something come over me, feeling like I'd fallen off the edge of the world, and then I saw you with your hand up ready to smack me. What was I mumbling? Did you hear it?"

"Yeah." Gooseflesh rose up Kyle's arms, and he stroked them as though warding off a chill. "You said, 'It's coming,' over and over again."

Maya's eyes and lips screwed up in confusion. "It's coming? What's coming?"

"I have no idea, but I don't think it's good."

"Why do you say that? Did you feel something too?"

Kyle wished he could answer no, but he couldn't. He didn't understand what had happened, or what it meant, but he knew lying about it – even to himself – wasn't going to help. "About a second after you stumbled, I felt this terrible sensation of falling come over me. Going over the edge of the world is close enough, but when it happened you described it more like we were being swallowed, and that's even closer. It was horrible. I felt lost and alone and powerless, like I was being consumed. But then it went away as quick as it hit me. With you...it lasted a little longer."

"I imagine it did," Maya replied, the confusion on her face changing to sadness.

Her words struck Kyle strangely. "What do you mean?"

Maya looked at him and chewed the inside of her mouth for a few seconds. "Back when you drove up the mine to talk to your dad I felt something terrible all around us, like a...a cloud of evil. When you left me in the Jeep it got worse. Then, like now, I felt like I was falling into some terrible monster as big as the world. This time it was so overwhelming I almost lost myself to it. If you felt it too, then something really bad is happening. If we're going to figure out what's going on, I'd say let's do it quickly. The sooner we're off this mountain, the better."

Agreeing wholeheartedly with her, Kyle nodded and led them forward again. A minute later they came to a clearing on the side of the mountain. On a good summer day it would have made for a nice view, with rising mountains on the left and a flowing river down on the right, but heavy cloud cover and rain diminished visibility and turned everything slimy and gray.

"Is that why we came out here?" Maya asked, pointing to their left.

Kyle followed her gesture to a hole in the mountain. Broken lengths of wood lay scattered around the area with nails peeking up from them. "Yep, this is it. They used to use this for ventilation before the coal seam turned east and they had to dig out a new one. The last time I was here this had been boarded up tight, which is why I brought the crowbar, but it looks like someone already broke it open for me. This, though... this is new."

He pointed at two lengths of pipe stretching from the entrance like fat metal snakes and running down to hang over the river embankment thirty yards away. Dark liquid poured from the ends of the pipes and fell into the river just a few feet below. Kyle's stomach flip-flopped at the sight of the river being polluted.

"What are the pipes for?" Maya asked.

Kyle walked over and bent down to take a look. The pipes, which were made of galvanized steel, were approximately a foot in circumference, and from a rough guess he figured the two runs were composed of twenty-foot lengths joined together with soft iron connectors and soldered. Putrid globs of dark fluid saturated the ground at the joints like oil spills. The smell of it pushed him back.

"I have no idea." He pulled up the neck of his shirt to cover his mouth and nose. "Shoddy work too. Look at these weld points. They've got...whatever this stuff is...leaking from the joints. And there aren't any anchors to keep it secure. Whoever put these here didn't give a shit about safety or codes."

"But what is that stuff?" Maya pointed at the black water gushing into the river. She took a step back from the pipes, her face losing color again. "It feels...evil."

Kyle stared at the ends of the pipes in confusion. "I know it's not coal sludge. That stuff's at the plant where the coal is processed, which is far from here. All that should be coming out of the mine is rock and coal. Well, unless they hit some kind of cavern or cave system."

The sound of his words barely died down when rocks scattered behind him followed by a very distinctive metal click. He'd been paying too much attention to the mystery of the pipes and had forgotten the greater reason for why they were there, and because of that someone had gotten the drop on them.

"That's a damn good question," a voice said. "It's too bad you'll never get the answer to it."

CHAPTER FIFTEEN

Screams ripped through the darkness like black lightning, dragging Taylor up from the depths of unconsciousness. She awoke on her side, rough ground pressing into her left hip and arm. When another scream tore the black she shoved herself up and scuttled away from the sound as quickly as her hands and heels could carry her. After a few shuffles a jagged wall slammed into her back and the base of her skull. Explosions of light erupted in her eyes like fireworks from the pain. Bile rose in her throat, and she had to lean over to keep herself from passing out.

"Somebody help us!" a ragged voice shouted. "Anybody!"

Taylor didn't recognize who it was. Then again, she had no idea where she was or what had happened. When she tried to remember the previous few hours, all she saw was a series of images that didn't make sense. The last real memory she had was getting out of her brother's car angry as hell and slipping into her room. After that, she saw only a montage of shadows and panic. If she'd woken up with her bed beneath her she'd have considered it the worst nightmare she ever had, but the comfort of her mattress and sheets were nowhere to be found. It was still a nightmare, but now it was one she was living.

"Why are they doing this?" another voice asked. This one was on the other side of her, closer, and distinctly feminine. She didn't recognize it either, but it seemed a tad more familiar than the previous voice.

"Because they're fucked in the head!" a male voice shouted. "I don't know if you saw who took you, but I saw my dad when he came for me, and he looked crazy, man. Crazy as shit. His eyes... It was like they were gone."

His words hit Taylor like a kick to the chest, and a memory rose up in her mind, a memory of her dad grabbing her, of his hands spreading like a tree's shadow over her, and his empty eyes so black and yawning. Another wave of nausea buffeted against her, and she opened her mouth to retch. Nothing but gasps of air came out.

"Who's that?" the first voice asked, her words shot out like she'd been hit with a cattle prod. "Who's puking? God don't make me puke too! Shit!"

"I'm not..." Taylor stopped to catch her breath. The dark felt like it had weight and pressed down on her. A nasty smell like an overflowing septic tank hung in the air, and her throat trembled in another bout of phantom gagging. The confusion and fear hovering over everything only made it worse. She knew if she started shaking she wouldn't stop until every atom in her body fell apart, so she curled her hands into fists and hit them against the ground as hard as she could. Pain flashed through her hands and arms, but it was better than the fear. It helped her focus, center herself, and she needed that. Finally she felt able to speak. "I'm not puking. I was just... I hit my head, and I don't know how I got here, and...What the fuck?"

Masculine laughter tumbled into the dark, but there was little humor in it. "Yeah, what the fuck."

Try as she might, Taylor couldn't place the voice. "Who is that? Who's here? I'm....uh, I'm Taylor Mason."

"I know you," the male voice replied. "I sit behind you in English."

"Brett Sobel?" A light went off in her head as she associated the voice with a face. Brett was a junior, like her, and he played on the football team. He'd seemed nice enough – for a sweaty jock – but he didn't talk much, which was probably why she didn't recognize his voice.

"Yeah. My little brother Alex is here too."

"Hey," a small voice said, the black making it seem even smaller.

Taylor turned toward where she'd earlier heard someone speak. "Who else is here?"

"Like it matters," the first female voice said, still ragged. "We're all gonna die."

"Shut up, Shelly!" the more familiar voice yelled, her words echoing painfully off the rocky walls. "Jesus Christ!"

Stillwater was a small town, and Taylor only knew of one Shelly in it who's voice could be young enough to match what she heard – Shelly Harris. Shelly's best friend was Hannah Gould, which sparked a connection in her head.

"Shelly and Hannah, that you?"

"Yeah," Hannah replied, a catch in her throat adding a hitch to the word.

All kids, Taylor thought. *What are a bunch of kids doing in the dark?*

To see if anyone knew the answer to that, she asked, "What's going on? Who brought us here?"

"I have no fucking idea," Shelly said. "One minute I'm laying down to go to bed, and the next thing I know I'm here and my head is pounding. I think I was drugged."

"How long have you been here?"

"A couple of days." Shelly didn't sound entirely certain, but Taylor couldn't blame her. "It's hard to tell when all you've got is the dark. Sometimes I'd hear what sounded like a door or something move, and then a plate of food would be dropped in front of me, or a bottle of water, but whoever brought it never said anything. I think I had two plates plopped down before Brett and his brother were tossed in with me."

"They said I was brought in just after them." Hannah sounded at her wit's end, a hair away from breaking down into either sobs or a crazed, murderous fury. "I think it was my uncle who... I've been living with him since my parents, ya know – or maybe you don't, I don't know – died last year. Things were going okay, given the situation, but the past few weeks have been rough. I thought maybe he'd started drinking, or doing drugs. Anyway, last night or... I think it was last night... I woke up with someone grabbing me. I only caught a glimpse of who it was before I was hit on the back of the head, but I think it was my uncle. Next thing I knew I was here, in the dark."

"And when was I brought in?" Taylor didn't like the similarities between Hannah's experience and her own.

"About an hour ago," Brett replied. "Shit, it could have

been ten minutes for all I know, though. The only marker of time in here is how long it takes between needing to pee again. I'd suggest finding a place close to you, by the way. You don't want to accidentally stumble into your own shit in here. Not a lot of handy wipes or Purell around to clean up with."

Taylor felt repulsed and faintly amused at the same time, but she put that aside to deal with the bigger issue. "Brett, did I hear you say it was your dad that brought you and your brother?"

There were a few seconds of silence, during which Taylor imagined he was nodding in the dark, but then he said, "Yeah, but...he looked all wrong. I know it sounds crazy, but his eyes were...they were black, and his skin looked diseased. I'm not lying either."

"I know," Taylor said quickly. "My dad grabbed me, too, and I think he looked the same way. And like Hannah said, my dad's been weird the past few weeks. Hell, both my parents have been weird, but my dad especially. It's like he gets home from the mine, but part of him is still there, or maybe part of the mine came with him."

"Yeah, same here." For the first time, Shelly didn't sound broken down. "About a month ago my dad came home from the mine drenched in water like he'd swam home down the river, and since then he's gotten more...unhappy, tuned out. I thought maybe he was coming down with the flu or something."

"Do all our dads work in the mine?" Brett's little brother Alex asked, his young voice quivery and high-pitched.

That's a damn good question. "Shelly, does your uncle work in the mine too?"

"Yeah," she replied, the volume of her voice increasing. "He's been weird too. This is fucked up, something's going on."

Taylor puzzled over the new information. All of them lived with someone who worked in the mines, and those someones had been acting weird for the past several weeks. Obviously something was going on, but what? And what did that have to do with them now being in the dark? "Do any of you know why–"

"What the fuck does it matter?" Hannah's voice fell just short of a scream.. "What does any of this matter? These questions are pointless, and I'm tired of listening to them! Now just be quiet! Someone has to know we're missing, so help will be coming soon!"

Taylor wanted to laugh at Hannah's naiveté, but she held herself in check because she knew it wouldn't help things. Not everyone had the same thought.

"Help, right." Sarcasm dripped off Shelly's words like acid. "I'm sure a S.E.A.L. team is on their way to save us, any minute now."

"You shut up!" Hannah's voice roared in the dark, loud enough to make Taylor wince. "Don't make fun of me! I'm sick of you always making fun of me! You're a goddam bitch, and I'm tired of you treat—"

The sound of stone being ground against stone rumbled over Hannah's words, stopping her in her tracks. Taylor felt the ground tremble beneath her, and her eyes swiveled to where she thought the sound was coming from as she scuttled sideways in the opposite direction. Seconds later she felt two sets of hands bump into her and heard a masculine "Ooff!" grunt against her ear as she plowed into Brett and his brother. She opened her mouth to apologize, but a sudden burst of light and silence cut her off.

"All of you better shut your mouths." A man's gruff voice came from behind a flashlight beam that shined like the sun.

Taylor instinctively closed her eyes to avoid being blinded, and in the bright haze she heard what sounded like two more people being thrown into the room. When she opened her eyes just the slightest bit, she saw Tamara Whitcomb and her twin brother Finn, both of whom she went to school with. She also knew that their dad worked in the mine. Which, judging from the rough stone walls around them, was where they were.

"If I hear any of you say another word." The man pointed his flashlight at all of them in turn, "I'm going to come back, and I'm going to chew one of your throats out and drink you dry. If you think I'm kidding, think again."

As he finished speaking he titled the flashlight up and shined it on his face. Decaying gray flesh, black eyes, and a misshapen mouth filled with razor sharp teeth shined into the dark. The nightmare her life had become now had a face to go with it, and a wave of madness towered over her, waiting to drop. All she had to hold it back were her screams, and those she let loose in a flood of tortured sound. When the light flicked off and dropped all of them back into darkness, her world became one long shriek of terror.

Even without seeing it, when the rifle's hammer clicked back, Maya knew what it was. She'd seen way too many TV shows and movies to not know what a gun being cocked sounded like.

"Stay right there," the voice behind them said, "and turn around."

When Maya obeyed, the first thing she saw was the rifle. She had no idea what type of gun it was, or who made it, but none of that mattered. It was long, dark, and capable of ending her life with one pull of the trigger – that was what mattered. The rifle looked powerful and in good condition. The same couldn't be said for the man holding it.

Leprosy was the first word to pop into Maya's head when she looked at the figure glaring at her over the barrel of the gun. His skin was sallow with hints of gray, like he'd been hiding in a disease-ridden cave for years, with tears and gaps marring his flesh as though something inside him struggled to get out. He seemed young, but he stood hunched over like an old man, and the fingers curled around the rifle were claws. He looked like a hundred pounds of shit stuffed into an ill-fitting meat suit, with a gun at the ready to end her life. As frightening as that was, though, something else scared her even more. It wasn't anything her eyes could see, or any of her other usual senses for that matter. It lurked beneath them, on a primal, spiritual level, and it had her psychic sensitivity meter pegging like crazy. He was a man, a person of flesh and blood and bone, but he was more than that. Shadows danced deep inside him, wisps of an ancient darkness that had taken root in him, changing him from the inside out, turning everything he was into something foul, something unnatural. In all her years of investigating the paranormal she'd never experienced anything like it.

"Dean?" Kyle said, his voice snapping Maya into the moment. "Dean Cotton, is that you?"

Dean raised his cheek from when it rested against the rifle butt, and then he flashed a gap-toothed grin as he laid it back. "Well now, your daddy said you was back in town, Kyle. I didn't think I'd be seein' you out here though. Last I heard, you were too good for these here mines. You change your mind, thought maybe you'd come see what you been missin'?"

"Not exactly." Kyle shook his head.

"Then why you here?"

Kyle looked at the man, then at his rifle, his eyes lingering on the long, gnarled finger pressed against the trigger. "'Cause something strange was going on out here."

"Strange?" Dean raised his head again, and one side of his mouth curled into a smile that made Maya's flesh crawl. "Oh yeah, somethin' strange is definitely goin' on. Somethin' glorious. It's been our little secret, but soon the whole world is gonna be in on it, and when that happens everythin' will change. And lucky you, you'll get a front row seat." He lowered his head and stepped to the right, away from the hole in the mountain. "Now, why don't–"

Before he could finish, Dean 's face hitched up in a strained grimace and his body twitched like he was being electrocuted. He dropped the rifle, and then dropped to his knees in a quivering fit. Maya barely had time to wonder what happened when gravity left her stomach and blackness spread across her vision, throwing her into twilight.

Nausea tickled the bottom of Kyle's stomach, and his vision dimmed for a moment, but it was nothing compared to the overwhelming sensation earlier. For the two people with him, though, it looked bad. Both of them were on the ground, their limbs twitching and their mouths chattering nonsensical words as their eyes rolled up until only the whites were showing.

He wanted to rush to Maya to make sure she was okay, but his instinct – honed by his years in the army – made him run for the dropped rifle. With practiced ease he unloaded it and pocketed the rounds. He then unhooked the thin leather shoulder strap, set the gun aside, and grabbed the jittering Dean Cotton.

He didn't want to touch the guy but he had no choice. Dean's arms and legs vibrated like he had a cattle prod jammed up his ass, but Kyle used his knees to hold his arms in place while he wrapped the leather strap around Dean's wrists, cinching it tight. He then turned, grabbed Dean's feet, and checked what shoes he was wearing. He was glad to see large laces crisscrossing their fronts. Using those he tied Dean's legs together at the ankles. Once he was properly trussed up, Kyle flipped him over so that his face wasn't mashed in the ground.

Satisfied they were no longer in danger, Kyle went to Maya. Halfway there she stopped shaking. She lifted herself up by her right arm as he squatted down next to her. "You okay?"

Maya shook her head and stared down at the bit of ground she sat on. "Not even a little bit."

"Did you hurt yourself?"

"I skinned my hand," she replied, holding up her left palm. Shallow, red scratches marred her skin, and thin streaks of blood dribbled from cuts where small rocks had nicked her.

Kyle untucked his shirt and tore a length of fabric from the bottom of it, then handed it to her. "Sorry. I wish I had something more hygienic, but it'll have to do."

Maya took it and wrapped it around her hand. "Thanks. What about—" Her eyes jerked over to where she'd last seen Dean, fear igniting her face like a lit torch, but when she saw him tied up on the ground she sighed and closed her eyes for a moment. Dean still trembled. "Oh thank God."

"Yeah, he keeled over the same time you did. Unless he turns into the Hulk or something, he's no threat to anyone now."

"Maybe he can shed some light on what's going on." Maya stood up and dusted herself off.

Together they walked over to Dean and squatted on both sides of his twitching body. His eyes were barely open, and all he saw were slits of white. His mouth moved and strange sounds tumbled out of him, but there were just that – sounds, nothing intelligible. He waited a few more seconds to see if Dean followed Maya's example and came to on his own, but when he didn't Kyle reached down and slapped Dean's cheek.

"Wake up, Dean. Come on."

The twitching didn't stop. Kyle slapped him again, harder, but nothing changed. Finally he pulled the man into a sitting position, then reared back and slapped him hard enough to send a crack into the air.

"Kyle!" Maya grabbed his arm.

Kyle shrugged her hand off. "Hey, he had a gun on us, remember? If it wasn't for this...seizure, or whatever this is...we might be dead right now. And my sister might be in danger too. If I have to kick the information I need out of him, so be it."

Kyle pulled his hand back to deliver another slap, but he stopped when Dean went silent and stared up. His pupils were so large they practically swallowed his eyes. A sick grin twisted his face.

"Your sister is just fine." The pitch in Dean's voice rose with laughter. "She looks as sweet as a plum. I bet she tastes as good too."

Kyle grabbed Dean by his shirt and yanked him close. The miner smelled terrible, like an animal that had been gutted and left to rot in the woods, but his need to protect his sister overrode everything. "Where is she? Where did you see her?"

"In the dark." Dean laughed and rocked his head from side to side. "Always in the dark. Everything's prettier in the dark."

"Do you mean the mine?" Kyle's head snapped up and he glared at the entrance in the mountain.

Dean pulled at his restraints, grunting and chuckling at

the same time. "It's not just a mine, dumbass. Never was. It just took us awhile to figure that out. And now your sister waits, her fear making her blood taste so sweet."

"Where in the mine is she?" Kyle shook the man in his hands like a ragdoll. He didn't know why he was asking. He wouldn't know one end of it from another. He asked out of instinct, out of fear.

"Not far, boy." Dean looked directly at Kyle. His eyes were almost completely black. "Just a little ways in, but it don't matter. Nothing does. Soon the darkness will rise, and we will all revel in his glory." Laughter and hoots burst out of Dean's mouth like crows fleeing a bell tower.

Kyle pulled on Dean's arms and struggled to his feet saying, "You're going to lead me to her, you son of a bitch," but Dean went limp and slipped from his grasp. He chuckled on the ground, bits of foam spotting the corners of his mouth as his eyes went white again. Dean wasn't going anywhere. "Shit."

"What do we do now?" Maya's tone was even and calm, but that didn't help Kyle's nerves.

"We're not doing anything." He stressed the first word. He then got up and walked over to where he'd set the night vision goggles down. "You're staying right here. We just have the one pair of these, so I'm going in alone. He said she wasn't far, and I'm hoping he's right."

Maya walked over and touched his hands as they held the goggles. "He's crazy, Kyle. Whatever's going on here is shredding his mind, and it might do the same to us if we give it a chance. I'm not saying we should leave – I mean, I am, but I know you need to do what you can for your sister – but you need to hurry. Careful, and quick, okay?"

Thankful for her understand, Kyle stepped close and tilted his head down toward hers. She tilted her own and pushed herself up into his kiss. Her lips were soft and warm, as were her hands when they touched his face. He felt much more calm when they pulled apart.

"Give me twenty minutes. If I'm not back by then, run back to the Jeep and haul ass out of town." He reached into his pocket and handed her the keys.

"You'll be lucky if I give you ten," she replied. He wasn't sure if she was joking, but a small smile pulled at her lips. "Now get going."

Kyle glanced over at the former man and frowned. He hated leaving her with him, but he didn't have a choice. He had confidence in his knots though.

"Okay. See you soon."

He turned and left before the fear building inside him could show on his face. Everything around him was falling into the Twilight Zone, and he had no idea how to even begin handling it. All he could think was that he had training, he had equipment, and he had a mission. If he could focus on those things, he'd be okay. As he neared the hole in the mountain, though, doubt crept into his chest like a sliver of ice aimed for his heart.

All alone on the side of a mountain hundreds of miles from home, Maya trembled. It wasn't just because she was alone. She was a big girl, she could handle that. And it wasn't because yards away from her was a trussed up hillbilly who minutes before had pointed a gun at her – she had grown up in Memphis, Tennessee, for Christ's sake. Those were valid reasons to be shaking, but as bad as they were they paled next to the evil she felt moving in the earth below her. It was like an ocean of malevolence and hatred and rage spread out beneath her feet, growing stronger and closer with every minute. It took every ounce of strength she had to not say, "Fuck it," run to Kyle's Jeep, and put all this crazy shit in her rearview mirror.

"It wouldn't matter even if you did." Little titters of laughter trailed after Dean Cotton's words.

Maya turned and looked down at the miner. His wrists were still bound tightly behind his lower back, and his feet were laced solidly together, but that didn't diminish his danger one bit. Not to her. What was wrong with him went straight into the yawning dark below them, and she didn't know if laces and leather straps could do anything about that.

"What wouldn't matter?" she asked, regretting the question even as she asked it.

Dean laughed again, and flecks of spit foamed in the corners of his mouth. "Running, you dumb bitch. Ain't nowhere to run *to*."

It took her a couple seconds to realize what he was saying, and why he was saying it. *He picked my thoughts right out of my head*, she thought, amazed and repulsed all at the same time. The idea he could see into her so fully and easily turned her stomach sour.

"It ain't hard," he said, continuing to reply to her unspoken words. "Not with you. You're old blood. I can smell it in you."

"Old blood?" Without even knowing she did it, she took a step toward him. "What do you mean, 'old blood'?"

Dean pulled at his restraints, grunting and laughing as his muscles flexed and strained. His gray skin, already marred by cuts, tore even further, and in the wounds she saw cords of black muscle quiver under the strain of his efforts. Liquid the color of bird shit oozed from the tears. Even from a distance she smelled the stink rolling off him, like a dead animal left to rot on the side of the road. Repulsive as he was, she didn't run away.

"Answer me." She picked up the rifle from where Kyle had tossed it. "Tell me what you mean by that."

Dean flopped around like a fish dragged onto shore, he shoulders bunching and his hips thrusting into the air. His movements were rough and spastic, and all the while he laughed his madman's laugh. After several seconds of wiggling and grunting, the laces around his feet burst apart, and with an agility she wouldn't have thought him capable of he flipped his torso upward until he stood on his feet.

"Stop right there!" She aimed the gun at his chest.

Hunched over, his chest heaving up and down in ragged motions, Dean tilted his head and looked at her with a smile on his face as empty as his black eyes. "You ain't got the guts, you stupid bitch nigger."

Blood drained from Maya's face. Her panic opened the

floodgates of her mind, shouting her every thought into the psychic ether, and the monster in front of her heard them loud and clear. "Don't get in my head! Stay out!"

"Your blood's so old." Dean stepped toward her. "You don't even know the honor you should feel at having it pump through your veins, the glory of the ancient ones that it came from. But I do, don't you worry, and I can't wait to tear your throat open and drink every last drop of it."

The smile on Dean's face widened until it tore the corners of his mouth, and pus leaked from the wounds, making him look like a clown from her worst nightmare. He opened his mouth wider and wider, roaring into the sky, and his shoulders and arms heaved at the leather binding his wrists. Maya watched in horror as his flesh tore and his muscles expanded, pulsing and bleeding a black thin liquid. He was changing, transforming right before her eyes, and deep inside her a voice screamed at her to run, but a terrible fascination kept her rooted in place. It wasn't until the leather strap broke and his arms flew up that the little voice finally was heard.

Dean snarled at her, a black tongue licking a ravaged mouth. "Too late," he said, his words nearly unintelligible.

With a speed that took her breath away, he leaped at her, covering the dozen or so feet between them in less than a heartbeat. She stumbled backward, barely missing his arms as they grabbed for her, and as she moved she threw the rifle at him. It hit his face but he didn't flinch. Instead he laughed and reached out, his clawed fingers scraping her skin.

In his touch she felt death, and she knew he would tear her open and make good on his intention to drink her dry, but suddenly his body seized up again and he dropped to the ground in a quivering pile. Relief flushed through her like cold water. She nearly shouted in glee when the same psychic thunderclouds poured into her brain too, and just like he did she collapsed into a spasming heap, her body falling like a felled tree right on top of him. When her skin made contact with his, terrible visions entered her mind, showing her a world she never could have believed possible. It was a world of darkest evil, as ancient as the light of the furthest stars, and she fell into it with eyes opened, sightless, and black.

Chapter Sixteen

A week ago Kyle had been up to his neck in supply requisition orders and boxes of tighty whities, glad to be back in the States but missing the smell of grilled kebabs wafting from carts on the streets of Kabul. Now, as he walked hunched over through a mine tunnel cast in varying shades of green by the night vision goggles he wore and searched for his sister, that felt like a lifetime ago. Since coming back home his world had been turned upside down, and ideas he'd once considered the stuff of fiction were all too real.

On the ground to his right were the pipes he'd seen running out of the mountain. He had no idea what was in them, but in the distance he heard the *chug-chug-chug* of pumps, so he followed them in the hope they'd lead to some sort of explanation. The mine's low ceiling forced him to walk in a crouch, and it didn't take long for his thighs and lower back to feel the strain. He hoped like hell Dean was right and his sister wasn't far.

He'd forgotten how oppressive being in a mine felt. Hewn out of the very rock of the mountain, every surface was rough, and grit sat piled in drifts on the floor and between the pipes. Even with the goggles on it was hard to see, the darkness like a mouth swallowing him bite by bite. It was the weight of the stone above his head, though, that really put the pressure on. The rocky ceiling looked thick and strong, but he'd heard enough stories of unsecured shale dropping on people and crushing them before they knew what was happening to keep a wary eye as he stepped further into the mountain.

Twenty yards in, the tunnel curved sharply to the right. Kyle pressed himself against the wall and leaned out slowly to see what lay ahead of him. All he saw was more rock and pipe before the tunnel ended at a T. The pumps grew louder as he edged deeper in, and as he neared the junction he could tell they were down the tunnel on the right, which was exactly where the pipes were headed. The tunnel to the left was featureless – just one long, dark walk.

A minute after turning right a new sound joined the pumps. At first it sounded like muffled talking, but after a few seconds he heard it for what it was – screaming. He tried to break into a run, but the low ceiling kept him to a hunched scurry. The goggles bounced around on his face despite the strap, screwing up his vision, but when a flash of light showed an opening in the rock wall several yards down on his left he saw it clear as day.

"I said shut up!" a deep voice roared through the opening. "Or I will gut every last fuckin' one of you!"

Envisioning his sister on the business end of that threat, he picked up the pace. When he finally came to the opening, he stopped and edged his face around to look. Inside the rocky chamber were seven people, all of them cringing against the far wall in fear. Even through the grime that coated their faces he could tell they were all kids. In the middle of the group, her eyes wide in terror, stood Taylor.

Between him and the kids stood a man holding a flashlight. He waved it around like a club, and his bunched shoulders said he was moments away from unleashing hell on whoever was closest to him. Kyle didn't give him that chance; he scurried as quickly as he could through the entrance and tackled the man from behind. The kids screamed even louder. The flashlight hit the ground, turning their shadows into monsters on the walls.

"Who the fuck?" the man asked as he threw an elbow backward and hit Kyle in the shoulder.

The blow was stronger than Kyle had been ready for, and he lost his breath as he stumbled backward. The miner twisted around, and in the skewed light he looked like a crazed beast. Kyle couldn't recognize him past the coal soot and snarling mouth. With a snarl, the miner rushed forward.

As his opponent closed on him, he stepped to the left and hooked his right arm around the miner's neck. Once he was locked in, Kyle hammered blows into the miner's side, hitting ribs, hip and arm as the guy tried to break free. They were solid hits, but the thick clothing the miner wore, along with the adrenalin, diminished their effect.

Swinging wildly, the miner got smart and sent a fist into Kyle's crotch. Most of his fist hit thigh meat, but enough of the punch went into his balls to make Kyle "Ooff!" and lose his grip. Now free, the miner reared up, grabbed Kyle by his shoulders, and threw him to the ground. What little air Kyle had in his lungs left him in a rush when he hit the stone floor, and he barely had a chance to draw new breath when the miner was on him, straddling Kyle's waist as his hands raked across Kyle's chest, somehow shredding his coat and shirt into ribbons. Kyle brought his arms up to defend himself, but his opponent took that as his opportunity to hit his shoulders and ribs. Each punch felt stronger than the last, and he gasped, not just at the pain, but also because he had to force air down his windpipe. When the miner twisted to drive a knee into Kyle's side, Kyle thrust his hips upward as hard as he could, ramming the miner's head into the ceiling. The miner staggered and fell off him.

Kyle scrambled to his knees and took a moment to catch his breath. He had time for one inhale before the miner regained his feet and came at him again, a strange light shining in his black eyes and his mouth slavering. Moving on instinct, Kyle leaned backward, drew his legs back, and kicked outward as hard as he could. The miner took most of the kick in his face and chest, and he stumbled backward several steps. Kyle got to his hands and knees, intent on finishing the fight – even if it meant bashing the man's head into the rocky floor – but he only moved a foot before the fight was finished for him.

Moving out of the shadows like a wild animal, a young man came at the miner from behind, wrapped him up in a bear hug, and threw him down with a roar. The miner hit so hard he bounced, but the young man wasn't through. As soon as the miner was down, the kid grabbed his head and smashed it onto the ground. The miner made a pained noise. The kid then jumped on his chest and pounded his fists into the miner's face like they were pistons in an engine well past the red line. He probably would have kept the beating going until the miner's head was bloody pulp, but after a few seconds a smaller boy left the shadows and ran to him.

"Stop, Brett!" the little kid said, tears streaming down his grimy face. "Stop it! You'll kill him!"

Brett ignored him and delivered another blow. "Why shouldn't I? He said he was going to kill us!" His eyes were hard as they looked down at the miner beneath him, but when he turned to look at the small boy next to him, they softened, and his fists uncurled to rest on his legs. His knuckles were raw and bloody.

"But you're not him." The boy laid a hand on the older kid's arm. "And I don't want you to be."

Kyle was impressed. *From the mouths of babes*, he wondered to himself. The fight now over, he waddled over to the downed miner and reached down to feel for a pulse. The miner's skin was incredibly cold, and the coal dust made him feel like he was a statue, but a vein still pumped beneath his fingers. The miner was down, but alive. How long he'd stay out, though, was anyone's guess.

"Kyle, is that you?" a voice asked from the shadows.

Relief flooded through his body when he heard his sister, and he turned to see her pick up the miner's flashlight and duck-walk to him. He grabbed her as soon as she was in hugging range, tears falling from both their eyes.

"What in the fuck is going on?" she asked as they parted.

"I don't know," he replied, wishing like hell he had something more to tell her. "There's...something going on, something strange, but right now what we need to worry about is getting out of here. Who all is here with you?"

Four new faces came into the light. Three were female, one male. They looked frightened to death.

"That's Brett and his little brother Alex." She pointed at the young man who'd finished off the miner. She then turned to the others and gestured for them to huddle in. "This is Shelly, her friend Hanna, and there's Tamara and her brother Finn. We're all in high school together. Well, except for Alex. He's in elementary school."

"He's still a smart kid," Kyle replied, giving the young

boy's hair a tousle and feeling old while doing it. "Okay, we need to get out of here now. Taylor, give me the flashlight and I'll lead the way out. The rest of you, grab hands and stick close. Ready?"

Seven scared and dirty faces nodded at him in the garish glare of the flashlight. He hoped he looked more confident. Once he had his sister's hand and saw that the rest of them were doing the same, he turned and walked to the exit, wondering when this nightmare would end.

Dark clouds hovered over the mountain like a wool blanket, sending down small spatters of rain in intermittent fits, but even that seemed like a burst of cheer compared to the oppressive darkness of the coal mine as Kyle and the kids came through the old vent opening. Shelly and Hanna dropped to their knees and wept, and their friends gathered around them, holding each other and glad to be in the light, muted as it was.

When Maya wasn't there to greet them Kyle looked at where he'd left Dean tied up. Dean wasn't there, but broken bits of leather sat on the grass in his place. Kyle's stomach twisted into a dozen small knots.

"Who's that?" Taylor asked, standing next to him and pointing to the right.

Kyle followed her finger until he saw a body lying on the ground. The sight of a red blouse and shock of dark, curly hair brought equal amounts of relief and fear charging up his throat. He ran over, hoping against hope that she wasn't hurt. It wasn't until he was a few feet away that he saw she was laying on something. When he reached her side, he saw what it was – an unconscious Dean. The hunting rifle was on the ground a few feet away.

"Maya!" He knelt down next to her. He took her shoulders and pulled her into a sitting position, but her head lolled to the side and her eyes were closed. He looked her over, checking for blood or wounds and finding none, then felt her neck for a pulse. It was slow, but it was there. He checked her skull, looking for a bump or gash showing that she'd hit her head, but he didn't find one. Her skin felt cool to the touch and had turned an ashy color.

Taylor hunkered down next to him. "Do you know her?"

He nodded, but he didn't know how true that was. He'd met her only a day ago, so could he really *know* her? Probably not, but he understood that in that time he'd learned a good deal about who she was, she'd taught him more than he ever wanted to know about his home town, and he'd had the best sex of his life. A lot had happened in that short span of time, and he wasn't ready for it to be over.

"Yeah, her name's Maya. I met her yesterday. She's here doing some research. I left her here with Dean while I went in looking for you. He... He was tied up. This shouldn't... I don't know what happened."

Taylor leaned over and took a long look at Dean. "He looks like shit, Kyle. Look at his skin. It's all split and gray, with this...pus-looking crap seeping out. He doesn't look human."

"That's part of what she's here investigating. I mean, not him specifically, but that there's something weird going on, and Dean looks to be part of it."

"And she's out?" Taylor asked, turning and looking the woman up and down. "She's hot. Much too damn pretty to be sticking her neck out around here."

Kyle scooped his arms under Maya and lifted her as gently as he could. As soon as she was away from Dean's body, it was like a switch was thrown in her body. He felt her begin to warm, and her skin returned to its natural creamy brown color. She didn't open her eyes or awaken, but it was a positive step nonetheless. Dean, on the other hand, moaned and started to twitch.

"Shit, he's waking up," Taylor said.

Kyle snarled as he looked down at the prone man. "No, he's not." With a savagery he didn't know he was capable of, Kyle hauled off and kicked Dean hard on the side of the head. Dean didn't make a sound as his head snapped to the right and he went still. His chest still rose and fell as he breathed, but he was knocked out. If the kids hadn't been around, he knew he would have gone even further.

"Let's go," he said, hugging Maya's body close and walking back to the trail that led to his Jeep.

Taylor called for her friends, then jogged to his side. "Go? Go where? We've got to find out what's going on. I think... I think dad is the one who brought me out here."

"*We're* not doing anything," he told her, his arms beginning to ache. "Right now the best thing you and your friends can do is hide out and sit tight. *I'll* be the one trying to figure this thing out."

"And where are we supposed to do that?"

Kyle looked over at his little sister, then hitched his head up the mountain. Understanding dawned in her eyes seconds later.

INTERLUDE
BLOOD AND WATER

With every foot the water lowered, the closer the sleeping God came to awakening. His heart beat in titanic pulses that grew closer and closer, and the water churned with the thrashing of his body as it stretched and unfurled. Ash watched from on high, anxious to see his Lord revealed in all his glory.

As exhilarating as the god's waking body was to watch, it paled next to the wonder of his waking mind. The psychic ether was vibrating from the power of the ancient being, quivering as dreams fell slowly away, revealing memories, desires, and hunger. Ash felt as though he lived in two worlds at once, one foot in a coal mine and the other on an ancient plain as his god strode across the world like a force of terrible nature. He knew that soon both those worlds would be one and the same, and that when it happened he would be standing next to the throne of a new Kingdom, his sole desire to serve the will of his Lord. Soon dreams would become reality, and reality would become a nightmare. His fangs dripped blood in anticipation. Nothing could stop what was coming.

The sound of huffing and puffing brought his mind back to the mine. As the ragged breathing grew closer, his annoyance grew with it. Heavy feet slapped at the ground, first one set, and then two more. Within seconds it nearly drowned out the sound of pumps.

"Sir, we got a serious problem," Gus said as he approached the chamber entrance. When he came to a stop, he bent over and breathed deeply.

Ash grit his sharp teeth. "I seriously doubt that. Our Lord rises. What problem could there be?"

"It's my boy. He...uh, he's been here."

Ash's black eyes widened, but after a moment he shrugged his bony shoulders. "So what? There's nothing he can do to stop what's coming."

"Beggin' yer pardon, sir, but he got the kids out."

Ash's bat-like nostrils face flared and his thin gray lips peeled back into a snarl as he whirled around. "He did what?"

Gus sucked in air and staggered back a moment, his own dark eyes as large as dinner plates. "I don't know how he knew they were here or how to find them, but he managed to sneak in through the old vent shaft and find his way to the room where the kids were locked up."

"And nobody stopped him?" Ash's shoulders bunched as frustration boiled his blood. In the grand scheme of things it wasn't a real problem – they would gather a new first meal for their god – but the thought that some punk asshole was able to enter his mountain and leave with his tribute was galling. The muscles across his upper back bulged, and the skin covering them split.

Gus shook his head and stepped to one side, revealing Dean Cotton and Sam Krauss. Dean had been tasked with watching over the old vent entrance, and Sam's job had been to deal with the kids. If what Gus said was true, then they both had failed. The bruises and cuts across their bodies proved it.

"Sam, come here and tell me what happened," Ash ordered, his lips moving but his teeth locked together.

Sam looked like he wanted to do anything but get closer, but after a moment of hesitation he stepped into the chamber, wringing his hands. "Sir, it wasn't my fault, I—"

Ash stepped forward in a rush and tore Sam's head off. Brackish blood sprayed into the air, coating the stone walls. A few drops of it landed in the water below, and the water churned as ropes of flesh lashed through the blood and drew it down. Ash brought the bleeding stump to his body, and while holding onto the head with one hand, he sank his fangs into the torn neck and drank his fill. He let the body fall to the ground, then he plucked the sightless eyes out and tossed them in his gore-covered mouth. They popped like ripe grapes when his teeth closed on them.

Gus and Dean stared down at Sam's dead body. Gus was still, his eyes taking in the scene like a man standing in fascination before a work of art, but Dean shivered and looked away before Sam's heart could pump out the last of his blood.

"What about you, Dean?" Ash asked, his black tongue licking blood from his thin lips. "Was what happened not your fault either?"

Dean flinched at the sound of his name, but he shook his head and managed to stand still. "I shoulda shot 'em, yes sir, as soon as I saw 'em. If one of 'em hadn't had old blood runnin' through 'em, I woulda done just that."

"Old blood?" Ash asked, his anger momentary pushed aside by wonder.

Dean nodded quickly, the gray skin of his neck waggling in the dark. "Yes sir. The nigger woman. I could smell it on her like perfume. I thought she'd make a special tribute, so I was gonna bring 'em to you at gunpoint, but I was... I was overcome by the rapture of our waking Lord before I could do it."

"I understand," Ash replied, the words entering the air just as he lashed out with his claws and decapitated the miner in one fluid motion. Dean's black eyes blinked as his head and body tumbled in different directions. "That don't mean I forgive."

Taking an ever so slight step backward, Gus glanced at the bloody ground, then said, "I'm gonna kill that boy of mine, rest assured, sir. Kill him slow and painful for what he done."

Ash considered Gus's words, then shook his head. "No, I need you here to monitor the pumps. They're work's nearly done, but nearly ain't the same as finished. We have others out there who can take care of this. Now go and do your job."

"What about the...Dean and Sam?" Gus couldn't help but glance at the bodies of his friends as he spoke, but they were fleeting glances at best.

"Leave 'em. I'm hungry."

Gus gulped, nodded, and walked away as quickly as he could without it being a flat-out run.

"If you want something done right, you gotta do it

yourself." Ash closed his eyes and reached out with his mind to find those who were eager and able to work his will. On his back, the tears in his skin widened into gashes as nubs of flesh broke through, pulsing and flexing. Dark blood dripped down his body to join that of the two dead men at his feet, turning the coal dust on the floor into a thick, warm mud.

Chapter Seventeen

Kyle found two bags of beef jerky and a Snickers bar in a cabinet. In the pantry next to it were sealed canisters of flour, sugar, dried beans, rice, and spaghetti noodles, along with some trash bags and cleaning supplies. He grunted in frustration.

"Hey, I found the water," Brett said. "There's ten gallons here. That should suffice, right?"

"Unless one of you decides to take a bath with it, yeah." Kyle closed the pantry and turned to see the teenage boy standing in front of the cabinets next to the stove.

Shelly and Hanna sat down on a blanket-covered couch, dust pluming into the air and the seat springs groaning as their weight dropped on it. They coughed and waved at their faces. The other kids settled on the floor by the fireplace and looked around blankly.

"Are you sure this place is safe?" Shelly asked when the air was clear.

"If by safe you mean no one knows you're here?" Kyle asked, looking around at the decoration free wooden walls and curtainless windows, "then yes. These old hunting cabins don't get much use out of season, and this one is far enough from town and the mine that no one is just going to happen by and see you're here. I wish I could take you all with me, but there just isn't room, so it's safer to keep you together here. All of you just sit tight, stay calm, and keep your heads down while I try to get help. No matter what, you guys won't be here more than tonight. The water Brett found will tide you over. Think you'll be okay?"

Half a dozen dirty, scared faces nodded at him.

"Okay. Good. I'll be back as quick as I can. Remember what I said – calm and cool."

When he got another understanding nod, he gave them the most confident smile he could muster and walked to the door. As he turned the handle, Brett hustled over to stand next to him.

"Hey, you sure you don't want me to go with you? I uh...I think I handled myself okay back in the mine. If things get hairy out there, you might need me."

Kyle couldn't help but think of Brett as a kid even though he was only seven years older than him, but kid or not he had a point. Kyle hadn't needed the help in subduing the miner in the cave, but Brett had jumped in without being asked, and because of that they had made it out in one piece. The kid had courage, and he had strength. Together that made him a potent ally. Unfortunately, it was because of those reasons that Kyle wanted Brett to stay right where he was.

"You're probably right, but look behind you. As much as I might need you, they need you even more, especially your brother. I can't be out there doing what I need to do if I'm worried about what's going on back here. I'm depending on you to take care of them. Are you up to that? Are you the man around here? Or do I need I ask your little brother?"

Brett frowned. "Yeah, I'm the man."

"With the way you kicked the shit out of that guy in the mine, I don't doubt you one bit." Kyle clapped Brett on the shoulder before opening the door and leaving the hunting cabin.

The rented Jeep waited just outside under a strand of trees that didn't quite keep the rain off it. Taylor sat in the back with Maya leaning against her, still unconscious.

"We ready to roll?" Taylor asked through her rolled-down window.

He nodded and went around to the driver's door. Once he was seated he started the engine and strapped himself in.

"I'm surprised Brett didn't come with you. Figured his male ego would demand he come along."

"Hey," Kyle said over his shoulder, "don't knock the male ego. It's what's keeping him in the cabin, watching out for your friends."

Taylor made a sound somewhere between a laugh and a cough. "They aren't my friends."

Kyle looked in the rearview mirror and saw Taylor staring down at the stranger next to her. Her dark hair was disheveled, her black eyeliner and lipstick was smeared across her face, and her Lady Gaga shirt was unrecognizable under the coal dust ground into it. Now, more than ever, she looked lost and alone. As though her life hadn't been hard enough already.

"I guess not," he told her, their eyes meeting in the mirror, "but right now they're sane and normal, both of which seem to be in short supply around this place."

They kept conversation to a minimum as Kyle drove down the mountain, the constant bumping and shaking from the poorly maintained roads too much for anyone to try and talk over. It reminded him of driving in Afghanistan. But, as soon as the gravel road ended at the blessed asphalt of Route 49, Taylor leaned forward and put her face between the two front seats.

"So where are we going?"

That was a good question. After getting the kids out of the mine, Kyle's first instinct had been to go to the police. That was what people usually did when the shit hit the fan. But, considering how changed so many others in town were, that didn't seem like a good idea. So, if the local constabulary was suspect, the next logical step was the county sheriff. Stillwater was in Mingo County, and the county seat for Mingo was Williamson, an hour's drive up Route 49. All he had to figure out now was what he was going to say. Stories about psychic visions and miners with black, soulless eyes wasn't going to get the cavalry a runnin'.

"Williamson." He flicked the wipers into their highest setting. "We need the county sheriff's department."

Taylor leaned back to cradle Maya against the door. "You saw what I saw, bro. That guy in the mine looked seriously fucked up, and I don't mean hillbilly-spending-too-much-time-in-the-dark fucked up. I mean Exorcist-skin-splitting-and-eyes-all-crazy fucked up. Same thing for the guy your girlfriend here was passed out on top of. Something weird is happening, and I don't think small town cops are gonna be much help."

"Then what would you suggest?"

"You're in the Army." She frowned at him in the rearview. "Get us some damn troops! Call in the National Guard! Something! Or call the Vatican and get us some priests. Or both! We need some big guns here."

He was impressed that she was keeping herself together as well as she was. For all his training and time overseas camped out in dangerous places, he'd never anticipated having to deal with anything as strange as what he'd seen and heard since coming back to Stillwater. His world had always been about rough people and hard facts. Now everything was being turned upside down, and all the things he'd thought he understood seemed like props on a stage, fake and temporary, hiding a truth he didn't want to know. His sanity was being tested, and he worried he was coming up short. Taylor, in spite of her age and inexperience – or maybe even because of it – was dealing better. He hoped like hell that held out, and that he could hold on with her.

"Sorry, but I don't have the president on my speed dial. And I don't have the pope either. We have to work with what we've got." He picked his phone up from the cup holder at his knees and looked at its reception bars. NO SERVICE stared back at him. "And right now we couldn't call anyone in even if we wanted to." He tossed his phone over his shoulder.

Taylor caught it and scowled. "Goddam it."

The rain fell harder, and Kyle turned up the wiper speed to its highest setting. The outside world was a wash of dull gray, the lush West Virginia greens muted and dour as water pounded down. As the road curved left around the mountain, he slowed down to avoid slipping on the wet asphalt. The sudden appearance of red and blue flashing lights on the highway ahead of him made him wonder if someone hadn't already crashed, but as they drew closer he didn't see any smashed cars or ambulances or road flares. Instead, two Stillwater police cruisers, parked bumper to bumper across the highway, blocked the road, their roof lights spinning like kaleidoscopes.

A hard, cold knot formed in the pit of Kyle's stomach.

Taylor leaned forward again, her face stopping next to his shoulder. "What the hell? This can't be good."

Kyle thought the same thing as he pressed harder on the brake pedal. At any other time and place, the sight of police cars and flashing lights wouldn't have been a cause for concern. This wasn't any other time or place though. He'd just been involved in the assaulting of two men, he had a minor with him, he'd hidden away half a dozen other kids, and he had an unconscious woman in the backseat. It was enough to make his palms sweat.

"I'd turn around." Taylor tapped his seat. "In case you forgot, I've got a knocked out chick next to me drooling on herself."

Kyle would have loved to have done just that, but his hands stuck in the direction they were held. "We can't turn around. We have to get to Williamson, and this is the fastest way there. Shit."

Taylor grunted, her head shaking in his rearview mirror. "Then you better come up with a good story."

"Yeah, thanks," he replied as he pressed down on the brake. The police cars were still a hundred feet ahead of him, two officers standing in front of them covered in yellow rain slickers, but in his mind they were already boxing him in, guns aimed at him by the dozen. Knowing that the worst thing he could do was act suspicious, he kept his hands steady and his foot smooth as he slowed the Jeep down, but in his mind he was frantically thinking of what he could say or do that might help get them out of Stillwater. By the time he stopped he had the beginnings of an idea. He fished his wallet out of his back pocket and opened it.

The officer tapped Kyle's window with his flashlight. Kyle looked up to see if he recognized who it was, but the darkness caused by the heavy cloud cover and the slicker's hood kept the officer's face in shadow. He pressed the button to lower the window. Rain pelted him, drenching his face before the window was all the way down, but he ignored it and held his wallet up, his driver's license and military ID facing out.

"Good afternoon, officer," he said in his best I'm-a-model-citizen voice. "Is there a problem with the road? I've got a sick friend that I'm trying to get to a doctor."

The policeman didn't respond. Kyle tried to find eyes to look into for what the officer might be thinking, but there weren't any. His entire face was lost to shadow. The cold hardness in Kyle's stomach expanded, chilling his entire body.

"Sorry you have to stand out in the rain like this," Kyle continued, hoping like hell some sympathy would things moving along. "Back when I was in Afghanistan rain was a blessing, but here it's just a pain."

Still the policeman said nothing. Meanwhile, another officer slowly approached on the passenger side of the Jeep, and two more exited the parked cruisers.

"So, should I turn around?" he asked, his lips numb and his tongue thick in his mouth. Every instinct told him they were in danger, that the darkness spreading in the town behind him was reaching out, but he just wasn't ready to give into that yet. In spite of everything that had happened, he still wanted things to make sense. He wanted his world to be normal. Running from cops was the opposite of normal, and despite the ice pick of fear pushing into the back of his skull, he refused to give into it. That wasn't how things were done.

"Okay," he said, " I've taken up too much of your time. I'll find another –"

As he drew his left hand back, the officer grabbed his wrist, and the intense coldness of his touch sent a shock through Kyle's system, making him drop his wallet. He gasped and stared at the hand holding him. The skin was ash gray, the fingernails black and split. The sudden movement caused the officer's hood to jerk backward, revealing a gray face with dark wells for eyes, and the mouth that sneered at him parted just enough to show teeth that would have been more at home in a dog's muzzle. Kyle flashed back to the men at the mines, seeing the same sallow skin and empty eyes. The situation was rapidly deteriorating into madness.

"Yer gonna pay for what you done." The frozen vise of

the officer's hand chilled Kyle's blood, but he forgot all about it when the officer pulled his pistol and shoved it in his face. The black depths of the gun barrel echoed the dark pits of the policeman's eyes, and in all of them Kyle saw his death. "You ain't fit for the glory that's comin'."

Over the next several seconds a great number of things happened, each event like a car crashing into the one in front of it, and the one constant was the screaming.

At the sight of the gun, Taylor cried out, grabbed Maya, and hurled herself onto the backseat floorboard. Moving quicker than he ever had before, Kyle jerked his arm away from the officer, leaned his head back, and grabbed the hand holding the gun. The dark skin felt clammy, but he didn't care as he pushed the arm forward and banged it against the steering wheel. Two-tenths of a second later, the gun went off, filling the Jeep with roaring noise and the stench of burnt gunpowder. The front passenger window exploded in a shower of glass as the bullet blasted through it, and the policeman approaching from that side dove to the ground to avoid being hit.

Taylor screamed, but the ringing in Kyle's ears almost drowned it out. The policeman next to him jerked to get away, but Kyle tightened his grip and jammed the cop's arm against the wheel several times in quick succession. The gun went off again, blasting a hole through the passenger door.

Fearing the next bullet would find flesh, Kyle balled up his right hand and punched at the fingers holding the gun. They spasmed open, and the gun tumbled to the floor mat beneath Kyle's legs. As it fell, the tiny part of his mind that the army had trained to not run around like a spooked puppy noted that the gun was a Smith & Wesson M&P40.

The policeman lunged into the Jeep and reached for Kyle's neck. The sickly cold fingers tightened on his windpipe when Taylor's screams finally broke through the ringing in his ears. "Go! Go! Go!" she shouted, the word coming out of her like a mantra.

Hearing her reminded him exactly where he was, so while he fended off the policeman with one hand he put the Jeep into reverse with the other. His foot slammed against the gas pedal, and the vehicle leapt backward in a rush of power. The policeman outside Kyle's window tried to hold on, even going so far as to lean through the window opening, but Kyle hit him in the side of the head with his elbow and yanked the wheel to the right, both of which combined to shake the officer loose and send him tumbling to the ground.

Tires squealed against wet asphalt, but that was drowned out by the sound of gunfire and shattering glass. A loud *bang* and a shudder told him they'd shot out one of the tires. He ducked and shouted for Taylor to stay down, then glanced in the rearview mirror. The Jeep's back window was a cloudy web of cracks, broken only by savage holes through which he could see the police taking aim for another round. He kept the gas pedal pressed against the floorboard and held the bucking steering wheel with an iron grip.

The swirling lights disappeared a few seconds later as they rounded the mountain. But, he knew they would be after him at any moment, so he took the first road to the right he saw, pelted down it at breakneck speed, and then took whatever turns came his way. Several minutes later he was far from the cops and deep in the back mountain roads of Stillwater, large stretches of trees and broken rocks hiding him away, at least for the moment.

"What the fuck was that?" Taylor asked as he pulled onto a narrow dirt lane and parked.

Kyle shook his head and stared at the trees flanking the road ahead of them. "That was shit going from bad to worse."

Taylor giggled for a moment, the sound so counter to the tension and fear that filled the interior of the Jeep, but then she let out a scream that curled the hairs on his neck. He turned around to find her banging her right hand on the seat and gripping Maya's left shoulder tightly. The dam had finally broken inside her.

"They shot at us!" she shouted, her eyes red and wide as they stared into him. "They fucking shot at us! What the fuck! Why... How are we..." She turned her dead from side to side as though looking for an answer somewhere in the backseat.

Finally she sighed and crumpled. "Shit."

"Yeah, that about covers it." Kyle didn't know what more to say. In less than a day the world had turned on its head, and in the wake of it he didn't have a clue what to do. His sister needed comfort – and hell, so did he – but more than that they needed a plan. He didn't know where to start with one, though, because he didn't have a clue what they were up against. In the Army they'd taught him that when he had an enemy his job was to point his weapon at that enemy and make them die for their country before he died for his. But who was his enemy here? The cops? His dad? Everyone? Or, was it something far more sinister and secret than a simple bad guy? No matter how evil a person was, their skin didn't change and crack and their teeth didn't turn into a dog's snarl. Something much worse than a bad cop and abusive father was at work in Stillwater, and Kyle didn't know how to even begin dealing with it.

"Shit isn't even the beginning of it." Maya's voice was weak and groggy, but the unexpectedness of it made Kyle and Taylor gasp. Maya leaned against the car door, her face a chalky brown color, and her eyes were red around the edges, but the look she gave Taylor and then Kyle through the rearview mirror was solid, grave, and unflinching. "You have no idea just how bad things really are."

CHAPTER EIGHTEEN

Maya felt like death warmed over. As she sat crammed up against the backseat driver's side door, she tried to pull herself together and gather what wits she had left back into her oatmeal bowl of a brain. It was easier said than done, and it didn't help that she'd woken up in the middle of a backwoods NASCAR race. How she'd gone from standing near the back entrance to the mine to being strapped into the back of the Jeep as it slalomed around country roads was a story she wanted to hear sometime, but at the moment there were more pressing matters to deal with.

Kyle pulled the Jeep onto a dirt road shrouded by trees, stopped, and turned around in his seat and looked at her over the headrest. "Do I even want to ask what you mean?"

"Does she know something we don't, Kyle?" the strange girl sitting next to her asked him, her skin and clothes chalky with soot.

Maya assumed from their resemblance, and from the way they talked to each other, that it was his sister Taylor.

Taylor stared at him like a drowning person stares at a raft floating just out of reach, desperate and afraid, then turned her frantic gaze on Maya. "What do you know? And how?"

Seeing the girl was on the verge of freaking out, Maya took a deep breath, calmed her face, and started talking in as smooth a voice as she could manage. She told Taylor an abbreviated version of her experiences as a child, about how that lead to her website and her writing, and how that had led her to Stillwater. Taylor looked skeptical at first, but as more of her story came out, the more Taylor's expression changed from a frown to vigorous head nodding.

"So then I'm not crazy after all," the young girl said with a sigh.

Kyle nodded without hesitation. "You're sure not. Something weird is going on, Piglet, and it's a far cry from normal."

"So you think there's..." Taylor looked around quickly, searching for the words she needed in the air, "shit, some sort of monster or...or demon loose in town, and it's causing all this?"

That wasn't exactly right, but it was close. Maya knew neither of them would want to hear what she had to tell them, but what other choice did she have? The truth was the truth, and no amount of hemming and hawing would make it less so.

"I hate to say this." Maya fixed each of them in turn with a hard stare. "But I think what we're dealing with is worse than that. Much worse."

"What could be worse than a demon?" Taylor asked, her voice taking on a brittle edge.

Maya sympathized with the girl next to her, but she couldn't hold back. "The thing demons answer to."

"And what does *that* mean?" Kyle looked at her in the rearview mirror with wide, bloodshot eyes. "Do you mean we're dealing with the Devil?"

"Not exactly." Maya struggled to convey what she knew without turning the conversation into a theological seminar. They weren't in a coffee shop, trading beliefs and ideas over scones. They were in a Jeep that had been shot up, hiding from people who'd been poisoned by an ancient evil. There wasn't time to get into the complexities of the spiritual realm. So, to keep things simple, she powered forward and just started talking.

"What you were taught in Sunday school isn't the truth. Neither is what people learned in their mosques or synagogues or temples. Every religion out there claims to have the truth, but they don't. At best they have a kernel of it, and that kernel's been buried in centuries of dogma and bullshit. The reality of the spiritual world is far stranger and more complex than you could ever imagine. And right now, here in Stillwater, we're sitting at ground zero of a supernatural apocalypse."

Taylor closed her eyes and took a deep breath. When her

eyes were open again, she asked, "And how do you know this?"

"Because I saw it," Maya replied, looking first at Taylor, then at Kyle. "When I fell on that man outside the mine, my skin touched his, and through that contact I saw some of what's been going on out here."

At the memory of those visions, Maya dropped her head and stared down at her lap. Visions were never easy things to experience, but what she'd seen outside that mine made every other experience seem tame. And it wasn't just images that had been trust into her mind. She'd heard things, smelled things, tasted... She'd been overrun with sensations, drowned in experiences that were terrible and dark. Even recalling it made the blood run cold in her veins.

"Just tell us what you saw." Kyle reached back to caress her arm. His touch was warm, a balm against the cold wet darkness closing in on her.

Nodding to herself in a you-can-do-this gesture, she looked back up and told them what she knew. "Evil, Kyle. So much evil. For thousands of years it covered the world in vast legions of darkness, fire, and blood. Demons walked the world, and mountains crumbled in their wakes. It was an age of evil that... I wish I could cut the memory of it out of my mind. No one should see what I saw. But then a flood came and destroyed them all."

Kyle reached into her lap and took her hand, his fingers warm as they stroked her skin. "A flood? Like from the Bible?"

"Not exactly," Maya replied. She soaked his warmth in and looked up at him. "The Bible isn't the only place you'll find a flood story. It's been told all over the world, in nearly every religion and culture. The Hindu, Mayans, Greeks, Native Americans, and more all have flood stories as part of their tradition. The details change, but the idea of water being used to purify the world runs through them all. I don't know who sent the waters, whether it was God or gods or...something else, but eventually the waters fell, and all the evil that plagued the world was drowned and washed away.

Well, *almost* all of it."

As the last words left her lips, she glanced out the window at the mountain rising up next to them, and a shudder ran through her body. Kyle followed her gaze, then frowned.

"Wait, are you saying some of that evil ended up in the mountain?"

Maya sighed and nodded. "Yes. Deep in a cavern at the heart of the mountain we're parked on is a creature of incredible evil and power. The miners worship it as a god, and who's to say they're wrong? It's been there for hundreds of millions of years at least, slumbering in the deep dark water that was supposed to destroy it."

Taylor coughed. "But I'm guessing something woke it up, right?"

"No." Maya shook her head, then stopped, nodded, and then shook her head again. "Yes and no. There's still enough floodwater remaining in the cavern it's in to keep it asleep, but it's waking up. Little by little, as those miners pump the water out, it stirs more and more. Soon the water will be gone, and I'm terrified to consider what'll happen next."

"How soon?" Taylor asked.

Maya shrugged. "I don't know. Hours at best. When people wake up tomorrow, it's going to be a very shitty day, I can tell you that much."

"Is that what those...psychic vibrations were?" Kyle asked. "That creature waking up?"

"Yes. That's how powerful it is. Even in its sleep it can reach out and touch your mind, affect the world, turn you into something vile."

"And that's what's happened to my dad and the other miners?" Taylor asked.

Maya hated saying yes, but she had no choice. "I'm sorry, but yes. About a month ago, according to the visions I got from that Dean guy, the miners were digging out a new tunnel when their machine broke through a wall and released some of the water in the cavern. They almost drowned from it, and...that might have been for the better. I know it's your dad, so I hate to say that, but that water cursed them."

"But I thought the water was supposed to kill evil," Kyle said.

"It was, but after millions of years of having that...thing...sleeping in it, the water changed, became just as evil as it was. And when it washed over your dad and everyone else at the mine, it in turn changed them."

Kyle looked down for a moment and made a "huh" sound, as though an idea had occurred to him. "Sorta like heavy water then."

"What's that?" Maya asked.

"The water that's used to cool nuclear fuel rods becomes irradiated over time, becoming what they call heavy water. Trust me, it's not something you'd want to fill your pool with."

Maya didn't have to understand the science behind what Kyle said to know that his comparison was apt. And, worse, he'd hit on another problem.

"Well, that leads to something else."

Taylor snorted and fell back against the seat, her red-rimmed eyes rolling. "Oh, right, like an ancient dark god under our feet wasn't bad enough?"

"I'm afraid not," Maya replied.

Kyle sighed and shook his head. "Shit. The pipe."

Were the circumstances not so dire, Maya would have smiled at his quick understanding.

"What pipe?" Taylor asked.

"The one leading out of the vent tunnel," Kyle explained. "The one we followed out of the mine. When Maya and I found it, it was spitting out some sort of dark, sludgy water. That was from the cavern wasn't it?"

Maya nodded.

"And it's going right into the river. The river that feeds into the local water utility."

"Wait," Taylor said, her lips screwed up in a disgusted sneer, "are you saying that we've all been drinking that evil creature's bath water?"

Maya nodded. "Everyone in Stillwater is consuming that thing, drop by drop. And the more it wakes up, the more its psychic influence is felt. People are evil enough as it is without its essences rushing through their bodies."

"But what about Taylor and the rest of her friends?" Kyle asked. "Why don't they seem to be affected like my mom and the people you met at the cafe?"

Taylor barked up a harsh laugh. "How often do you see kids drink water, bro? If it ain't comin' out of a can or bottle, we don't drink it."

"So then…" Kyle started before pausing to digest everything he'd heard. After a moment he continued. "We think we know what's happening. The next question is what do we do about it?"

"And there you come to the real problem." Maya leaned back in the seat like Taylor. "I don't have a single damn idea."

"Can we…I don't know…throw a grenade at whatever this monster is?" Taylor asked. "Get some deep core drillers to drop a nuke on its ass Michael Bay style? Something?"

Maya wanted desperately to know what to say, to have a definitive answer, but she didn't. "Maybe. None of my visions came with a list of its weakness or vulnerabilities. We might be able to shoot it or blow it up, but then again all that might do is piss it off. Please understand, it isn't purely flesh and blood. It's as much a being of psychic terror as it is physical, a creature whose every fiber is made of the darkest evil. For all I know a cross or a stick of sandalwood incense might be more useful than bullets or bombs."

"Then let me simplify things." Kyle fixed them both with a hard look. "We don't have a grenade, or a nuke, or a proton pack, or anything else like it. Right now all we've got are a bunch of ghost stories and a shot up vehicle. The best thing we can do is to try and get to Williamson again, or – fuck – anywhere other than here, and let people know what's happening."

"What about Hanna and the rest in the cabin?" Taylor asked.

"They're good for now. They've got plenty of bottled water, and they're far from the crazies. Right now they're better off than we are."

Maya bit her lower lip. Kyle was correct. There wasn't anything they could do in Stillwater to stop what was coming. There likely wasn't anything they could do anywhere else, either, but every mile they put between themselves and the evil under the mountain, the better she would feel.

"Then we need to get my car." She knew it meant going back into a town that was probably getting crazier by the moment. "It isn't much to look at, but it'll get us farther than this Jeep will."

Kyle sighed, but the look on his face said he knew she was right. "Alright, if that's what we have to do, then let's do it. The sun is nearly down, and I don't want to be here when darkness falls."

Maya couldn't agree more, so she nodded and patted Taylor's leg. Taylor took her hand and squeezed it.

"I don't know you from Eve," the young girl said, her soot-streaked face solemn and her skin clammy cold, "but I'm glad you're here."

"Me too," Maya replied, not meaning it in the least little bit. If she'd had a genie in her pocket, her one and only wish would be to have never heard of the town of Stillwater, West Virginia.

Getting through the backwoods to town on three tires was a slow, arduous process, and it hadn't been made easier by the rain continually pouring from the sky, turning dirt roads into bogs and asphalt into Slip 'n Slides. The lone upside to the rain was the lack of traffic they had to avoid while circling around the edge of town. At least, Kyle hoped it was the rain that kept the townsfolk out of his hair and not something more monstrous.

When they finally rolled to a grinding halt in a dark corner of the parking lot next to The Basement, Kyle parked and killed the engine. His eyes flicked from shadow to shadow, from the bar to the motel across the street. The hairs on the back of his neck stood up, telling him something was wrong, but he didn't know if that was due to something in particular or the general sense of FUBAR that permeated the town. He felt eyes on him from every quarter, and in his mind the eyes were black and pitiless.

"Why did we park over here?" Maya asked, craning forward and cramming herself into the space between the front seats.

Feeling the sudden heat of her against his arm pulled some of the clouds of paranoia from Kyle's head. Glancing over at her, the distant parking lot lights barely lit her face, outlining her beauty like an artist using chalk on black paper. It seemed crazy that less than a day ago they had been entwined in each other's arms, the sheets damp with their sweat as they gave themselves to each other.

"Because there's a distinct possibility they know where we're staying."

"They?" Maya angled her head to peer at the motel's parking lot.

"The police, for one."

"How?"

Kyle rubbed at his left wrist, the one the cop had grabbed with his freezing cold hand. "Well, there aren't a lot of places we *could* be staying at other than here, but even if that wasn't the case, I dropped my wallet when we were stopped trying to leave town. A quick search on my credit card history would be all they needed."

"Shit," Maya replied with a sigh.

"On the plus side, they dropped something too." He reached into the tight space between the seat and plastic console that bisected the front of the Jeep. When his hand came up, he held a gun. Taylor and Maya drew back like he'd pulled out a snake.

"Where in the hell did that come from?" Taylor asked.

Kyle shook his head at the fearful way both women looked at him. "I knocked it out of the cop's hand. I forgot all about it until we headed this way. Damn thing slid under my feet. I managed to tuck it away when we stopped at a stop sign."

Maya leaned forward again. She wasn't as close as she'd been a few seconds ago, but some of her fear had worn off.

"Is it loaded? Does it still work?"

"It worked well enough earlier," he replied as he pressed a button and the magazine dropped into his hand from the grip. Small brass casings were neatly lined up inside it. "It's a .40 caliber Smith & Wesson with a standard fifteen round mag. The cop shot twice, so we have thirteen rounds left. It's in great shape, too. Frankly, right now I'd rather have this than my wallet, so I'd call it a fair trade." He slapped the mag back into place as he finished speaking and tucked it next to the seat again.

"So if you think they might be waiting, should we risk getting Maya's car?" Taylor asked.

Kyle's head tilted from side to side as he considered how to answer her words. "Do I want to risk it? Hell no, but I need to. Unless either of you knows how to hotwire a car, that is." When all he got were blank looks, he nodded and chugged ahead. "That's what I thought. Maya, give me your keys."

Maya reached down to the floorboard where she'd put her purse earlier in the day, rooted around inside it for a moment, then gave him a jangling set of keys with a small, green ghost figurine dangling from the key ring. Kyle recognized it as Slimer from Ghostbusters.

"While you take care of that, I've got my own mission to take care of." Taylor reached for the door handle next to her.

Kyle jerked around and hit the LOCK button on the door console next to him, then turned back around. "What in the hell are you talking about? You're not going anywhere. I need you to stay here."

"You don't get to tell me what to do," Taylor replied as she pulled on the door handle. It snapped out of her hands and the door remained closed. She hit the UNLOCK button with a stiff jab of her finger, but Kyle relocked it before she could get the door open. She tried to get out again, and then again, before slamming herself backward against the seat and hitting the door. "Goddam it, Kyle! You're not Dad!"

"No, I'm not!" Kyle said. "Dad tried to kill you. I'm trying to keep you safe. I don't know if you can tell the distinction, but trust me, it's there. What could you possibly have to do that's so important?"

Taylor huffed and pulled uselessly at her door handle. "I need to go find Morgana. Her house is only half a mile from here. I can't be so close to her now without trying to find her."

Feeling some of the wind taken from his sails, Kyle ground his teeth. "Sis, I understand how you feel, but—"

"No you don't!" Taylor gave an exaggerated wave of her hand. "You don't know shit. While you were off running away from all this, I was stuck here, trying to figure out on my own who I was and why I was so different from everybody else. Do you know how many times I thought about running away? How many times I considered killing myself? No, you don't, 'cause you weren't here. Morgana does. She saved me. She's the only bright spot in my whole world, and I love her. So, pardon me if I want to find her and get her out of this fucking mess."

Kyle's face numbed as blood drained away. He couldn't believe what his little sister said, the naked truth of what his leaving had meant, and the terrible pain she'd had to go through alone. The tongue-lashing she'd given him the night before seemed like nothing compared to what had come out of her now. In the face of that truth, how could he deny her?

"Okay, you made your point. I don't have the right to tell you what to do. But, as your big brother, can I at least ask you to stay until I get Maya's car? Once I have it we'll go together to see about Morgana. Safety in numbers, okay? Can you do that?"

Taylor's nostrils flared, and her fingers tapped against crossed arms, but after a few seconds she nodded. "Okay."

Kyle gave her a slow nod. "Thanks, Piglet."

"Fine. And stop calling me that. I'm a little old for it."

"You'll always be my Piglet," Kyle told her with a pat on her leg. "No matter how old you get." He then reached down and pulled out the Smith & Wesson. "Okay, you two wait here and I'll be right back."

Before he could unlock his door and open it, Maya said, "You actually think you're going to run off and leave me behind again? In case you don't recall, that didn't work out too well for me last time. Where you and that gun go, so go I."

"Jesus H." Kyle closed his eyes and set the gun down on the center console before his twitching fingers could pull the trigger and blow his balls off. "Why can't you two just do as you're told?" He took a moment to breathe deeply, filling his lungs with cool, calm air. "Fine. Fuck it . Whatever. Taylor, I hope you wait here. If you do, keep your head down and the doors locked. Maya, if you're coming, all I ask is that you stick close and stay behind me. Okay?"

Maya nodded, her face all business.

"Alright, then let's do this." Kyle checked the .40 cal out of habit, opened his door, and exited the Jeep. As his feet touched asphalt, the skies opened up and poured buckets of wet misery down on his head. "Perfect."

INTERLUDE
COME THE SHADOWS

For days Ash had stood on the ledge that hung over the deep mountain cavern, the sole marker of time he cared for being the water level as it dropped inch by aching inch. Problems big and small reared their heads, but through them all he'd never left the cavern. At his feet, discarded remnants of who he'd used to be piled up slowly – a nose here, an ear there, a fingernail or tooth to add some texture. He was barely human anymore, and he couldn't have cared less. The only thing that mattered was the shrinking pool of water below him.

Small ripples spread across the pool's surface as things moved beneath it. His black eyes gazed in fascination, anxious to see signs of his god's awakening. Tendrils flicked through the water, but he knew the Dark One was still in the grip of its millennial sleep. That grip was slipping, though, and as consciousness slowly returned, the god's monstrous body moved.

As more flesh writhed in the water, suddenly bubbles boiled to the top, and what little remained of Ash's prick hardened. The dark dreams of his god receded from his mind, the glorious visions of the past lifted like a heavy fog, and a hum took their place. The droning noise sounded like a hundred voices all singing as one from a great distance. He could barely hear it, but it was there, and the dark song was as beautiful as it was dreadful.

The Dark One was nearly awake!

A tear fell from his midnight eyes, the droplet slowly making its way across cracked skin to hover like poisoned rain at the corner of his mouth. But, before it fell, a light shined from the depths of the retreating water. It was scarcely able to filter through the muck and shifting tentacles, but the greenish-red light gleamed from the depths and sparkled against the teardrop. Ash looked down in wonder at the shimmering light, and as it filled his black eyes, the voices sang louder in his head.

"It's coming," he said to himself. "The Dark One rises."

Ash trembled in the glory of his awakening god, and he knew that beyond the mountain Stillwater trembled too as its people transformed into monsters under the Dark One's will. In the distance, through miles of twisting tunnel, he heard men screaming in pain, wailing like babies torn from their mothers' desiccated wombs. They were being reborn, remade from the inside out, and the process was as painful as it was magnificent.

In the receding waters below, massive tendrils lashed and spasmed, churning the dark water into foam. A body was becoming visible beneath the tentacles, a bloated twitching mass that – even from what little could be seen of it – seemed colossal. Ash couldn't begin to understand what event had transpired to force its bulk into the dark belly of the mountain, but as he gazed down on it he decided it didn't matter. Soon it would rise, and the mountain would crumble around it. The Dark One would be reborn, and then the world would be reborn with it, birthed in fire and blood and screams.

A laugh fell from Ash's mouth, but the sound became a scream when a terrible pain exploded in his chest, driving him to the ground. He was on fire, every cell of his body vibrating so quickly he could feel himself burn. His gums burst, filling his mouth with brackish blood as the last of his teeth were pushed out by jagged fangs. Hard claws the iridescent color of a beetle's shell shredded the ends of his fingers, the pain of it so intense his hands curled into tight fists, driving the claws into his palm. The wounds seeped blood the color and consistency of molasses, but they rapidly healed. His bones throbbed, shattered, reset, shattered again, and then reformed into twisted versions of themselves, as strong as they were deformed. Layers of doughy white skin sloughed off his body, revealing mottled gray flesh like the underbelly of a fish that had never ventured from its murky depths.

The greatest pain, though, came from his back. The knobs of flesh growing there burned as if a flaming tree fell across him, each one a bright spot of pain. He tried to reach behind him to grab the knobs and tear them off, but his arms wouldn't reach, so he turned his face toward the cave ceiling and howled until the lining of his throat burst and his cry became a gargle of blood. Seconds went by like hours, each beat of his heart sending vibrations into the stone beneath him. The pain increased until it nearly undid him, but with a large burst of flesh it ended, and in the sickly light he unfurled a broad expanse of grisly wings. As they spread from his shoulders he knew his rebirth was complete.

His god had forged him, remade him as a reward for his diligent service and faith. His ascension was at hand, and his reign as the demon prince of the world was about to begin.

CHAPTER NINETEEN

Kyle and Maya had just stepped out of the Jeep when the sound of breaking glass and voices raised in anger shattered the still night. As they rounded the corner of The Basement they saw half a dozen cheering people standing in a loose circle in front of one of the bar's large windows, now broken into a million glittering pieces and scattered across the handicapped parking slots. Two figures rolled across the glass shards, their legs kicking and their fists swinging wildly, and the crowd looked down with manic smiles as they roared their approval.

"I'm gonna kill you, ya son of a bitch!" one of the men on the ground said. He wore leather pants and a leather jacket with a stylized falcon stitched on its back. Kyle didn't recognize the voice, and blood seeping from multiple cuts on the man's face and forehead made recognizing him impossible.

The man he pummeled was dressed in a shabby blue suit, torn and wet from both rain and blood. He looked older than Kyle's dad and terribly out of shape, but the desperation of his situation gave his kicks and punches extra viciousness. Streaks of red around his mouth and on his hands made Kyle think back to the night before, when he'd seen the same guy sitting by himself enjoying a rack of messy barbeque ribs.

"You ain't killin' shit, asshole," the man in the torn suit said as he rammed his dark loafer into his opponent's crotch. "And I wasn't looking at your woman, but once I'm done with you I'm gonna fuck her in her ass and make you watch."

"Don't let him talk that way to me, baby!" a woman cried. She was one of the throng urging the fight on. Despite her words, the smile on her face said a good ass fucking would be right up her alley. She was dressed in leather similar to the man fighting for her honor, and another memory of the night before rolled through Kyle's mind. The same couple had been in the bar, eating at a table several feet from Mr. Ribs. Apparently dinner at The Basement was a regular event, but tonight things had gotten out of hand. Kyle hoped it was an isolated incident.

Taking Maya's hand, he ducked at the corner of the bar and whispered, "Keep your head down and follow close."

Maya tore her eyes away from the fight with a struggle, then looked at him and nodded.

Keeping low, they scurried from the dark corner of the bar to a big Dodge diesel pickup, moved from there to an old Mercury sedan that looked to be held together by religious bumper stickers – LIFE IS A GIFT, NOT A CHOICE and IN CASE OF RAPTURE, VEHICLE WILL BE UNMANNED just two examples. The road crossed in front of them like a black river, the asphalt gleaming wetly under the streetlights arching over it in lonely islands of light.

After giving her hand another squeeze, they scurried from the parking lot and crossed onto the highway. They were halfway into the far lane when a squeal of tires stopped them in their tracks. Kyle looked to his left and saw a truck speeding around a corner toward them from the direction of town. Between its speed and the wet road, the car didn't have a hope in hell of making the turn, and it crashed into a streetlamp with a chunky metal *thud*. More broken glass spilled into the night, and the light flickered out. Several seconds later the driver got out of the truck and staggered around it, presumably looking at the damage. After doing a shambling circuit, the driver reached into the truck and pulled something out. Without the streetlight to illuminate the situation Kyle couldn't tell what was going on, but the point was moot when the driver shouted, "You stupid piece of shit!" and unloaded a shotgun blast into the truck's grill. Steam burst into the air from the ruined radiator. The driver pumped the shotgun, shifted to the right, and blasted a load of buckshot into the truck's tire, which burst like a watermelon being sledgehammered.

"This town has lost it," Maya said, stating the obvious. "If we don't get out of here soon we'll lose it too. That dark thing is closer to waking up, and I can feel its mind reaching out for all of us."

The desire to get out of Stillwater back when he'd graduated had been huge, but that was nothing compared to what Kyle felt now. His hometown had always felt like it sat balanced on the rim of a vast toilet bowl, ready to fall into the shit at any moment. He'd figured that, sooner or later, it would slide over the edge, and when it happened it would be bad, but he'd never imagined it would be this bad. Then again, he'd never considered the possibility that Stillwater's demise would come from the rising of an ancient evil buried deep in the mountains around it. Somehow that idea had never struck him.

"Yeah, come on." He waved her on.

Once they were across the street, Kyle scurried to the far corner of the motel and ducked into a patch of shadows that looked out over the parking lot. There were half a dozen cars parked before various rooms, Maya's red Honda among them. He scanned each one, looking for people seated inside, but from where he stood they all looked empty. He also couldn't see any sort of colored lights or decals that would indicate a government vehicle.

"See anything?" Maya asked.

Kyle shifted his eyes around, checking motel windows, the roof, shadows around the edge of the building, and the area behind the far side of the motel before shaking his head. "No, it looks clear."

"I guess the police have other things to worry about." She gestured toward the crashed truck and bar fight.

Kyle shrugged. "I don't think they give a shit. After the way they came after me, they're probably as crazy as the rest of this shithole." He reached into his pocket and felt the metal of Maya's key ring bite into his hand reassuringly. "Come on, let's do this."

Maya's room was near the middle of the U-shaped motel, but he didn't want to cross the openness of the parking lot, so Kyle skirted the edge of the building and walked them down the inside of the eastern edge. The motel didn't have many lodgers, so most of the rooms were dark and silent, but a few here and there lit up. The sounds that came from them were disturbing. Normally he'd have seen it as his duty to investigate, but not here, and certainly not now. So long as the noises stayed behind closed doors, he was fine leaving them there.

A scream erupted behind the door two feet in front of them, Room 106, and Kyle barely had time for his blood to chill at the terrible sound of it before the door flew open. It hit the wall next to it so hard it shattered the window. Kyle raised his hands and jumped backward. Maya yelped and stumbled back too, then screamed and pointed at the parking space in front of the room. Kyle followed her gesture and saw a woman lying on the ground, half-naked and beaten to a pulp. Blood ran from her face in thick red streams, and she scarcely had the strength to turn her head so she didn't drown in the rain.

"You lying fucking whore," a man said as he walked out of the room. He wore brown and white striped boxers, and nothing else. Blood spattered his pale chest and stubbly face. He rubbed at his bruised knuckles.

"Please, Bobby," the woman on the ground said, her voice barely louder than the rain beating down on her. Her red panties and yellow bra looked almost as rough as she did. "I didn't mess around on you, I swear."

Bobby stormed forward and kicked her in the side like a punter going for a field goal from fifty yards out. The woman on the ground tried to roll away, but that only exposed more of her back, and Bobby's bare foot hit her with enough force to send her tumbling further into the parking lot. She screamed and reached for her side reflexively when she came to a stop.

"I didn't, Bobby!" she cried into the storm. "I didn't, I swear!"

Bobby was having none of it. He stomped over to the woman, grabbed her by her mop of blonde hair, and hoisted her to her feet. The sheer unrelenting violence of the moment transfixed Kyle, locked him in place, but when the woman screamed again and beat at Bobby's fist as it clutched her hair the spell broke, and Kyle ran to stop what was happening before it could go any further.

"I'm gonna beat your lying ass straight to hell." Bobby drew the woman close and balled up his fist. "And then I'm gonna go do the same to that sonuvabitch you been fuckin' behind my back."

"Let her go, man." Kyle drew close.

Bobby kept his grip on the woman. "This ain't none of your concern, asshole. Not unless she's fuckin' you too." He gave the woman's head a savage shake. "Is that so? Huh? You fuckin' him too?"

The woman opened her mouth, but no words came out, and her eyes rolled up. The sight of it broke Kyle's heart. In her he saw his mother, back when she was good and loving; he saw Taylor and everything she'd had to go through without him; and he saw Maya, alone in a dark and uncaring place. It broke his heart, and he swore to himself he wasn't going to let anyone else get hurt, not while he could do something about it.

"I said let her go," he told the man, reaching around to grab the .40 caliber tucked in his jeans. "I'm not going to say it again." He flicked off the safety and let the metallic click emphasize his point.

Bobby snarled. "You want this bitch?" he asked, shaking the woman's head by her hair again. "Then fuckin' have her."

Kyle didn't understand what Bobby meant until the man heaved his arms and flung the woman at him with a savage pull of her hair. The woman didn't scream, even as handfuls of her hair ripped out, and she tumbled toward Kyle like a sack of broken sticks. Kyle reached out with his left arm to grab her as she fell against him, and Bobby's eyes lit up when Kyle stumbled under the sudden weight and impact. Kyle fell to one knee, the woman's bloody body a dead weight against him, and Bobby rushed toward them with both fists raised and ready to deliver more pain. The tactic would have worked against most people, but Kyle – even though he spent most of his time going over supply lists and shelves of gear – had been trained for combat, so even with the woman pressed against his left side he was able to keep his gun arm free and his head clear. The rain seemed to stop for a moment as he lined up his shot and fired, each drop hanging motionless in the air. When the gun barked, it was one more peal of thunder in the storm. A ragged hole appeared in Bobby's left chest where the pectoral muscle met the shoulder. It spun him around, and then he fell, just as Kyle had hoped he would. But, Bobby had just hit the ground when he threw his head back and yelled like a berserker at the clouds overhead, then thrust himself up and came toward Kyle again. Another shot rocked the night, this one hitting Bobby in the meat of his right thigh. Bobby hit the ground again, this time with a thud as his legs swept out from under him.

"I'm gonna kill you." Spit flew through Bobby's clenched teeth. "I'm gonna break your head open and fuck yer skull, gonna fuck your brains and shit on 'em."

Bobby jumped to his feet, wobbly but powered by something beyond the flesh, and stomped forward again. His pale skin had an ashy pallor Kyle recognized.

"Make this stop!" Maya shouted, her voice ragged. Kyle couldn't see her, but he could imagine her face streaked with tears and her mouth twisted up in fear and panic. His heart broke all over again. "Just make it stop, please."

Knowing he had little choice, Kyle took aim one last time and pulled the trigger. When Bobby hit the ground, this time it was with a hole in the center of his chest and blood pumping out of it in a thick syrup that soon slowed to a trickle. He didn't get back up again.

"Are you okay?" Kyle asked the woman he held in his left arm. When she didn't answer, he gave her a slight shake and put his mouth close to her ear. "Hey, it's okay. He won't hurt you anymore."

When she still didn't say anything, he bent over and lowered his arm until she lay on the ground. Her eyes were open, but they were motionless and unblinking, even when rain drops splashed against them. He knew what he'd find when he reached to take her pulse, but knew he had to do it anyway.

"Is she alright?" Maya asked, stepping close and bending over his shoulder.

Kyle shook his head, then reached down and closed the woman's eyes. "She's dead."

"Oh my God." Maya had to grab his shoulder to stop herself from falling over, and the tears that fell on his skin were warm, unlike the cold, unceasing rain. "This is terrible, Kyle. So terrible. What... What are we going to do?"

Despite the rain that tumbled down on them, Kyle had never seen more clearly in his life. The dead man and woman before him had cleared up any reservations or confusion he'd felt before. In their emptiness he found his resolve.

"We're getting the fuck out of here as fast as we can, that's what, and we are never looking back."

He took Maya's hand from his shoulder, gave it a kiss, and pulled her toward her waiting car. The gun was still in his hand, its weight reassuring in the storm, and he vowed to use it as many times as he had to in order to get them all to safety, no matter who stood against them. When they reached her car, he unlocked the passenger door, and as she got in he walked around the back his eyes looking for anyone who might come toward them. No one appeared in the wet darkness, and he reached to unlock his own door, but Maya had already pulled the knob up, so he opened the door and settled into the driver's seat.

After days of driving the Jeep and months riding in supply trucks, the little Honda felt like a go-cart, but within seconds he had the engine revving and the wipers at max speed. Once they were both buckled in, he stuck the gun between his right leg and the center console, then backed out of the parking space. When they crossed the highway he saw that the crashed truck and its driver were still going at it, but he must have run out of ammo because he had taken to beating the vehicle with the shotgun like a bat.

The fight was still going on in The Basement's parking lot, but now everyone was involved. In the stark light of the bar's exterior signs the mass fight looked like a single gray beast made up of many arms and legs and mouths, all of them reaching into the center mass to do as much harm as possible. Kyle recognized their waitress in the mix, and the bikers and rib eater were still in it, but most of the rest were a blur of ashen, angry flesh. He stayed as far from them as he could while he drove to the damaged Jeep. When he pulled in next to it, Taylor slipped out of it and dove into the Honda's waiting backseat.

"Man, it's getting crazy out there," his little sister said.

Maya grunted and stared straight ahead. "You don't know the half of it."

Taylor ran her hand through her wet hair, slicking it back and away from her face. "I bet. Did I hear gun shots?"

"Don't ask." Kyle reached for the gearshift to put it in DRIVE, but before he could a familiar wave of nausea rolled over him. It was enough to make his stomach sour and his eyes ache, but other than that he was fine. Maya, though, vibrated in her seat. Her hands were vises on her armrests, and she grit her teeth so hard the cords in her neck jumped. He reached over to sooth her, give her some sort of help and comfort, but when he moved over he saw Taylor was jittery too, her fingers thrumming against her pants and her eyes fluttering.

A dark pit opened in Kyle's stomach, and he felt his world slipping into it, never to return as he watched the two women he cared about spasm in the grip of an evil he couldn't begin to understand or hope to stop. All he could do was wait.

Chapter Twenty

Maya inhaled sharply and sat up in the back of the jeep like a woman struggling to swim to the surface before she drowned. When she opened her eyes she recognized where she was, but it didn't feel real to her. Her brain struggled to wake up from the nightmare overwhelming her. It seemed like hours ago when the dark dreams crashed down, but from the darkness outside and the familiar lights of The Basement's parking lot she could tell it had only been minutes, if that. She sat awake, in her car, but part of her remained in the nightmare, and she worried she'd never fully leave it again. She felt slimy, coated in blood and filth.

"I don't feel good." Taylor groaned, smacked her lips, and rubbed at her arms like she was trying to brush herself clean.

"I know what you mean," Maya replied.

"What happened?" Kyle asked. He looked at each of them like he feared they'd shatter at any moment. "Are you okay now?"

Maya shook her head. Deep down she knew a terrible truth, and keeping it hidden wouldn't help anyone, especially herself. "No, we're not. That thing in the mountain... It's changing us. Taylor might not drink much of the water, but she still lives here, and the proximity has infected her with it anyway, just more gradually. My psychic sensitivity is connecting me to it too. The longer we stay here, the more it'll get inside us, transform us into what the rest of the town is becoming. We have to go, Kyle. Now."

Kyle stared deep into her eyes, and she felt his thoughts reaching out to her, so warm and soft compared to the dreams of the dark god. His entire world sat in the backseat of her car, and his desire to protect them was fierce.

"Okay then. Let's get the fuck out of here."

He turned and reached for the gearshift, but Taylor cried out and grabbed his shoulder.

"Wait! You said we'd go get Morgana!"

Kyle shrugged her off and shook his head. "Sorry, Piglet, but things have changed."

"You promised!" Taylor grabbed his arm and shook it savagely. "You promised me we'd get her, and goddammit you're going to do it! If you don't, so help me God I'll break this window out and get her myself!"

Kyle released the gearshift and looked over his shoulder. "You wouldn't dare."

Taylor's jaw muscles bunched as she stared back at her brother, her eyes steady and hard. "Then you don't know me as well as you think you do."

A staring contest broke out between the siblings, and Maya felt their conflicted emotions shooting back and forth like gunfire. After a few tense moments Kyle blinked. "Alright. I guess I've let you down enough for one lifetime. Which way do we go?"

Taylor opened her mouth, but her words were cut off by a horrible wailing sound outside the car. When everyone turned to look through the front windshield they saw a group of people coming around the corner of the bar. Their bodies twitched, their steps halting and jittery. When they shambled into the Honda's headlights, the true horror of what was happening in Stillwater was revealed. Taylor screamed, and Maya felt terror claw its way up her throat at the sight of the convulsing figures. Their clothes were torn and useless, scarcely covering skin that looked covered in rancid puss, so gray and shiny in the light. Their eyes were black, nearly lost in the doughy folds of their faces that barely looked human. The claws, though, nearly drove Maya mad with horror, the black claws that arced from their hands as they stumbled closer and closer. They'd once been people, but now as the ancient evil awoke they were shambling monsters, moaning their pain and hunger into the rain-choked air.

"Head to Barker Road!" Taylor grabbed the seat in front of her and shook it. "Back around The Basement and on the right!"

Kyle's head nodded at the sound of his sister's voice, and

he reached down like he wasn't sure where he was. But, as one hand shifted the car into reverse and the other curled around the steering wheel, he nodded. "Hold on!" He hit the gas and sent the car rocketing backward, away from The Basement and the mass of twitching bodies.

Maya was thankful when the headlights slid away from the townspeople, their monstrous appearances like battering rams at her sanity, but when the darkness of the mountains filled the windshield, she knew it was just the beginning. Stillwater was a small town, but there were a lot of miles left to go, and each one would be more dangerous than the one before. For the first time in her life she knew what true terror felt like.

Stillwater burned. In spite of the rain, fire raged through the small West Virginia coal town, and those homes and buildings that weren't burning were being torn apart by beings who might have once been people but had now become decidedly less. Screams pealed through the air like thunder, but for every call for help that broke through the Honda's windows came a dozen angry growls and bellows. The people of Stillwater were as damned as the buildings they'd spent decades trying to coax through winter after winter, through good times and bad. Though Kyle hated the place, he felt sick in his stomach seeing it spiral into hell.

"Take the next right," Taylor's soft voice reflected off the window she stared out of.

Kyle didn't give the STOP sign a second look as he turned the wheel, but when the Honda's headlights splashed across two gray figures tearing at something on the ground, he hit the brakes so hard they fishtailed on the wet road. The gray creatures didn't turn or stop what they were doing, their arms and upper bodies moving up and down in a mad rhythm Kyle felt in his heart. A grim curiosity made him look at what they were doing, but when a length of shiny intestine wiggled into the air like wet reddish-green tubing he swallowed back his gorge and hit the gas. The gray monsters heard the engine roar and turned to see him barreling toward them. When Kyle saw the victim at their feet – a kid barely old enough to sport a few feeble whiskers on his blood-splattered face – turn and give him a desperate look, he gunned the engine and veered into the creatures. They jumped out of the way, more agile than they looked, but Kyle felt the tires hit the kid and hoped he'd given him a quicker death than what the beasts who'd been pulling his insides out had promised. That didn't stop him from hating himself though.

"Oh my God," Maya said behind him.

Kyle wasn't sure what her words were aimed at. The fires? The roaming transformed townsfolk? The kid he'd run over? Maybe she'd been hit by another psychic thunderclap. But he didn't ask her to clarify. He was busy enough dealing with his own horror.

"How much farther?" he asked when he came to an intersection. More houses burned up Midwich Street.

Taylor slowly turned forward and looked at where they were. "Two more blocks down, last house on the left."

Grunting, Kyle accelerated. The engine whined, in bad need of a tune-up. He babied it as best he could.

"What's that?" Maya asked, her arm appearing next to his head and her hand pointing to the far right side of the street.

Kyle focused his eyes, and at first he thought he was looking at some wobbling ball of jelly rolling up the sidewalk, but as his headlights got closer he saw a pack of gray creatures running in a knot so tight it was easily mistaken for one body. They were howling at each other, their claws and teeth tearing at one another as they lopped along the sidewalk. Kyle's blood ran cold as the Honda neared them, but his heart nearly stopped entirely when he saw what the creatures were chasing after – two kids peddling like mad on bicycles.

"What are those stupid kids doing out on bikes?" Kyle said.

When one of the bikes toppled over, spilling the kid on it to the ground, he instantly regretted calling them stupid. In his head he calculated how quickly he could get to the bike and get the kid in the car, but he hardly had time to think about it before the gray creatures pounced and made the matter moot. Screams exploded into the air.

"At least one of them might get away." Maya pointed at the other bike, whose rider hadn't slowed for a second.

Not wanting to look at the carnage, Kyle drove past the creatures and their kill without slowing. He couldn't close his ears, though, and the cries and howls shook the car. When they came close to the still-peddling bike, Taylor gasped.

"That's Morgana!"

The Honda was ten yards back from the bike and its rider, and between the rain and the swaying of the bike he didn't know how anyone could tell who was riding it. "How do you know?"

"I'd know that hoodie anywhere! Hurry up before those things get her!"

He hadn't thought to notice it before, but on the back of the rider's coat was a white smiley face with fangs poking down and a glittery red bow sitting perfectly above the round eyes. He wasn't sure if it was funny in spite of the horror going on around them, or because of it.

As they drove up next to Morgana, the poor girl steered away from them and gave them a panicked look, not unfairly assuming they were going to run her down, but before she could get a few feet into an alley between houses Taylor rolled her window down and reached a hand out.

"Morgana, stop! It's me! Taylor!"

That caught the fleeing girl's attention. Her feet locked in place and the bike's rear tire swerved as she came to a quick stop. "Taylor?" she said, squinting as she looked at the Honda.

"Yeah, it's me, baby." Taylor leaned out the window, letting the rain soak her upper half. "Hurry and get in! We gotta get the fuck out of here!"

Morgana looked at Taylor, then back the way she'd come, and then at the destruction ahead of her before she let the bike hit the ground and jumped into the Honda's front passenger seat. Taylor hugged her from behind before her door even closed.

"What in the fuck is going on?" Morgana asked. Her eyes, which were circled by so much eyeliner she looked like a drowned raccoon, flicked between everyone in the car. "I mean seriously, what the fuck?"

"That's the question of the day, isn't it?" Kyle wasn't sure where to even begin.

Morgana shook her head and hit her knees with closed fists, the veins on her pale hands standing out like road maps. "I don't understand. I've been... I've been getting these visions in my head, felt these strange feelings in my chest, and now people are... Jesus Christ, they're becoming monsters! How is this happening?! Are we going to become like that too?!"

"Not if we can help it, baby," Taylor said, her voice stronger than it had been minutes before. "We're getting the hell out of this town."

Kyle wished he felt as sure as his sister did. Every second sent them spiraling down the toilet bowl faster and faster, and he felt the force of it dragging at him. His foot hit the gas like a hundred pound weight, and the Honda took off. In the rain-streaked rearview mirror the pack of monsters finished off the downed biker before shambling after fresh meat. Rain already started washing the blood away.

"Leaving town?" Morgana asked. "We need to go to the police!"

Kyle steered left onto Toluca Avenue and shook his head. "If they haven't already...changed into whatever the fuck those things are...we couldn't trust them anyway."

Morgana looked at him like he was speaking gibberish, but before she could protest Taylor wrapped her arms around the girl .

"We already ran into the cops," Taylor said. "They tried to kill us. Whatever's going on, they're part of it. The only help we're gonna get is outside of Stillwater. Far outside it."

"Do you understand what's happening then?" Morgana's pale face seemed to float in the shadows created by her dark cloths and flowing black hair.

Maya nodded in the rear view mirror. "We don't know all of it, but we think we..." She trailed off, her eyes unfocused as if suddenly in deep thought. She tilted her head first to the right, then the left, and then looked out the window next to her. Taylor leaned over and patted her shoulder. Maya didn't respond, but a few seconds later she took a quick breath and leaned forward. "We have to get out of here! Go! Go!"

"We are!" Kyle replied. "What's wrong now?"

"He's looking for us!" Maya's eyes lost focus again as her fingers drummed on the side of his seat.

"Who?" Kyle asked.

Maya looked into the rearview and fixed him with a hard glare. "The devil's prince."

Interlude
Dreadful Lights

The creature once named Ash felt warmed in the light of his waking god as the dreadful waters ebbed. The Dark One's mind woke more and more, his thoughts filling the air like a glorious whirlwind, and Ash felt lifted from his reborn shell.

Ready my world, a voice said within his mind, the words a fusion of pain and ecstasy. *Prepare the way for my coming.*

Ash ached at hearing his god speak, yearned to serve him, please him. "Yes, my Lord," his cracked, gray lips said as his consciousness rose from the cavern. He passed through coal, rock, dirt, and grass until he was high above the mountain and looking down at Stillwater. What he saw pleased him. The cavern's water had done its job – all over town people were changing, the essence of the Dark One unlocking the shadows hiding inside them, freeing their bloodlust, their desires, transforming them into what they truly were deep down in their souls.

And it was just the beginning. Tonight it was Stillwater, tomorrow West Virginia, and the day after that...the whole of the world, all of it in flames and drowning in blood, all in service and sacrifice to the dark god in the mountain.

But, as Ash's mind surveyed the town, not everyone bent to the dark's will. They were the unwashed, tiny points of light defacing the black canvas below. They weren't of immediate concern being so few and spread apart, but then he noted several clustered together. Their mutual proximity made their light shine balefully bright.

Incensed, he sent his ethereal body toward them. As he flew close he felt a troubling distinction in one of them, a power that none but he and his lord should have possessed. In that shining mind was the vestige of a primal soul, a soul older than man, and as he observed it he was reminded of the woman he'd been told about earlier. Yes, he remembered her. The nigger bitch with the old blood.

Well now, he thought, *I figured you'd have been put down already. I guess if you want something done right, you gotta do it yourself.*

Smiling a razor sharp grin in the growing gleam of his rising god, Ash sent orders into the night, preparing the world for what was to come by removing what little trouble remained. One old blood bitch and a few kids weren't much to worry about, but he supposed it was best to be careful and get rid of them all the same. After that, nothing would stand in their way.

CHAPTER TWENTY-ONE

Kyle hit the brakes and brought the Honda to a skidding halt. "What do you mean 'The devil's prince'?"

Maya stared at him through the rearview, her light brown face growing lighter by the second. "I mean—"

She broke off mid-sentence and gasped like she was about to choke. Kyle twisted around in his seat and reached out to her, but as his hands came close her wide eyes turned black and a sick grin slithered over her lips.

"She means you're fucked." Maya's voice rumbled deeply.

Taylor and Morgana screamed, but Kyle barely heard it. All he could do was look into the dark eyes of the woman he was falling in love with. No matter what the person in the backseat looked like, Maya wasn't there anymore, of that Kyle was certain. But even with that knowledge he didn't know what to do about it, how to make it right, bring her back. Despair beat against his chest with cold fists, but before he could give into it, Maya smiled again.

"Don't look so sad." Her words sounding like stones smashing together. "You'll all be dead soon, and then you'll have nothing more to worry about."

Maya raised her hands and lunged forward. Lost in the moment, Kyle didn't realize what was happening, and she had him by the throat before he registered he was being attacked. Her fingers were freezing cold, and when they locked around his neck they burned his skin. He grabbed her wrists, but the flesh felt like iron in his grip and he didn't budge them a bit. The girls screamed again, but then Taylor threw herself against Maya, hitting at her arms in a flurry of motion.

"Stop it!" Taylor yelled. "Let him go!"

Morgana grabbed Maya's right arm and yanked on it. Kyle watched them try and help him, but the icy burn of her fingers clamping down on his throat and the lack of new air in his lungs shrunk his world down to the space between him and the thing using Maya's body. Dark red splotches peppered his vision, and black fog narrowed his world more and more. He pulled at her wrists, grabbed her forearms, and tried to rock her back and forth, but she seemed welded to the car frame, as immovable as steel.

"Why fight it?" she asked, her mouth curling at the edges. "There's nowhere you can run to, nowhere to go. The dark god of the mountain is rising, and soon the world will sing his song. You're doomed, you stupid shits. Give in, die now. Take what small mercies you can find before we burn them all aw—"

The blackness in Maya's eyes swirled like oil being sprayed off pavement, and the smile on her lips faltered. Kyle felt her grip on his throat relax just a touch, but it was enough for him to take her wrists again and pry them loose. Taylor grabbed Maya's arms and tackled her into the seat, holding her down with all her strength.

Strange sounds erupted from Maya's mouth, a mixture of rocks cracking, dogs barking, and crazed laughter. The blackness returned to her eyes, then swirled away again. She lunged upward, then fell back, over and over until Kyle feared her neck would snap from the pounding, and then it all stopped. The calm silence that followed was almost as terrible as the chaos that came before it because Kyle expected it to shatter at any moment. It wasn't until Maya coughed and looked into his eyes, her face sweaty but her expression relieved, that he sat back and breathed again.

"What the fuck was that?" Taylor asked. She kept her hands on Maya's shoulders and didn't look away for a second.

"I think that son of a bitch got in me," Maya replied without moving or trying to get free. "I don't know how, but...that was awful. He was in my head like a...a diseased dog, dripping with filth and death."

Kyle shook his head and took another deep breath. "It wasn't exactly a party out here either."

"Is he...it...gone now?" Morgana asked.

Maya nodded. "I think so, yeah. He had his claws in pretty deep, but this is my goddam head, and I'll be damned before I let him have it."

"From the sound of it, we're all damned." Taylor let go of Maya and sat back.

Exhaling in a blast of air, Maya nodded again and looked at all three of them with a quick turn of her head. "Probably, yeah, but...maybe not."

"What do you mean?" Kyle asked. Maya looked exhausted, but there was a small glint in her eyes, and it sparked an echoing light in his heart.

"I mean... That fucker was in my head, but I was also kind of in his. The water that's kept that beast asleep for so long is nearly gone. When the cavern's empty, it'll rise up and do exactly what that son of a bitch said. That I saw clearly enough. But, I also saw something I don't think he wanted me to – we can stop it by refilling the cavern. I think the beast will return to its sleep if we can drown it again and block it up."

The flittering glimmer of hope in Kyle's chest dimmed. "Oh, is that it? And how are we supposed to do that? It's not like we can flip the pump's direction since the pipe leading out of the caves doesn't dip into the river, and though I'm sick as hell of this rain, it's not enough to fill a mountain with. For a flood like that we'd need..."

Kyle's face went numb, and his mouth stopped moving as ideas and plans suddenly filled his head. After another few moments of contemplation he cleared his throat and tried to explain the craziness that had popped into his brain. It was a long shot, but it was all they had. First, though, he needed to get his sister and Maya to safety.

"Need what?" Maya's eyes were intense as they stared into his.

He shook his head and turned around. "It doesn't matter right now. After I get you three out of here, then I'll deal with it."

Maya jolted the back of his seat. "There isn't time for chivalry, Kyle. If you have something in mind, then let's get to it. The end is pretty seriously nigh."

"But—" Kyle could only get the one word out before Taylor hit him on the shoulder.

"Dude, it sounds like there's nowhere we can run to that this evil old bastard won't eventually catch up to us. If you know a way we can stop it now, then get on that shit!"

Kyle wasn't so sure about his plan, and Morgana didn't seem all that convinced either in the rearview mirror, but Taylor's conviction swayed them both.

"Okay, but when this doesn't work and we're all dead, don't say I didn't warn you."

He pulled out his cell phone.

INTERLUDE
POWER OF THE BLOOD

Deep in the mountain, Ash knelt on knobby knees, holding his head and cutting his skin with claws he wasn't accustomed to yet as pain throbbed through his skull, courtesy of the nigger bitch. He hadn't anticipated she'd have enough power to resist him. The power in her blood was old, but there was strength left in it that would have to be reckoned with.

After a few moments he rose to his feet and contemplated his next move. But, as he considered his options, distant voices whispered into his ear. He listened to them, listened close, and he smiled as he realized that – though the cunt had taken her mind back – he still had a connection to her, and through it he heard the heathens talking in the distant Honda. When she spoke about the cavern and the water he relished feeling her fear, but his enjoyment turned sour when Kyle spoke. Gus's son was young, but he wasn't stupid, and the plan he formulated had merit. Too much merit, in fact.

Since finding the dark god in the mountain, Ash had felt like he'd found his destiny, and the dreams of the sleeping beast had promised him power beyond measure, power to shake the world and burn the heavens. He'd not had reason to worry or fear since that moment, but as Kyle spoke, anxiety again touched his heart.

Ash turned so quickly the dust on the ground whirled into a small cyclone, and it didn't have time to settle before he was gone, calling for Gus and the rest of his minions. The moment of their ascension was close, and Ash wasn't about to let anyone stand in their way, especially some black bitch and Gus's wayward son.

CHAPTER TWENTY-TWO

Far in the distance chaos ruled, turning Stillwater into flaming ruin of what it used to be, but the back roads were still calm, and as Kyle pulled the Honda off a gravel road onto an empty asphalt parking lot everything was quiet. No one stirred, nothing moved. All was shadow and silence.

"Your friend said he'd be here, right?" Taylor's eyes darted around in quick, furtive glances. She sat in the front passenger seat, her hand gripping his leg.

Kyle nodded and turned off the engine. "He lives on the other side of the mountain, about as far from town as you can get and still be in the county. Give him a couple of minutes."

"And you told him to stick to the old trails?" Taylor asked as she rolled her backseat window down. The outside air, wet and cold with rain, slapped their senses awake. "Told him to avoid the main roads?"

Kyle sighed. "You were sitting right here when I called him."

Morgana, who'd moved to sit next to Taylor, grabbed Kyle's headrest and pulled herself forward, causing him to sink backward a couple inches. "And did he sound...ya know...okay? Normal?"

"He sounded half drunk, so yeah, I'd say normal."

Maya rolled her eyes and shook her head.

Several sets of eyes gleamed behind a fence at the edge of the parking lot, each pair moving left and right in low, slinking motions. Kyle's heart jumped into his throat and his hand twitched toward his pistol, but then one of the pairs of eyes loped near a security light shining down from a tall wooden pole and a German Shepherd appeared from the shadows. He would have laughed if his heart weren't crammed into his throat.

Soon headlights turned into the parking lot. They belonged to an ancient Ford truck that looked like it should have been put down years ago, and its springs squeaked liked stepped on mice as it crossed onto the asphalt. Kyle smiled, remembering all the miles and dents he'd helped put on the truck when he was younger.

"Is that him?" Maya asked.

Kyle unclipped his seatbelt and opened his door. "Yep, that's him. Come on."

The four were out of the Honda and huddled together against the rain when the Ford stopped next to them. A figure rushed around the truck and came toward them, arms up and arched toward them like a vampire from an old black and white movie. Taylor and Morgana took a half step backward, but Kyle laughed and opened his arms.

"Thanks for coming, man." He clapped the figure's back and then releasing him.

"Jesus H," Dirk replied, his face pale in the glow of their headlights. "What in the goddamn hell is going on?"

Kyle frowned, unsure of where to begin answering that question. "What do you mean?"

Instead of replying, Dirk ducked his head and walked toward a metal building ten feet from the parking lot. Several dogs whined from the cyclone fence circling it. With a jangle of keys he unlocked the fence and gave the dogs vigorous scratches behind their ears and a few calming words before waving everyone else in. The dogs immediately inspected the group as they passed through the gate, their noses sniffing like vacuum cleaners and their tails wagging in propeller motions behind them. Once everyone was cleared by the four-legged guards Dirk walk to the office door and unlocked it. A sign over it read CHAPMAN CONSTRUCTION - MAIN OFFICE. Everyone stamped their feet and shook the rain off as best they could once they stood on a rubber mat inside the office. The dogs stayed outside to maintain their vigil.

Dirk closed the door behind them. "I mean just what I said. My dad called me earlier today, giving me an earful about how terrible a son I am and how much he wished I'd never been born and how I've tarnished the proud Chapman name. He's a shitty dad and all, but what he said was extreme, even for him. When I tried to call him back after calming down and all I got was a busy signal. I drove by a convenience store to get an extra sixer to polish my day off with, and there was a fight going on by the pumps – just a whole group of people beating the shit out of some sad son of a bitch – so I said fuck it and left. When I came over the hill to get here I saw a couple of fires in town, but I didn't see a single fire truck, or ambulance, or even a police car. Not one spinning light, anywhere. And here you're calling me asking to meet you at the construction office because you need me to get you something, yet you won't say what over the phone." Finished with his recounting, Dirk sidled up next to a desk and sat down on the front left corner of it. "So, I ask again, what the fuck is going on?"

This was the moment Kyle had been dreading. Dirk had every right to ask the question, and he had a right to an honest answer, but would he believe it when they gave it to him? Kyle wasn't sure, and he wouldn't have blame Dirk for not believing it either. Had he not seen things with his own eyes, heard what he'd heard and felt what he'd felt, he would have scoffed at stories about hidden devils and people being transformed by evil. But, if he wanted Dirk to help him, then the truth was the only thing that would do, because what they were going to have to do was so extreme that nothing short of the destruction of what slowly awoke in the mountain would be worth doing it.

"Dirk," he said as he sat down on a tattered couch close to the entrance door, "I know what you're about to hear is gonna sound unbelievable, but trust me when I say every bit of it's true. All those things you mentioned, all those strange goings-on? There's a reason why it's happening. And the real bitch of it is that it's about to get worse. A lot worse." He then looked over at Maya and nodded for her to begin.

Over the next several minutes Maya talked without interruption. Most of it Kyle knew, and what little he didn't came as no surprise. Taylor had heard some of it before as well, but hearing it all laid out in one long spiel was tough, and she joined Kyle on the couch. Morgana and Dirk, though, knew almost nothing, so Maya's speech hit them the hardest. They alternated between looks of shock, disbelief, wonder, understanding, and fear – mostly disbelief and fear. By the time Maya finished they looked as white as washed bed linens drying in the sun.

"So...okay." Dirk shook his head and stared at the ground before he looked up and stared at Kyle. "Okay, let's say I believe all this shit – and fuck me for even thinking it – what do you need from me? It sounds like we should be running out of town like our feet were on fire and our asses were catching."

Kyle took a deep breath and calmed his face as much as he was able. If he was going to have a chance in hell of getting Dirk to go along with his plan he needed to seem as reasonable and thought-out as possible. "Well, if Maya's right, then running won't save us. At best we'll get another day of safety, maybe two. After that it's all over no matter where you are. So if we can't run, then our one alternative is to fight back, to stop it."

"And how do you propose to do that, Dr. Venkman?" Dirk asked, crossing his arms and leaning back on the desk.

Keeping his face straight, Kyle replied, "We flood the mine."

Dirk stared at him, then glanced out a small window to the rain falling outside, then looked back at him. "I know you didn't do all that well in science class, man, but the rain out there ain't gonna flood anything more than the ditch at the end of my driveway."

"I'm not talking about rain," Kyle said. "I'm talking about the river."

"The river?" The right corner of Dirk's mouth twisted up and his eyebrows teetered on his forehead. "Shit, man, even with all the rain we've gotten, the river is too low to crest the bank."

Kyle nodded in agreement. "That's true, but what if we blew the dam?"

"What?" Dirk slipped off the desk and had to catch himself before he plopped onto the floor. "Are you fucking insane?"

"No." Kyle forced himself to remain calm and not rise to Dirk's reaction. "I'm just a man without any other options."

Dirk snorted and sat back down on the desk, then pushed away and paced the floor in front of it. "You call blowing the dam an option?"

"The only one we have, man. Like you said, we don't have time for the rain to do it, and there's no other way to get the river high enough to spill over the bank and get to the mine."

Dirk spun and pointed a finger at Kyle. "It'll do more than flood the mine, dumbass! It'll flood the entire town! Who knows how many people would die?"

"The people of Stillwater are already lost," Maya said. As soon as she opened her mouth Kyle wanted to leap over and shut it because he knew what she was going to say – he'd thought the same thing too – but he knew Dirk wouldn't want to hear that. Not yet anyway.

"This ain't your town!" Dirk replied. "You don't get to make that call."

"Then who does?" Kyle asked, plunging ahead since all the cards were on the table. "You? Me? Neither us is exactly Stillwater's favorite son. But it's not even about that. I've been down in it, I've seen what they've become, what others are becoming right now as we speak. They're monsters, Dirk. It's not their fault, and it's a fucking terrible shame that it happened, but right now we don't have the luxury of beating our chests and crying over the inhumanity of it all. As shitty as it is, we've got worse problems to deal with, and that has to be our primary concern." He paused for a moment, took a deep breath, and then looked Dirk square in the eyes with all the severity he could muster. "If we don't stop that thing in the mountain from rising, what happens to Stillwater won't mean fuck-all.

Dirk sighed as he glared at the four people arrayed around him. Kyle knew that if just one of them had come to Dirk with their story, he would have understandably blown them off, maybe even if two had come, figuring he was getting punked. But all four of them had seen the monsters, three of them had been to the mountain. Collectively it had to be hard not to believe them, no matter how hard Dirk wished he could.

"Shit." The word cut through Dirk's teeth in a hiss. "Shit, shit, shit. Alright, so... Fuck, if you want to flood the river, the best way to do it would be to blow the dam's sluice gates. The dam itself is too thick to blow without a couple days of preparation and planning, but the sluice gates are just metal plates. Put explosives on each one, set timers, and boom – instant flood. We've got stuff that'll do the trick out in another building. Which, I guess, is why you called me."

Nodding, Kyle got up and grabbed Dirk's shoulders. "Yeah, it is. Trust me, I'd rather have let you get your usual Friday night drunk on, but we're the only ones who can stop this, and we need your help to do it."

A sad laugh shot from Dirk's lips. "If I'm your ray of hope, then you must really be buried in shit. I –"

The dogs, which had been quiet the entire time they'd been talking, suddenly barked up a frenzy, cutting Dirk off. Kyle ran to the nearest window and looked out. He didn't see anything, but something had riled the dogs up because they were running around the fence, barking like crazy. "Dirk, I think the party might be coming our way. You know where the stuff is we need?"

"Yeah." Dirk jangling his keys again.

"Good, 'cause we need to get it and go." Kyle looked at Maya and his sister, and panic was writ large across their faces. "Stay right here and look after each other. This shouldn't take but a minute." He gave each of them a smile he didn't feel, then turned to Dirk. "Okay, let's do this."

Dirk opened the office door and Kyle followed after him. Rain sputtered down on them, seeped into their clothes. Arrayed around the parking lot were several metal buildings with signs like LUMBER, PLUMBING, and DRYWALL secured over large, roll-up doors. Dirk ignored those and went toward a smaller building bearing a sign with red stripes painted on it and the words RESTRICTED MATERIALS in black. Behind them, the dogs continued to bark and run back and forth along the fenced area.

Once he reached the restricted building, Dirk unlocked it and rushed inside. Florescent lights sputtered to life overhead. Kyle followed him in but stayed neared the door and kept one eye outside. The louder the dogs barked and the faster they paced the fence, the more the small hairs on the back of his neck stood up.

"I can't believe I'm fucking doing this." Dirk unlocked another door, this one leading to a cage made of thick metal wire mesh. "Dad would throw a shit fit if he knew what we were up to."

"I imagine he has other things going on right now," Kyle replied.

Dirk was out of Kyle's line of sight, Kyle could hear him opening lockers. "Yeah, I guess so. He... Do you think the same thing's happening to your folks?"

"I know it is." Kyle felt numbness pass over him at the thought of his parents. As much as he'd hated his dad and was disappointed in his mother, he'd never wished them ill. They were as their parents had raised them, and to their credit they'd managed to raise a couple of good kids. To see them undone, to know his parents were for all intents and purposes dead, it chilled him. Without knowing it he'd forced himself not to think about it, but Dirk's words pressed the issue. "The last time I saw my mom she was raving like a... psycho or something, and my dad...his eyes were black. Not like he'd been punched, but no whites, no irises, no pupils. They were shiny lumps of coal in his face. I don't even want to think what they're like now."

"Black eyes, huh?" Dirk snapped something closed in the cage. "Yeah, I think I saw something like that with my mom this morning. I stopped by the house to drop off my dirty clothes, and she tore into me like I'd taken a shit on her dining room table. When I left she just stood in the doorway, glaring at me. When I looked back to tell her I loved her, it was like her eyes were gone. I thought it was shadows at the time, but now...maybe not."

Dirk grunted, then came out of the cage carrying two large metal boxes. He set them down with a *thud*, closed the cage, and then locked it. Kyle smirked, not seeing the point. If they succeeded, this place would soon be underwater. If they didn't, everyone would be dead.

"Need any help with those?" Kyle asked as Dirk turned back and lifted the cases.

Shaking his head, Dirk said, "They're not heavy. You ever mess with explosives in the Army?"

"No. Boxes of uniforms and field gear were more my area of expertise."

"As clumsy as you were as a kid," Dirk said with a smile, "that's probably a good thing. Eh, then again you could take this case of C4 and drop it off a cliff, and it wouldn't do a damn thing but splat. Hell, you could even throw it in your fireplace and use it as kindling. For it to go boom, you need this." He shook the case in his left hand.

"What are we bringing? Blasting caps or detonator cord?"

Dirk raised his right eyebrow. "Oh, so you know just enough to be dangerous. Wonderful. Since speed is of the essence we're bringing timed blasting caps. They're easier to set than an alarm clock, and they slide right into the explosive like a hotdog in a bun."

Kyle started to smile, but the dogs launched into a fresh round of barking, which then turned into howls. He jerked around and stared out the open door. A pack of gray-skinned monsters crossed into the parking lot entrance, howling just as loudly. Claws and fangs flashed in the night.

"Oh my fucking god," Dirk whispered over his shoulder. "You weren't lying. Sweet Jesus, you weren't lying. I'd hoped y—"

"Come on," Kyle said. "We gotta go."

Kyle ran from the supply building and dashed to the office. The door opened as he approached, Maya's hand holding onto the doorknob like it was the only thing keeping her from flying off into the dark. Taylor and Morgana stared out the window, their already pale faces almost bloodless.

"There's so many of them." Maya's lips barely moved as

she spoke..

He saw her fear, knew it was inside him too, but his training refused to let him give into it. "A dozen or a hundred, we still gotta go. Get ready to run to the Honda." He pulled the Smith & Wesson from the back of his jeans and looked over at his sister. "You two ready?"

Taylor nodded, then pointed out the window. "What is Dirk doing?"

Kyle glanced behind him and saw his friend run toward the fence gate. As soon as he reached it he lifted the latch and swung it open. The dogs, already in a barking frenzy, surged through the opening and ran toward the approaching monsters. Kyle winced, knowing what lay in store for the animals, but hoping at the same time they'd give him and the people with him an extra few seconds.

"Come on!" Dirk yelled as he picked up the metal cases. "Move your asses!"

"You heard the man." Kyle stepped out of the doorway. "Go!"

Maya moved to the other side of the door, and between them Morgana and Taylor dashed for the Honda's back doors. Maya stepped close to Kyle, touched his face, then gave him a quick kiss before following after them. Kyle didn't care to close the door as he stepped into her wake.

Moving like an avalanche of fur, the four German Shepherds tore across the parking lot and leapt at the creatures. Kyle counted ten of them as he neared the Honda's driver's side door, though that was only a guess. The creatures stumbled back a step when the dogs crashed into them. They barked and growled as their teeth and claws sank into graying flesh. Blood spurted into the air, driving the dogs further into a frenzy, but soon the growls became yelps of pain, and the monsters surged forward again. Kyle winced as the dogs cried out, the sound of it eerily like screams.

"You better use that thing if you want to get out of here!" Dirk said, his eyes flicking at Kyle's gun. He then reached into his truck and pulled the Mossberg shotgun they'd once slaughtered countless bottles and cans with from the rack mounted on the rear window.

With the dogs now nothing more than meat staining the parking lot, the pack of creatures split in two. One group headed toward the Honda, and the other toward the truck. Kyle gauged how rapidly they approached, then calculated how fast he could get in the Honda, engage the transmission, and flee. Math wasn't his best subject, but it wasn't hard to put two and two together and get four dead people. The creatures would be on them and pounding at the Honda's windows before he got the car into reverse, and he didn't think it could take much of a pounding. His only real option was to fight.

A loud boom to his right told him Dirk was way ahead of him. The shotgun sounded like a cannon as it sent buckshot into the half dozen or so creatures headed toward him. One fell to its knees, a spray of bloody holes turning its upper body into a gory mess, but the others around it didn't miss a step. He pumped the shotgun and fired again, this time hitting several at once, but they didn't flinch, and it only slowed them for a second.

Kyle raised his .40 cal and took careful aim. One squeeze later and a creature fell, blood spurting from a ragged hole above its black right eye. Kyle gave a quick, silent word of thanks to his drill instructors, then lined up his sights and shot again. The second bullet hit a creature in the throat. He didn't know if he killed it, but it dropped to the ground and flopped around like a fish pulled out of the river to drown in fresh air, and that was good enough. Dead was good, but down and out was a close second. His third shot either missed or didn't hit anything vital because none of the creatures reacted, but the shot after that hit the leading creature in the chest, spinning it around and dropping it.

A flash of light in the far periphery of Kyle's vision drew his attention, and with a quick look he saw Dirk step away from his truck and back toward the office. His shotgun boomed, sending a creature flying to the ground on its back. He pumped, shot, pumped, and shot again, turning another creature into ground chuck. "Running out of ammo!" He took another backward step. "Got more in the off—"

Dirk flinched and stopped in mid sentence, then looked down. Kyle followed his gaze. A blunt, dark object stuck out from Dirk's chest. When it opened, Kyle recognized it for what it was – a fist. Dirk coughed. Blood jetted from his mouth in a thick stream that splashed on the ground. The fist disappeared, and Dirk fell. Behind him stood a nightmare vision of a man, the broken lips of its twisted face turned up in a grin that made Kyle's stomach flop in his abdomen.

Part of Kyle's mind reeled at the sight of his dead friend, but he shut those thoughts down and brought his pistol up. As the gun rose, the nightmare grew larger. A flapping sound hit the air as wind buffeted Kyle's face. He scarcely had time to register what happened before the dark monster lifted into the air and flew at him. Kyle dove to the right to avoid being driven into the Honda and fired two shots. The nightmare didn't flinch or stop, and a heartbeat later it hit the car right where Kyle had been standing. It flipped over the hood to disappear over the other side. The Honda rocked on its wheels, and the women inside it screamed.

Dread coiled in Kyle's chest as Taylor and Morgana scrambled to exit the Honda's back door on the near side, terror lighting up their eyes like stadium lights. Maya, though, was in the front passenger seat, and the dented metal of where the shadow had hit the car held the door shut, so she had to scramble across the gearshift and driver's seat to get out. Her feet just hit the ground as the nightmare appeared behind her.

Kyle opened his mouth to yell out a warning, but he was too late. Maya screamed in a high, keening sound as the monster lowered its head next to hers and sank its teeth into the flesh of her neck and shoulder. Kyle's instinct told him to shoot, but with Maya in the way he couldn't risk it, so he ran around the car to try and wrestle her away. He circled the rear of the car, but a gust of wind slapped against him, pushing him back and driving stinging rain into this face. He closed his eyes for a moment, and when he reopened them, the nightmare was ten feet in the air, Maya in its arms, and great bat-like wings holding them aloft.

"Oh yes!" The winged nightmare's voice felt like nails

pounding into his ears. "The ancient blood. She will hasten the raise of my dark lord, her blood the spark that will light the world on fire. Now let the darkness come!"

Though he hated hearing the monster speak, he thought he recognized the voice. When he looked up at Maya's terrified face as she struggled to get away from the arms that held her, he knew from where – it was the voice Maya had spoken with in the car, the voice of the spirit that had taken her over. Now here it was, in the flesh, taking her body yet again.

"Kyle!" she shouted, reaching out for him. "Help me!"

Kyle brought his pistol up and aimed down its sight, but the jerking motion of the wings made an accurate shot impossible. "I can't!"

Maya bit down on the arm holding her, and she dropped as it jerked away. Kyle ran forward to catch her. Before she fell more than two feet, the shadow grabbed her again, and the wings beat fiercely to lift them away. Within seconds they were lost in the dark sky, Maya's fading screams all that remained.

"Kyle, they're still coming!" Taylor shouted as she grabbed his arm, jerking him back to what was happening around him.

With the nightmare monster gone, the gray monsters shambled forward again, their feet tearing through the gravel of the parking lot. They were so close there wasn't enough time to get Taylor and Morgana back in the dented Honda. Kyle dashed for Dirk's dropped shotgun, picked it up, and turned to Taylor.

"You remember how to use one of these things?" he asked, handing her the pistol.

Her eyes were as large as the moon as she looked at it and then at the monsters now just a few yards away. She nodded, her face bloodless.

"Then use it!" he said, shoving it into her hands.

Taylor took the gun, gulped, and started firing. He stood next to her, their shoulders nearly touching as they created a wall of ammunition and sound. Gray creatures that had once been people jerked and sputtered, brackish liquid seeping and spurting as they fell one by one. The monsters drew close, Kyle and Taylor stepped back, Morgana already in the office doorway behind them. The shotgun boomed and the pistol barked, over and over again. Pallid flesh exploded away from bones and muscles to splatter on gravel. Growls boiled the air.

A claw lashed out and ripped through Kyle's shirt, scratching his chest. He shoved the shotgun in the creature's mouth. Chunks blew out of the monster's head when he squeezed the trigger and emptied its skull.

"Kyle!" Taylor screamed as two monsters lunged forward.

He kicked the one nearest him and drove it to the ground. The thing at the end of his boot thrashed and grabbed at his leg, then took his foot and gnashed on it. The steel toe covering saved him from losing his toes. He mashed down, pressing its skull into the gravel, and gave his boot a vicious twist. The creature's head split in half, spilling blood and broken fangs.

Next to him, the other monster grabbed his sister and pulled her down as it leaned in to eat her face. As she fell her arms bent, and the gun in her hands pressed against the creature's ashen chin. When her knees hit the ground, the shock of it made her entire body twitch, and a bullet blasted through the monster's head. Bits of brain and skull rained down around her. Blood splattered her face.

Kyle barely had time to be thankful she was still alive before more creatures pressed in on them. He stepped close to her and helped her up with one arm while swinging the shotgun around with the other. They fired again once they were standing side by side, but dry, metallic clicks soon replaced the sound of gunfire. By the grace of a God Kyle was begrudging to believe in, only one monster still stood. Feeling his heart pound in his chest like a wild animal, Kyle ran forward and kicked it to the ground, then smashed the butt of the shotgun into its head like a lumberjack trying to chop a tree down. His arms heaved up and down, up and down, and in the back of his mind he heard himself bellowing in rage and fear as he turned the gray creature's head into mush. He didn't stop until Taylor's cool hands grabbed his arm and pulled him away.

"Kyle, stop it!" she yelled, tears streaming from her eyes. "It's dead already! Stop it!"

Kyle's lungs ached as he gulped in air, but then his throat burned when vomit flew from his mouth to spatter the dead creature at his feet. His knees trembled, threatening to drop him to the ground, but he locked his legs and forced himself to stay upright. If he fell he wasn't sure he'd be able to get back up again.

"We gotta go." Taylor's voice was high pitched and pleading.

She was right, but he didn't know where they should go to. Without Maya and Dirk, their plan lay in ruins. Nowhere was safe, not in the whole wide world. What was happening in Stillwater was just the beginning. Once the ancient evil in the mine rose, all of them were dead. But, as he thought of the mine, he knew what he had to do. Shutting down his mind, he walked over to Dirk's body, bent over it, and patted his dead friend's pockets. When he felt metal, he reached in and withdrew a ring of keys. Finding the one with a FORD logo on it, he removed it from the ring and held it out to his sister.

"Taylor, I need you to go with your girlfriend to the cabin where the rest of your friends are at," he said. "Go there and hunker down until I come to get you okay? It should be safe enough."

"No," she replied, shaking her head. "We're getting out of here. All of us. Together."

"I can't. Not yet."

Taylor's facial muscles flexed as she clenched her jaw. "Why not? There's nothing we can—"

"There is," he said, cutting her off. He took her shoulders in his hands and stared into her eyes. "We could run all the way to other side of the world and it wouldn't matter. Think about it for a second, and you'll know I'm right. Either we do something to try and stop this, or we wait to die. I still have a chance to stop all this, but I can't do it and keep you safe at the same time. So go, take Morgana, and wait with your friends. Can you do that for me?"

Taylor shook her head and glared at him, but he just looked at her. After a few seconds she cried and threw her arms around him.

"I never thought you'd leave me twice." Her tone was soft, but her words still cut deep.

"Last time I left for myself," he whispered into her ear. "This time it's for you. Now go. As soon as I'm done, I'll come get you, and then we'll put this town behind us once and for all. Okay?"

Taylor nodded and stepped back. "Okay."

Kyle leaned forward and kissed her cheek. "Good. I love you, Piglet."

"I love you back, big brother," she replied, tears still streaming down her face.

They hugged once more, and then Taylor waved Morgana over as she walked to Dirk's truck. Kyle watched both girls get in, not moving a muscle until the taillights vanished in the distance. Now with nothing with silence and the stench of carnage around him, he went into the office and opened desk drawers. In the lower right one he found a box of 12-gauge shotgun shells and took as many as his pockets would hold. He then walked back outside to the two crates holding the explosives and detonators. They were lighter than he'd expected as he carried them to the Honda and put them in the trunk. He took one last look at his dead friend. "I'm sorry, man, I really am," then got in the car and started the engine. As he pulled out of the parking lot he turned the wheel to the right and crossed onto the road that would take him to the dam. He just had one stop to make on the way there.

CHAPTER TWENTY-THREE

The ventilation tunnel for the mine opened like a wound on the side of the mountain. When Kyle and Maya had been there earlier in the day, with the rainclouds backlit by the sun and the true nature of what was happening still unknown, it hadn't seemed that ominous. It was just a hole dug into the rock. But now, in the dark, alone, knowing what waited at the heart of the mountain, the vent opening had a dreadful feel to it, and it took every ounce of his strength and courage to cross into the mine.

The darkness inside the mountain was absolute. He felt it on his skin, like wool stretched across his face and limbs. Before he could stumble into a wall and break his nose, he stopped, set Dirk's shotgun down, and lifted the night vision goggles he'd taken from Maya's car over his head. Once they were in place and powered on, the mine went from twilight to dusk. The roughly hewn stone of the tunnel and the pipes that ran along the floor were vague greenish shadows within shadows, but half blind was better than no sight at all. Now able to at least keep from smashing into the rock, he picked up the shotgun, ducked his head, and scuttled forward.

The chug of distant pumps echoed through the tunnel like monstrous mechanical hearts, their competing rhythms beating the air mercilessly. With every second and every gallon, the world came closer to ending. The beat of the pumps drove Kyle forward, urging him deeper into the darkness.

After a minute of scuttling he came to the chamber Taylor and her friends had been held in. The dead miner lay in the middle of it, his face smashed and his gray mouth open in a Jack-O-Lantern grin of broken, jagged teeth. His sightless black eyes stared up at the shale roof above him in unblinking wonder. Dried blood crusted his chin, cheeks, and the crumpled hunk of flesh that had once been a nose. Kyle shivered at how close he'd come to being the one dead on the dusty floor, and then turned to trudge further into the mountain.

As each foot fell, the chugging of the pumps grew closer and louder. His back ached from bending over for so long, but he grit his teeth and tried to ignore it. Maya was somewhere ahead, and God only knew what danger or pain she was in, so he picked up his pace. Soon the air vibrated from the nearby power of the pumps, the sound of their gas engines hammering against his eardrums as the tunnels carried their unceasing clamor like the horn on an old phonograph right to his head. Half a minute later the tunnel ended, and the darkness beyond it was as deep and wide as outer space. Things moved in it, though, shuffled in the dark, and he stopped before he stumbled amongst them.

To the far right and about ten yards out were the pumps, and several small lights blinked on their control panels like stars. The hoses leading from one end of each were clamped onto pipes running past his feet, while the hoses from the other end led to a wide opening in the rock to their right, the cave's mouth rough and uneven, as though it had been clawed into the rock. A glow emanated from inside the opening, the light wavering as though reflected off water. Something about it made his heart skip a beat, so he averted his eyes to look elsewhere, but he knew that eerily lit cave was where he needed to go. That was where the water came from, where the ancient evil slept, and if the winged monster was to be believed, it was the most likely place he'd have taken Maya.

Bodies littered the dark stone floor outside the cave and out past the pumps like trash that had been tossed aside and forgotten about. Some looked like normal people, and some were twisted, distorted shells of who they used to be, but all were bloody and savaged in some way, and all gazed out at the world with midnight eyes. A shiver ran up Kyle's back like a frightened cat.

A large machine sat to the left. Kyle had never seen one in person, but he'd heard of them – a continuous miner. Its massive tungsten-tooth covered front end sat still and quiet.

The rock floor around it was washed clean by the water it had released when it breached the cavern on the right and flooded the tunnel. Those the water hadn't killed, it had changed. Kyle didn't know if the miner still worked, but on the floor to its left sat a man with its controls in his hands, his gnarled fingers flicking the switches like a child with a toy too advanced for him. The man's face was twisted, his shoulders far too hunched forward to be healthy, and drool hung in thick ropes from his fat, gray lips.

Beyond the miner and the cavern opening lay a long, wide tunnel that led into the rest of the mine. Kyle couldn't tell how deep it went, but what little he could see looked exactly like the mines he'd been in before as a kid. Tunnels crisscrossed the one leading away from him at regular intervals. Several miners moved about in the dark, most of them alone and shuffling around in small circles on twisted legs, their gray heads cocked like they were listening to music he couldn't hear, but they didn't have ears to hear with, just nubs of flesh. Others stood in small, fidgety groups, their bodies stooped as they leaned toward each other talking. Occasionally one of them would look his direction, but their eyes never lingered, and they never gave a sign that they saw him. Their bodies were too misshapen and covered in coal dust to recognize any of them.

Knowing he had to move, and quickly, Kyle checked the miners nearest him to make sure none were looking his way, then duck-ran to the lit cavern opening. His stomach tightened with every step, and nausea drove bile into his throat in a burning trail of sickness, but he kept going. Within seconds he crossed through the opening. The light from the cavern was too bright for the goggles, so he shifted them up to his forehead and blinked to clear the spots that suddenly filled his eyes. After a moment his vision cleared, and he found himself in a short cave. It was taller than the mine tunnels, but much more narrow. It ran for about twenty feet from the opening before ending at a cliff edge. Maya stood barely a foot from the dropoff, a monstrous beast of a man at her side. Their backs were to him as they gazed down at whatever wretchedness sat in the cavern below.

Kyle tightened his grip on the shotgun and took a cautious step. As his eyes continued to adjust he saw the winged beast held Maya by the back of her neck. She hung angled out over the cavern with her arms hanging down and blood dripping from her fingers in a steady drop-drop-drop that matched the beating of his heart. The pumps were loud behind him, but as he neared the end of the tunnel he heard the beast speaking, the massive wings on his back twitching as he spoke.

"You should feel honored." The beast's voice rumbled like an avalanche. "You have the blood of the ancients in you, and now that blood will hasten their return. You will be the mother of a new dark age. Isn't that wonderful?"

Maya's head twitched and her arms shook for a moment, but beyond that Kyle didn't see her respond. The beast pulled her toward him and leaned in, his misshapen head so close he could have kissed her cheek. After a moment he chuckled with the sound of ice breaking and held her back over the abyss.

"You have fire in you, I'll give you that."

Kyle crept forward, treading as lightly as he could. The beast shook Maya as if trying to shake loose the last drops of water from a bottle, his eyes locked on the cavern and the monster within it. When Kyle was within a few feet of them and still hadn't been discovered, he breathed a silent thanks to whatever was looking out for him.

That was when a voice behind him said, "You shouldn't have come back, boy."

Several things happened in very short order.

Kyle turned and found his father standing in the opening. He looked worse than before, like a corpse left to bloat and wrinkle in a river, his flesh gray and shriveled. His eyes were black pits, yet somehow still disapproving. When he stepped into the cave he raised his clawed hands and growled low in his throat.

Maya yelped, catching Kyle's attention and dragging him back around. The beast, now alerted to his presence, glared down at him. He'd seemed so monstrous before in the construction company's parking lot, but he seemed even bigger now, a foot taller than Kyle and twice as massive. Maya looked like a toy in his hand as she hung over the cave floor, her blood turning the dirt on the ground to mud. The beast's eyes were wide empty pits, and his cracked lips pulled back in a sneer that turned Kyle's insides to water.

Moving without thinking, Kyle reached out with his left hand, grabbed Maya by her shirt, and pulled her toward him. The beast's hand didn't loosen from her neck, and she barely moved halfway between them before he yanked her back. His snarling lips opened, but whatever words he'd been about to utter were lost when Kyle lifted the shotgun in his right hand, jammed it in the beast's face, and pulled the trigger. The boom resounded in the tight space of the cave, but the buckshot that exploded from the barrel was far worse, and the beast's grip on Maya went slack as he flew backward into the cavern, brackish liquid spraying into the air in a rancid mist. Kyle lunged forward and grabbed her again before she could follow the beast's screams into the cavern's depths.

"No!" a voice cried out, reminding Kyle that he was far from alone.

Turning as quickly as he could with a half conscious woman in his arms, Kyle turned halfway around when clammy hands curl around his throat and tighten. Reacting on nothing but instinct he threw his free hand out and bashed what had once been his father across the head with the shotgun. His father staggered backward, his claws cutting Kyle's neck as his grip loosened and pulled away. Kyle hissed at the sudden burning pain at his throat.

"Fight all ya want, son." Blood oozed like oil from a gash on his father's gray cheek. "You're all still gonna die."

"Don't call me son," Kyle replied, pumping the shotgun. A spent shell casing flew from the weapon and bounced off the cave wall.

His dad laughed and humor danced in the inky depths of his eyes. "Sorry to tell ya, *son*, but there ain't shit you can do about what's comin'. Not a goddam thing. You're useless, as always. Your momma should have aborted you like I told her to."

Kyle winced. He hadn't thought his father capable of still hurting him, but the depths of the man's vileness were beyond measure. The twisted monstrosity standing before him was the full expression of the darkness that had been inside him, the truth revealed. Perhaps that's what the cavern's poisoned water actually did. It didn't sow evil so much as it exposed that which was already there. Looking into the twisted face of his father, gray skin and black blood and bottomless eyes, he knew whatever goodness the man once had was long gone.

"I hate you." Kyle raised his shotgun and pulled Maya close.

His father snarled, but before he could do or say anything, a loud roar erupted from the cavern's depths, and the mountain shook like a fault line under it was finally giving way. His father screamed and clutched his head. Maya moaned and trembled against him. Kyle tried to keep one eye on her, one on his father, and one on the cavern behind him, but he couldn't watch all three at once. A second later the choice was made for him.

"Arrgh!" his father bellowed as he let go of his head and ran at Kyle.

For a moment all Kyle saw were claws and sharp teeth, but as he leveled the shotgun and aimed it, he couldn't help but see the father Gus Mason had been once upon a time. What rushed at him in the cave with hands stretched out for murder wasn't his father though, so when he pulled the trigger it was with little regret. What remained of his dad hit the cave wall, then slumped to the ground, his chest now a mess of ruptured organs and bone splinters. He didn't move again.

In his arm Maya began to shake, and a loud moan escaped her lips. Kyle looked down to find her head turned behind them and her eyes wide. His stomach sank as he turned, fearing what new terror came. A massive black hand reached over the cliff's edge, its claws digging furrows in the rock, and a second later another hand joined it. A shadow rose up, which turned into wings that spread and flapped in a savage motion. When the beast sprang up and landed on the cliff, it looked even more terrible than before with its face pitted in deep scars. Buckshot glittered in some of the wounds. The beast was hurt, but alive.

"I will eat your soul, boy." The gigantic black creature ducked its shoulders and rumbled toward them. The darkness of its eyes hid none of its rage, and the fangs filling its mouth glistened in the light like knives. Each step sent a tremor through the floor.

Before Kyle's terror could steal all his faculties he pumped the shotgun and sent another round of buckshot at the beast before tightening his grip on Maya and dragging her with him the opposite direction. If the cave had been bigger they wouldn't have stood a chance, but the beast was too large to get a full head of steam going. Slowed as he might have been, he was relentless, and he didn't let the buckshot impede him one bit. Kyle knew deep in his quivering gut that nothing would stop the beast from tearing him apart. Not distance, not time, and apparently not even a shotgun blast to the face.

He noticed a large chunk of shale on the roof. As he ran past it he raised his shotgun behind him and shot it. An avalanche of stone rumbled down, blocking off the cavern. He doubted it would stop the beast, but it would at least slow him down.

Once out of the cave and back into the mine, one glance was all it took to know they'd gone from the frying pan to the fire. Gray shapes loomed out of the darkness, their growls adding to the din of the pumps to create a cacophony of noise that shook Kyle's eardrums and made his insides quiver. Hands, claws, and gnashing teeth came at him from the dark in every direction, and as they came Maya grew heavier and heavier on his arm.

Knowing little else to do, Kyle looked for the nearest wall and carried Maya over to it. He lowered the goggles back over his eyes. Gray claws came at him from the right. The shotgun fired, filling the mine with a brief flash of light and a rolling roar. In the sudden bloom of light he saw a monster right behind the one he'd just shot, so he pumped the shotgun and fired again. Hands reached for him from the left, he fired. Growls and a foul stench came at him from directly ahead. He fired again, the strobe light effect of the shotgun and sound turning the mine into a hellish nightclub. His hands tired as they aimed, fired, and pumped, over and over again, reloading from his pockets after every sixth shot. Gunpowder filled the air and his ears rang.

When his pockets finally came up empty he turned the shotgun around and swung it like a bat. The hot metal barrel burned his hands, but he didn't let go. His arms ached as he bashed in one gray skull after another. When the stock broke off he curled his left hand into a fist and prepared himself to fight hand to hand.

But there wasn't anything to hit.

For the first time in what felt like forever he found himself alone in the dark save for Maya, who sat on the ground.

"Maya," he said as he stooped down next to her. "Maya, wake up!"

She stirred and looked up at him, her face pale and her eyes unfocused. "Wake up?" she asked, her lips barely moving and her voice nearly drowned out by the pumps. "Was I asleep? Was I dreaming?"

"I wish. Now come on, get up. We need to go."

Maya groaned and pushed herself up, but as soon as she reached her knees she hissed and jerked away from him. A bloody scar tore across her wrists, the skin puckered and pulled back. Blood trickled from the wounds. She needed serious medical attention, but he didn't have an ambulance in his back pocket, so instead he took off his outer shirt, tore several long strips from it, and tied them clean side down tightly around her wounds. It wasn't much, but it was all he had, and it would stop the bleeding.

"Ow, that hurts," she said in a childlike voice as she picked at the impromptu bandages.

Kyle smacked her hands away. "I know, but it's better than bleeding to death. Now we—"

Rocks exploded from the tunnel leading to the cavern,

and a loud roar chased the tumbling stones. Kyle grabbed Maya and pulled her to her feet as, at long last, the beast emerged from the cave and looked around, his ruined face swiveling from side to side like an automated turret seeking a target. It only took a moment for it to find them.

With the beast between them and the way out, Kyle looked around for something – anything –he could do. Even with the night vision goggles he didn't trust that he could find their way out of the mine before the beast ran them down, so fleeing wasn't an option. His shotgun was broken and useless. After a quick glance around all he could see was the continuous miner, its front and rear lights pitifully small against the dark of the mine. Even unpowered it was a formidable object, weighing several tons easily, and if nothing else he could try and keep it between them while he thought of something. He pulled Maya close and ran with her to it just as the beast roared and took off after them.

The miner was even bigger up close, like someone had taken a bus and squashed it, then put a gigantic barrel covered in metal fangs larger than his fingers on the front. The tungsten-carbide teeth were coated in coal dust, dulling their shine but losing none of their wicked promise, and as Kyle and Maya hobbled their way between the miner's front end and the rock wall it sat parked in front of, he made sure to stay as far from those mountain eating choppers as he could, though there wasn't much room to work with.

Maya screamed, and Kyle turned to find the beast reaching the miner and following them around its front, powerful gray arms outstretched to grab her before they could get clear. Kyle yanked Maya close, and a second later they were on the other side of the miner.

Like an enraged bull, the beast roared and lunged toward them. He was too big to easily squeeze between the miner's drumhead and the wall, so metal teeth dug into his flesh, infuriating him even more. His massive black arms rose up, and then he slammed his fists on the drumhead. To Kyle's dreadful shock, the machine actually shook. The beast hit it again, and then again, all the while roaring loud enough to overwhelm the pumps, and the continuous miner trembled with each blow. But, the miner's treads didn't move, and the more the beast thrashed, the more it wedged itself in.

Seeing faint hope, Kyle pulled Maya around the far side of the miner, his eyes locked on the pipes that led out of mine and back to Maya's car. As they stepped past a gray body sprawled on the dirty floor with dark chunks of brain slowing sliding out of its shattered head, Maya stumbled, just avoiding falling on the body. Adrenaline coursing through his body, Kyle caught her with a lightning fast grab, then looked for what tripped her. The continuous miner's control panel lay on the ground behind her feet. Kyle's heart rate increased as his gaze flicked to the beast, its black skin bulging as it tried to muscle its way from the machine's vicious front end.

"Hold on." Kyle stooped over. The controller was heavier than it looked, and there were a dizzying amount of buttons and switches on it, but after a few seconds he spotted a large red button with the word STARTER written above it on tape peeling at both ends. He didn't have a religious bone in his body, but he uttered a quick prayer, crossed his heart, and then put his finger against the button. "Here goes nothing."

Heat rushed through Kyle's body when the miner rumbled to life and bright lights lit up to push the darkness back. The beast's roars, which were already loud enough to shake the mountain, somehow became even louder, and its thrashing reached a fever pitch. When the miner's treads jittered, Kyle didn't know if it was the transmission warming up, or if the beast was actually shifting the several ton hunk of metal. Either way, precious seconds were slipping away, so he looked down at the controls and searched for any button or toggle that might be useful. When his eyes hit on a switch labeled DRUM CONTROL across the top and the words ON and OFF etched next to it, he immediately flicked it to ON. The sounds that followed were the stuff of nightmares.

The miner's drumhead spun to life with a thick, mechanical chugging noise, and the metal prongs arrayed across it became a blur of motion. The beast's bellowing turned to shrieks. Suddenly pain lanced through Kyle's skull, and Maya screamed. The monster lashed out, pressed against the miner to push it away. The pain in Kyle's head increased. Chunks of dark flesh and sprays of blood jetted into the air as the beast thrashed. To Kyle's horror, though, the beast was almost free.

Kyle wasn't about to let his one chance at victory slip away, however. Two small joysticks sat on the edges of the controller – the one on the right labeled DRUM HEIGHT and the other labeled STEERING. Hoping the many hours he'd spent playing his Xbox hadn't been in vain, he pressed up on the left stick. The miner's treads kicked to life and rolled the machine forward.

The nightmare creature roared, sending fresh pain into Kyle's head. He kept his left thumb pressed against the control stick. The drumhead rolled, its teeth now slick with blood, and bits of dark flesh flung into the air. The treads churned against the ground, pushing against the beast who somehow still fought. Sweat broke out on Kyle's forehead at the thought that not even the miner could stop the beast from killing them. But, after a few seconds, the miner moved forward an inch, then a foot, then a yard. The beast's howling turned into a sloshing gargle, and then Kyle could no longer see it over the spinning drumhead. A few heartbeats more and the miner hit the wall and dug into mountain rock. The air soon became thick with dust. A second later the pain in his head disappeared.

A dark hand reach up and touched Kyle's arm. He jerked in surprise and dropped the controller, but when Maya's pale face appeared next to him he gulped and tried to slow his rampaging heart.

"I think it's dead," she said over the sound of the miner. "We need to go."

Kyle looked at her and then at the continuous miner as it sat in place and churned at the air. Nothing else moved. "Yeah. Let's go before shit goes from bad to worse."

Taking her hand, he guided her toward the tunnel leading out. At every turn he expected gray hands to reach for his neck, and every puff of wind that touched his throat felt like the breath of some creature as it bore down on him, but after several minutes of scuttling they eventually made it out of the mine and into fresh air. Never in his life had he ever felt so thankful to be standing in the rain.

After taking a moment to enjoy the cool drops against his skin, Kyle took Maya's hand and started toward the parked car, but he barely took a step before he was stopped. Maya didn't move with him.

"Come on," he said, "we gotta go. The end is nigh, remember?"

Maya nodded, but she didn't move her feet. "I remember. Better than anyone."

"Then let's go." He put as much urgency as he could in his words, but her feet stayed planted. He wanted to grab her and shake her, wanted to slap her and throw her over his shoulder, but the look in her eyes wasn't obstinacy. It was acceptance.

"That thing," she said, " in the cavern, it... My blood worked. It's about to wake up. I can feel it like snakes in my head. Whatever power you thought you felt before, it's nothing compared to what's coming. You won't make it to the dam before it's fully awake and tearing the mountain down. When that happens nothing else will matter. It'll be over for all of us. But...I think I can slow it down. If I stay here and concentrate, I think I can get into its mind and keep it suppressed long enough for you to do what you need to do."

Kyle didn't know what to say or think of her statement. Until recently his life had been – while not exactly a rose garden – at least normal. Now suddenly he had dark gods and flying monsters and psychic battles to deal with, and he didn't know where to even begin trying to process it. But the explosives were solid. The dam was solid. Those things he understood. Slumbering ancient evil and telepathic fighting? He didn't know shit about those. One thing he knew for sure was that Maya was a woman with her mind made up, and he wasn't about to step in front of that train.

"All right," he said. "If I knew how to argue with you or thought it would actually make a difference, I would. But please, get a little higher before you settle down. When that dam breaks this place is going to get really wet really fast, and I don't know how high it'll get. Go up a bit, and when you think you've gone high enough, go a little higher. I'll come find you as quick as I can afterward. Okay?"

Maya nodded, then leaned forward and kissed his cheek. "Thanks."

Figuring they'd both earned more than that, he cupped her cheeks in his hand and drew her in for a proper kiss. Her lips were cool, but they warmed as he pressed against them, and her tongue felt hot as it slipped into his mouth and slid against his own. He breathed her in as deeply as he could, surprised at how she could still smell like cinnamon and oranges despite everything they'd been through. She pressed against him, curled her fingers through his hair, and returned his kiss with passion. When they finally parted, the rain seemed to fall a bit more gently.

"Gotta go," he said.

She nodded. "I know."

"Be safe."

"You be even safer."

Kyle smiled, intending to do just that, then gave her a final quick kiss before turning to leave. The warmth of her against his lips gave him the strength he needed to do what came next.

Green light filtered through dust in wavering beams, crossing breezes shifted the coal soot one way and then another, and the only sound was the miner as its engine rumbled like a giant cat purring in the night. But, as the dust settled, a bloody hand as black as the heart of the mountain burst through rubble and pressed against the ground. Soon a battered and bleeding body dragged itself free. Once out, the great black body lay still, its chest heaving as air wheezed in and out. Gaping wounds laid the body open and blood seeped to the floor, but as the seconds ticked past and more dust settled, the wounds stitched themselves closed. Eventually the beast rolled over and pushed itself to its knees. More wounds healed, and as they did the beast's heart beat faster and stronger. Within moments wings unfurled and shook the air in a mighty flap, swirling more dust into the air behind it.

Dark eyes looked forward, the gloom of the mine laid bare, and far in the distance it saw the opening that led out to the mine's parking lot. With a grunt Ash lowered his head and ran. His fight wasn't over, and he was going to make damn sure the world's long night was just getting started.

CHAPTER TWENTY-FOUR

Maya's muscles and bones ached with every step up the mountain, her parched throat burned, and spasms gripped her empty stomach. She couldn't do anything about most of her problems, but she tried to slack her thirst by tilting her head back and swallowing the rain that fell into her mouth. It wasn't as good as the cold glasses of sweet tea she used to enjoy on her grandmother Mozelle's back porch, but every drop helped.

As Maya passed between a pair of trees her feet slipped on the wet grass. She reached out and grabbed the tree to her left to stop her fall. The rough bark bit into her hands and tore the skin of her palms, but that was nothing compared to the fire that suddenly burned up her forearms from her wounded wrists. When she was stable again she looked down, and the strips of cloth Kyle wrapped around them were spongy with blood. Seeing the moist red bandages weep crimson tears onto the mountain made her dizzy, so she looked away and tried her hardest to push it from her mind.

In the distance, lights moved through the trees as Kyle turned the Honda around and drove away. As the red taillights dimmed, a feeling of utter loneliness closed in on her and squeezed her heart. Even when that monstrous black beast had grabbed her and taken her to the mine, then tore her arms open with its claws to drip feed her life into its master at the bottom of the cavern, she hadn't felt hopeless, because she knew Kyle was out there and would come for her. Even though they had known each other for only a short span of time, they had forged a bond between them, and it had given her hope. Now he was going away, and all her hope went with him, leaving her none for herself.

Tilting her head down, she focused on the ground right in front of her, and like a mule she went up the side of the mountain until she felt like she'd gone high enough to avoid the floodwaters to come. Remembering what Kyle said, she went a little higher still. When she felt like she'd reached a safe distance she hobbled over to the nearest tree and sat down with her back against it. The soggy ground soaked her butt, but it was better than being out in the open.

"Okay, Maya," she said to herself as she crossed her legs and put her aching forearms on her knees. "You can do this. You're not alone. Focus, do your job, and then you can throw Kyle in the backseat and take him home. So put your big girl panties on, and let's do this."

Using those words as a mantra, Maya closed her eyes and concentrated on her breathing and heartbeat. When both were steady, she said a silent prayer, then pushed her consciousness down through her body and into the darkness of the mountain below. At first she met resistance, as though the layers of rock and coal that had been thrust into the sky over hundreds of millennia were trying to keep her out, but she forced her way through and pushed deeper, and then deeper still. As she burrowed, the resistance dissipated, and soon she felt herself being pulled down. The change sent a jolt of fear through her, but when she tried to slow her descent the pull increased. The harder she fought it, the worse it got, until she feared it would tear her mind apart.

Suddenly she burst through the earth and found herself floating in the ancient cavern, but it wasn't as she'd seen it with her physical eyes. Here she didn't see rock, or water, or caves. Instead she saw blackness stretch away from her so thick and complete that the idea of anything else had no meaning. Even space had stars to break up the infinite dark, but not here. The darkness just...was. But then, as her astral body turned to face the direction she was being pulled, she saw the true face of the evil that woke in the mountain. Her mind shrieked. It was terrible, the most horrible thing she'd ever seen in her life. The elder god was a mass of psychic energy, its thoughts like snakes rolling over each other, slimy and pulsing with dark power. The water was a faint white light surrounding them in a halo that felt like a gentle fire warming her face after too long in the cold, but the light dimmed with every passing moment, and the cold pull of the god took its place.

Maya didn't want to get near it. Not even a little. The evil radiating up at her sickened her to her core. Not for all the money or fame in the world would she go near it. But she wasn't there for money, or for fame. She was there for Kyle, for his sister, for Darius wherever he might be. She was there for her friends, her family, and all the friends and families of people she didn't know. For them, she would do it. For them she *had* to. Maya let the dark gravity of the ancient god pull her close, and when she was next to the boiling black mass she dove in.

As the snake-like thoughts engulfed her, her distant body screamed until her throat tore and blood flecked her lips and chin. The ground beneath her trembled, and the tree at her back shook.

The Honda's headlights were ghosts caught in moonlight as the car rumbled down back roads. Kyle sent gravel flying into the air as he rocketed from one corner to the next, trees whipping by on both sides of him like horrified bystanders who could only stand and watch. A clock ticked in his head with the sound of thunder as the second hand moved, moved, moved, and his body shook from the urgency threatening to overwhelm him.

A flash of white lit the darkness in front of the car. It shone as bright as the sun, and grand white wings spread out, filling his eyes with light. For a moment Kyle thought an angel had appeared before him, its wings shielding him from what was to come, and for those few beats of his heart he no longer felt afraid. He'd never believed in God before, never prayed a second in his life, but with that vision in front of him – and with everything else that had happened the past two days – he took it as a sign that he wasn't alone, that someone or something was watching out for him and wanted him to know. The relief washing over him made him shiver. He would be okay.

A second later a loud thump reverberated through the car

as the angel became an owl and hit the top of the windshield. The blow wasn't enough to damage the tempered glass, but the small spray of blood on the window and the tumble of gray feathers in the rearview said the owl wasn't so fortunate. Kyle wasn't sure whether to laugh or cry, so he did both. A sharp left turn suddenly appeared ahead of him that he was going too fast to make. He hit the brakes, gripped the wheel tightly, turned, and then hit the gas halfway through the corner. The back wheels slid into the ditch, and the frame dragged across gravel, but then he was through it and rolling down a straightaway.

A right turn jumped in front of him a few seconds later. He dropped his speed again, sloshed around the corner, but as he hit the gas pedal the road turned left again, and he yanked the wheel around while letting off the accelerator. The world shrank to a narrow stretch of gravel twisting between fortress walls of tree trunks that threatened to smash the car's front end with every swerve. After several tense seconds and hard turns of the wheel he broke free of the mountain and its trees. Several dozen yards ahead of him gravel ended as asphalt cut across it, and off to the far right stood Stillwater Dam.

Maya floated in darkness, but a darkness that was wet and hot and moving. She felt smothered by it, buried, drowning, dying. She'd been stupid to think she could do anything against the ancient evil, so stupid, and now she was going to die, barely a mote in its eye.

As her life faded, she once again thought of her grandmother Mozelle. How disappointed the old woman would be in her for being so foolish. The thought scarcely formed in her mind before a small dot of light appeared in front of her, so small and fragile yet it was like a star in the vast emptiness, and in it she saw her grandmother sitting in her old chair, her hands working her crocheting needles as sunlight streamed through a window to warm her bones. The darkness retracted the tiniest bit, and that gave Maya hope she desperately needed.

Suddenly, as though to crush her spirit before it could gain strength, the darkness took on form and crashed into her. It pushed against her, rough and hurtful. It pressed against her mouth, her nose, her ears. Then it pressed between her legs, wanting to penetrate her, rape her with shadows. She tightened her astral body and pushed at the dark, fighting for even an inch of space to breath, to be free. The gloom closed around her, but after several panicked seconds it pulled away. She was relieved, but then a voice spoke to her, and that was somehow even worse.

"Such a frightened little thing," it said, the voice like thunder and ice and murder in the dark. *"You quiver in the face of what is to come, but in you is the blood of all the terrors that once were. We are kindred, you and I. Soon your dark blood will echo my song as we reclaim our world. Look, and see what delights you have in store..."*

The darkness held her effortlessly, as if she were nothing, and her mind filled with the evil it once knew, the world it once held dominion over. The images were so alien to her they could have come from another planet entirely, but she knew they were of the world around her, the world that once was and would be again.

Nightmare images hit her in rapid succession – Fire striding on black hooves, creatures scurrying from the sea to throw their slick green flesh against beasts from mountains that crumble behind them, driving them to their death. Deep within bloody oceans great shapes lumber slowly, and monsters large enough to eclipse the sun float in the sky. Obsidian ziggurats rise from cracked plains in worship of Dark Powers, and sacrificial crimson paints their stones as the faithful prove their worth. Everywhere is death and pain and torment.

But no horror is as great as the evil lying in a volcanic caldera, its swollen body blackened by the heat of the earth's molten blood but strengthened by its pain and isolation. Massive tentacle arms sprouting from its body like malignant tumors scoop earth and lava together to shape foul beasts that it fills with its seed to give them life so it can then send its children off to destroy and terrorize. No evil is too minor, no torment too small. It wages a campaign of darkness it believes will never end.

But then came the rain and the lightning and the wind, a storm created by forces it didn't know or understand, and the tempest swept the world until every trace of those who'd once strode it was no more.

The ancient evil had more work to do, though, and as it raged against its death it struggled to find a way to save itself. When the raging flood slammed it against a mountain, the Dark God used every bit of power it had to pull the mountain down on top of it and hide. By the time it was done the evil had nothing left, no power or strength. But the water couldn't kill it, no matter where it came from or how powerful it was. All it could do was suppress it and contain it with sleep.

Until now.

"*So you see, little one, our time has come again. I will rise, and your blood will burn as I send you into the world as my emissary of darkness. You need resist me no longer.*"

Maya didn't want to believe it, yet part of her knew it was right, that it spoke the truth. But she wasn't ready to give in to the nightmare, no matter how persuasive it was, so she summoned what courage she had and sheltered it like a candle against the wind. "You don't know anything. Time is running out for you, and you don't even know it. My love is out there, and he'll end you."

She wasn't sure what reaction she'd hoped to get, but the laughter that rumbled around her wasn't it. "*Nothing can stop my rise. The sacred water had power, but now it is gone. A new dark age is at hand. See what I see, and accept the new world order.*"

Before she could guess what the voice meant, her vision clouded like static on an old TV screen, and seconds later she found herself flying high above the town. Flames twinkled in the night, and a rhythmic sensation flexed the muscles of her back. Maya realized her mind was now a passenger in another body, one that had recently held her in its claws like a doll and tried to drain her dry. In the far distance were the lights of her car as it came to a stop next to the dam. Panic filled her heart like a million frantic butterflies, and the evil pressed against her harder, tightened around her throat to still her screams.

The parking area on the south side of the dam stood empty, so Kyle pulled into the closest spot and parked. When he let go of the steering wheel his hands trembled fiercely enough to rattle his fingers, so he grabbed the wheel and squeezed it.

"You're okay," he told himself, the tremor in his voice betraying him. "The fucking world is depending on you, so get your shit together. Don't think about the fact that your hometown has turned into a goddam horror movie, and that you just killed your dad, and that your sister..." Kyle closed his eyes, took a deep breath, and let it out in a long exhale that left his lungs empty and the windshield fogged up. "Fuck it, let's do this before I shit myself and run for the hills."

Kyle shoved the door open and stepped into the cold rain. After filling his lungs he circled around to the Honda's trunk and opened it. Sitting to the right of the flat tire were the two cases from the construction building, which he set on their sides and opened. In the first were four bricks of C4, each one wrapped in foil and easily mistaken for meatloaf a kindly wife would wrap up and send with her husband to work for lunch were it not for the fact that they were set in molded foam and had warning symbols all over them. In the other case were four detonators and a remote trigger. He pressed the power button on each to make sure they still had a charge. Small red lights blinked.

Looking at the detonators and then at the C4 bricks, he wondered how hard it would be to put them together when he reached the sluice gates. Carrying around explosives with the detonators plugged in and ready to blow wasn't what he'd call a good idea, but it beat trying to do it when all he had was a ladder to hold on to, so after making sure the remote trigger was turned off he took a brick in one hand, a detonator in another, and pressed the metal prods into the C4 like a kid pushing his finger through clay. Once it was secure he powered up the detonator and set it to RADIO, then did the same thing three more times.

Finished with that delicate operation, he went around to

the rear passenger door, opened it, and looked around for the backpack he'd seen earlier. A few seconds of rooting through the pile of crap in the floorboard rewarded him with a green canvas bag. After everything in it was dumped out, he carried it back to the trunk and set the primed C4 in it, then put the trigger in a his front pocket, careful that the plastic guard was secure over the trigger button even though it was turned off. Better safe than sorry. He was taking enough risks already. The backpack went over his left shoulder a moment later.

The walk from the car to the river side of the dam was twenty yards at best, but it was the longest twenty yards of his life. Every step seemed to push it two steps away, and the crunch of gravel beneath his feet sounded like gnashing teeth. Even the rain seemed to push him back, slow him down, but eventually he made it to the ladder embedded in the concrete that led down to a sluice gate. There were three other ladders just like it further down the dam, all of them blocked by a loop of chain and a "DO NOT CROSS" sign that anyone over the age of seven could get around.

Kyle grabbed the raised ladder rail and swung around the chain. When his foot hit the rain slicked top rung it shot out from under him, and he found himself dangling over a hundred foot drop by his right hand. The backpack slid down his left arm and nearly went into the drink before he caught the strap. His arms burned and his legs were jelly, but after he caught his breath he reached over and pulled himself onto the ladder. How long it would take his balls to drop back down was another matter entirely.

No longer taking his grip for granted, Kyle went down the ladder one careful rung at a time. When he got to the sluice gate he found it partway open and spilling reservoir water in a thick gush that made the rain seem paltry. The lowest rungs were covered by the flow, so he had to bend as he reached into the backpack and pulled out a C4 brick. On the back of it was an industrial adhesive covered by a layer of waxy plastic, which he peeled off and let flutter away in the wind before reaching out as far as he could without risking another fall, and slapped the C4 brick onto the middle of the sluice gate. The detonator's red light stayed lit.

"One down, three to go."

Kyle climbed back up, the clock in his head ticking louder than ever, and went to the next ladder, repeated the process, then went to the third. With the ladders as precarious as they were, he focused his mind on the rungs in front of him like a laser, blocking out nearly everything else around him.

As he stuck the third C4 brick in place, a strange whistling sound niggled at the back of his mind, but it wasn't until the adhesive hit the sluice gate that he pulled out his focus enough to see what made the weird noise. His eyes barely turned away from the dam when he saw a black shape fly at him. It was so large it blocked out the flaming town in the distance behind it. Kyle tried to gauge its speed and distance and how far he was from the top of the dam, but his body reacted without conscious thought and swung him around to the tiny ledge in front of the sluice gate. Water pounded his legs and feet, threatening to send him flying, but half a second later the flying beast hit the section of ladder he'd just be hanging from hard enough to dent the metal and crack the dam's concrete.

An impact like that would have killed any normal creature, but the great black beast was anything but normal. Catching itself before it could bounce away or fall, the monster clung to the ladder with one hand and growled, then reached out with the other to claw Kyle's face off. Kyle fought against the water pouring behind him and took a step backward, taking him just out of reach, but not so far that he didn't feel the wind buffet him as the claw raked past his face. He looked from the hand to the black face that growled at him from the ladder, and a bomb went off in his stomach when he recognized it. The face and body beneath it were mangled, shredded hunks of dark flesh hanging in stripes, but the fury that emanated from its black eyes was unmistakable. It was the creature from the mine. How it had survived the continuous miner's ravenous drumhead Kyle didn't know. If being shredded by a hundred whirling carbide teeth couldn't kill it, then what would?

The monster took another swipe at Kyle and howled

loudly, but the sudden scream of tortured metal was even louder, and Kyle cheered as the ladder it clung to snapped where it had hit it and pulled away from the concrete like a banana peel. The beast tried to clamber over the tilting ladder, but his movements only hastened its fall, and in seconds he and it were plunging into the river far below.

Feeling the clock's ticking in his bones, Kyle wasted no time in leaping for the rung still connected to the dam. It hung at head height, but he made the leap with little trouble. Like a monkey climbing up a tree he scrambled to the top and turned toward the fourth and final ladder. Just one more explosive left.

He was halfway there and gaining confidence when the dark monster rose up from the dam and flew straight for him. Kyle lunged out of the way into a shoulder roll. The beast was fast, though, and blocked the way as he got to his feet. The ladder Kyle needed lay behind it, but it might as well have been on the moon. Kyle knew he wouldn't be able to get to it, go down, and plant the last explosive with that thing attacking him every step of the way. It would slice him to ribbons before he even made it to the ladder. Figuring three explosives were better than nothing, Kyle changed direction and ran for the Honda.

Moving faster than Kyle thought possible, the monster flapped its wings and zoomed past him, then landed, blocking that route as well. The look on its ravaged face was that of a cat who wanted to play with his food a bit before eating it. Kyle's fear turned to anger. He wasn't a fucking mouse, and he refused to be played with. He looked past the beast, then behind him, then to either side, looking for any advantage, any way out. His review yielded him only one option.

Moving before his mind could lock him in place, Kyle pivoted to his right, ran half a dozen feet, and leapt into the air. The fall wouldn't be a long one, and the river was deep, so he knew he'd survive the fall. His worry at that moment was getting far enough away from the dam before he blew the gates. Once he did that, the water would come fast and furious. He didn't want to be anywhere near the river when it did, so he—

Something large smashed into him. It wasn't the river below, as he'd expected, but something behind him. Claws gouged into his sides, and a foul stench clouded around his head. He didn't have to look over his shoulder to know what had happened.

"I'm going to kill you so slowly." The monster's words, rank and cold, slid past his ear. "You'll beg me to end your life, scream for it, and then I'll just go slower. Your soul is mine."

Kyle didn't doubt the beast's words. Not for a second. The pain of the claws pressing harder and harder into his sides as the beast flew into the sky was proof enough, but it was the chilling certainty in the voice that cemented it. Whatever hope Kyle had had of getting away to safety was gone. Now his future had become a grim inevitability of pain followed by a slow death. Even that would be a mercy compared to what the rest of the world had in store for it when the mountain's evil heart fully awoke and pulled itself into the night. He thought of Taylor and her girlfriend, of the guys in his unit, of the kids he'd pulled out of the mine, and of Maya, who even as he was carried higher and higher sat on the mountain and waited for him to pull the trigger.

Kyle's head jerked as the image of the remote trigger entered his brain, the trigger that was in the backpack dangling from his arm. Time was running out for him, but it wasn't for everyone else. Moving as quickly as he could, he reached over, unzipped the pack's side pocket, and withdrew the radio detonator. As he shifted the pack its top opened, and in the dark interior he saw the red light of the last primed C4 brick. He shook his arm to get rid of the backpack, but the winged nightmare holding him ripped its left claws from Kyle's side and grabbed the pack before it could fall.

"What's this?" the beast asked with a thick chuckle. "You should know by now that I am eternal. Whatever little weapon you've got in here won't save you or this world. It's over."

As the beast squeeze him tighter, all feeling left Kyle's body. He felt numb, yet he was glad. He knew what he had to do, and the singular purpose to which his life narrowed had a certain comfort to it. The beast was right – it was over. But for the rest of the world and for those he loved there would be another dawn. When he flipped open the trigger guard and pressed the detonation button, he smiled.

Stillwater River glowed red and gold as a small sun filled the sky above it.

Maya and the dark god screamed as Kyle sacrificed himself, and Maya was hurled from its raging mind. Horror filled Maya as the echo of what she'd witnessed resounded through her head. The new love in her heart was scarcely a day old, yet the pain of it being torn from her hurt so badly she wanted to open her chest and take it out, smash it, be free of it. Through everything she'd suffered, none of it hurt as much as watching Kyle take his life so others would live.

But, as the evil in the mountain continued to rage, she realized his sacrifice held a deeper meaning. Kyle had given his life in a selfless act of love, and in so doing he'd given the oncoming water a power it wouldn't have had otherwise. His sacrifice sanctified it, and the evil in the dark knew.

"*No!*" it screamed in her mind as the mountain beneath her shuddered. "*I will sleep no more! My time has come!*"

With terrifying speed the river swelled and water spilled over the banks, overtaking everything in its path. As the water surged into the mine, the evil buried within it raged and thrashed. Tentacles the size of trees smashed against stone as it struggled to free itself. Great slabs of stone fell, and the mountain's peak quaked as it fell inch by terrible inch. A hole suddenly opened in the cavern's ceiling, and with a titanic lurch the ancient evil heaved itself upward.

"*The world is mine! I am free once more, and all will suffer for my pleasure!*"

Thoughts of victory rolled away from it in great red psychic waves, overwhelming Maya's fevered mind with images of dark bodies being tortured as they screamed and burned. But, before the ancient evil could reach the top, the flood reached the cavern and it was drowned again, buried in water along with the bodies of dead miners, scattered equipment, and rocks torn from the walls and ceiling. Within moments the cavern was filled and sealed shut. Ever so slowly the dark one's terrible thoughts drifted away, its mind still raging but growing more and more faint, until eventually it wasn't there at all.

Standing on the mountain and looking down at water that was much closer than she'd ever believed possible, Maya felt the primordial power return to its long slumber. An echo of Kyle's smile flitted across her face, but tears framed it, adding their own power to the swollen river. The danger was over, for now at least. Kyle had bought the world a second chance.

To the east, storm clouds broke apart, and thin streams of early morning light fell, turning the water around her gold.

EPILOGUE

"I can't believe he's gone." Tears flowed down Taylor's face. She stood next to Maya, the two of them looking down at what had once been the town of Stillwater. Behind them stood the rest of the kids Kyle had saved, all of them crying over those they'd lost, what had been washed away. None of them entered the dawn unscathed, and their tears flowed for a good long while.

The weak light that filtered through the thinning clouds was more than enough to show the devastation. Roofs and buildings poked up like islands, and debris was everywhere. Bodies floated here and there in the distance.

"I wish I could say that his death..." Maya didn't know what to say, how to bring comfort to someone she barely knew when her own pain nearly brought her to her knees. "He did it for us, Taylor. It doesn't make it easier, I know, but in the end his only thought was of us. He saved the world. Goddammit...it hurts like hell, but he's gone, and we have to go on. Maybe in a few years we'll appreciate that."

Taylor nodded, and the two women leaned against each other. Shared pain was better. It wasn't until one of the kids stepped up and spoke that Maya wiped her tears away.

"So what do we do now?" Hanna asked. "I don't... We don't have homes anymore, or parents. What are we supposed to do?"

In the back of her mind Maya wondered the same thing. "You stay here, I guess. Someone has to have noticed what happened. They'll probably have the National Guard out here before the day's out. They'll take care of you...somehow."

"But what do we tell them?" Brett asked, his eyes wide and looking around for answers. "I mean, I know shit is all fucked up and all, but what happens when we tell them about...you know...the crazy stuff in the mine?"

Maya squared her shoulders, and for the first time that

morning the pain of Kyle's death took a backseat. "You don't tell them anything. At most you say...you were all hanging out together, maybe you wanted to party at the cabin, let some steam off. If they press you, tell them you don't know what happened. If you say it enough you'll believe it too. Trust me, we all live with lies we don't remember the truth of. You were here, together, there were some strange noises off in the distance, and you woke up to find...that." She pointed at the flooded town.

"Is that what you'll tell them too?" Taylor asked.

"No," Maya replied, shaking her head. "It would be better if I wasn't around. You kids live here, so you're expected. They'll believe you if you all stick together. But I'm different. Me being here will raise a lot of questions I don't want to answer. I can't answer."

Taylor lowered her eyes and nodded. "Yeah, I guess so. I guess this means your book is out too."

"Yeah, it is." Maya had come to the same conclusion earlier. It wasn't that she was afraid people wouldn't believe her, that they'd think she made it all up. She was more afraid someone *would* believe her, and that they'd come to Stillwater, search around, and somehow unleash the evil all over again. There were very bad people in the world, and some of them would love nothing more than to get at the evil in the mountain. No, no one needed to know what had really happened here. It was over, and that had to be enough.

Taylor nodded again, as did the rest of the kids. After a few minutes of sporadic conversation, the kids started drifting apart, each one wrapped up in their own grief and confusion. Maya saw that as her cue to go, but as she turned toward Dirk's truck parked further up the mountain Taylor walked over to her and touched her arm.

"I know this might sound weird," the young woman said, her face pale as snow in the sunlight, "but I was wondering if Morgana and I could come with you. We could...I don't know...be your assistants or something. We'd earn our own way, help you however you needed. Just...take us with you."

Maya looked down at a pair of eyes that were mixed in

sadness and hopelessness, and her heart thudded in her chest. "But what about your homes? Your lives here?"

"What life?" Taylor replied, her hand sweeping out toward the lake where Stillwater used to be. "What home? We've got nothing here anymore. No parents, no homes, so school, and barely any friends. The only thing we've got are lives my brother died for, and we're not going to waste it picking through the rubble in this fucking place. I want to do something with my life. And, frankly, when I look at you I...I feel like Kyle is close by. Maybe that's sad or stupid, but it is what it is, and I don't want to give that up."

A warm weight pressed into Maya's chest, and even though she staggered under it, it gave her hope and finally a sense of something other than sadness.

"It's not stupid," she said. "I see Kyle in you too, and right now keeping his spirit with us sounds like the best idea I've ever heard. Come on. If we're going, we need to go now before the authorities show up. And no offense, but I have seen all of Stillwater I can stand."

Taylor and Morgana laughed. It was a small sound, barely enough to brighten their eyes, but it was enough.

"No offense taken," Taylor replied. "Believe me, we are *so* done with this town. Let's get as far away from it as that piece of crap truck will take us."

It was Maya's turn to laugh, and when she did she felt a tiny piece of her sadness break off and fly away into a sky that was clear, and bright, and warm.

THE END

About the Author

Justin Macumber is the author of Amazon Bestsellers HAYWIRE (Gryphonwood Press) and A MINOR MAGIC (Crescent Moon Press). When he is not hard at work on his next novel he co-hosts the Dead Robots' Society podcast. He and his lovely wife live in the Dallas/Fort Worth Metroplex with a crazy pack of dogs and cats that run them ragged. You can find him online at justinmacumber.com and deadrobotssociety.com. He is also a co-host and reviewer for the popular Hollywood Outsider podcast, which is located at thehollywoodoutsider.com.

38078336R00156

Made in the USA
Middletown, DE
12 December 2016